THE RAVINE

THE RAVINE

PAUL QUARRINGTON

RANDOM HOUSE CANADA

www.randomhouse.ca

This book is a work of fiction. Names, characters, places and incidents either are the product of the author's imagination or are used fictitiously. Any resemblance to actual persons, living or dead, events or locales is entirely coincidental.

LIBRARY AND ARCHIVES CANADA CATALOGUING IN PUBLICATION

Quarrington, Paul
    The ravine / Paul Quarrington.

ISBN 978-0-307-35614-7

    I. Title.
PS8583.U334R39 2008   C813'.54   C2007-906157-5

Jacket and text design: Terri Nimmo

Printed and bound in the United States of America

10 9 8 7 6 5 4 3 2 1

*There's nothing in the dark that's not
there when the lights are on.*

ROD SERLING

"*Distress Hotline. Carlos speaking.*"

"*Carlos? Phil here.*"

"*Phil! How's it hanging?*"

"*How's it hanging? Is that really an appropriate way to greet callers to a distress centre?*"

"*Phil, we've talked about this. You are not really in distress.*"

"*Says who?*"

"*Says all of us. You're depressed, you've got this self-destructive drinking thing going on, but you don't pose any true threat to yourself or others.*"

"*I beg to differ. I pose a* huge *threat to others. Why, look at what I've already done to them! And I wasn't even trying.*"

"*Phil, some of what you're going through is just life, you know. I mean, I've gone through some of this stuff.* My *marriage fell apart . . .*"

"*Really?*"

"*Big time. Mirella just decided she was in love with somebody else. She decided at, I don't know, eleven o'clock in the morning, she was out, she was fucking* gone, *before dinner.*"

"*Do you have kids?*"

"*A boy and a girl. Six and three. And now there is this really bitter custody battle, she keeps dragging up all this heroin stuff that is like years old.*"

"*Hmm. Heroin, you say?*"

"*I've been clean for twelve fucking years. She's a ruthless bitch to even mention it. And it's not like she was a fucking Girl Guide. I mean, there's been some shit in her body, you can bet your ass on that.*"

"*Uh-huh.*"

"*And like this sexuality stuff. I mean, whose goddam business is that?*"

"*Whose sexuality are we discussing?*"

"*Mine. There has been a little confusion. A little ambivalence. But who among us is absolutely one hundred per cent hetero?*"

"*I see. So I take it she's making a strong case for sole custody.*"

"*It breaks my fucking heart, Phil. Some days I don't know how I'm going to go on.*"

"*Well, you know. Baby steps. Right? One little step after another little step, before you know it, you've covered vast distances.*"

"*Didn't I say that to you?*"

"*And you were right.*"

"*I guess so. Look, Phil, sorry, sorry, I mean, you called me, we should talk about . . . so? What happened tonight that made you pick up the phone?*"

"*Well . . .*"

"*Aside from drinking four bottles of wine or whatever it was.*"

"*I just called to say, um, I won't be calling any more. I mean, it's been pleasant getting to know you all, but maybe it's taken up a little bit too much of my time. And I need time, now, I need lots of it.*"

"*How come?*"

"*Because I'm working on a* book.*"

"*Really? A book about what? Your career in television?*"

"*Well, I might mention that.*"

"*People find television very interesting.*"

"*I have noticed. But I think my book is going to be a bit more general.*"

"Like about how you screwed around and did all these things which you think are so bad but really aren't? Things that when you get right down to it are a little bit boring?"

"Yeah. And of course there'll be quite a bit about my career in television."

"What are you going to call this book?"

"Umm . . . The Ravine."

"The Ravine? How come?"

"Because it seems to me, Carlos, that I went down into a ravine, and never really came back out."

PART ONE

THE RAVINE

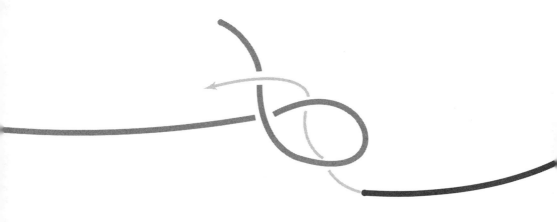

1 | THE RAVINE

WHEN I WAS ELEVEN, AND JAY WAS TEN, WE JOINED THE WOLF CUBS. I was actually too old to be a Cub—at eleven a lad should be a proper Boy Scout—but there is apparently a kind of apprenticeship that Lord Baden-Powell insisted be undertaken, symbolically represented by placing two little stars in your Cub beanie, which means you then have both eyes open. This has to do with the wolf imagery, you see, the baby cub growing until the birth-gook clears from his eyelids and they pop open with self-realization. I adored all that wolf stuff, I loved sitting around in a circle with the other boys and chanting—praying—to the plastic wolf's head that our scoutmaster held mounted on a staff.

"Akeyyyy-la! We'll do our best! Dib dib dib, dob dob dob!"

Jay and I still do this, after several too many at Birds of a Feather, the hateful bar at which my brother has been resident pianist for lo these many years. At least, we *used* to do this, but haven't for months now, because Jay and I aren't talking. He's mad at me for screwing up my life. He should talk. But before this estrangement (and often) we used to stumble out onto the street and find a suitable object for our veneration—the moon, a comely hooker, a two-fingered man playing the ukulele—and we'd snap to attention and begin the Grand Howl.

"Akeyyyy-la! We'll do our best! Dib dib dib, dob dob dob!"

Despite my enthusiasm for the Wolf Cubs, I never did get both eyes opened. I managed a solitary gold star and then quit the organization, or was forced out, I have forgotten exactly what happened. Anyway, one gets one's eyes opened by achieving badges in various disciplines—arts and crafts, outdoorsmanship, map-reading—but I was a failure at all these things. The only thing I was ever any good at was knot-tying. For some reason, I was a whiz at tying knots, despite chubby little fingers and spectacularly bad eyesight. (I'm legally blind in my left eye, and my right is only marginally better.) But when the scoutmaster handed me lengths of rope, these handicaps faded away; indeed, they may have been a benefit, my sense receptors overcompensating for the little cocktail sausages that housed them, some inner sense making crystal clear what my eyes rendered indistinct. The scoutmaster always called upon me to demonstrate new knots. I would hold two lengths in front of me, one white, the other darkened (still far away from the pitch-black second strand featured in the manual), and announce the knot—"Garrick's Bend"— before grabbing a standing end and setting things into motion.

Setting out on this novelizing journey, I have some doubts about my visual memory. I read an interview with Alice Munro once (despite my low standing as a television writer, I maintain an interest in such things), who said that when she was shown a black-and-white photograph of her grade two (or something) class, she could recall the colour of everyone's blouse, sweater, skirt. Shown a picture of my grade two class, I would be challenged to pick out myself, were it not for the huge clue of my spectacles. However, I can conjure in my mind the sight of Jay in his Wolf Cub uniform. Clothes have always been ill-fitting on Jay, none more so than those huge shorts and green shirt. His legs and arms stuck out like pins in a voodoo doll. Jay was always a small fellow, undernourished—if you saw the two of us together, as children, you might conclude that I had been stealing the food from his plate. (Which may have been true, now that I think of it. He never cared all that much for food.) He was and is a small fellow, except for his hands (which aided in his career as concert, and subsequently cheesy, pianist) and his head (which has since birth seemed too great a weight for him to bear).

There was another Cub, named Norman Kitchen, who desperately wanted to befriend me. I don't know why, exactly. He attended another school in the district, but even so, I can't believe he was unaware of my ranker status. After all, he'd seen me several times at the Galaxy Odeon in the company of my brother and Rainie van der Glick. Kitchen was a plump lad, with blond hair that was obviously his mother's pride and joy, as I can't believe either nature or a ten-year-old boy could come up with such an elaborate display of curls. Norman Kitchen had dark, hooded eyes and a nose that seemed to have been carved for a marionette. His lips were thick, and pursed much of the time, as though he lived in constant expectation of having to buss a dowager aunt on the cheek. Norman was quiet, although when he did speak, he spoke very loudly. He tended to draw too near to people, as if wishing to speak conspiratorially, and then open his mouth and blast away. This is an irritating habit, so I rejected his friendship, although I think in retrospect that I spurned Norman Kitchen only to exact a tiny amount of revenge for the way I was treated by most people.

Wolf Cub meetings were held twice a week, Wednesday nights and Sunday afternoons. They were held at the Valleyway United Church, which lay across the field from the back of our house, a couple of hundred yards away from the school. The church, I mean the building itself, exerted a strange influence upon me. I never went there to take part in services, because my mother was not a religious soul. I had never been inside the church until I went for Wolf Cubs, but as soon as I entered I felt a strange familiarity creep over me, as though I'd returned to a place that I'd missed very much. At the end of the lobby was a huge stained-glass window, Jesus standing with his hands spread before him, as though he were saying, "The fish was yay big, swear to Dad." I liked to arrive at the church early, and mill around the lobby, absorbing salvation. But my brother would grow impatient; he'd tug my sleeve and we'd descend into the basement. We'd join a circle of boys and chant, "Akeyyyy-la! We'll do our best! Dib dib dib, dob dob dob!"

One Sunday afternoon Jay and I cycled over to the church, even though in order to do so it was necessary to follow the streets (Langstaff to Juniper Way up to Dunedin and across) and it would have been much quicker to just walk across the field. But it was a glorious late spring/early summer day, so Jay and I jumped on our bikes and pedalled over. By coincidence, Norman Kitchen had done the same thing, so after the Cub meeting the three of us met up by the bike stand. Kitchen hollered at me, "Hey, Phil! Let's do something!"

"Jay and I are going for an adventure," I said. I was fascinated by the concept of having an adventure, which was what all the boys on television had. They had adventures effortlessly, all they had to do was walk outside, but I understood that this was make-believe, and that if I wanted to have an adventure I was probably going to have to bike somewhere. "You can't come."

"Why not?" demanded Norman at a pitch. "I could be your sidekick!"

"Jay is my sidekick."

"I'm not your sidekick," muttered Jay, who had busied himself with some bicycle maintenance, namely, readjusting the clothes pegs that held the trading cards that were purred by the spokes. "I'm your brother."

One of the reasons Jay had busied himself was to get distance from me and my nastiness to Norman, so I drew a breath and reconsidered. "Tell you what, Kitchen. You can't be the sidekick. But you could be the fat guy who drinks too much and does the cooking and gets killed."

"Okay!" he agreed.

I pulled my bike out of the rack and leapt into the saddle. "Let's ride!"

The area where I grew up is now simply part of Toronto, but when I was a boy it was a separate entity. It lay a few miles to the north of the downtown core and was separated by wide tracts of undeveloped land. Don Mills (Canada's First Planned Community!) and the city were connected by the Don River, which once teemed with salmon, although nowadays a fish would have a better chance of survival in a cheap motel. Anyway, as you all remember from your Earth sciences, rivers form valleys over vast stretches of time, even a sluggish thing like the Don. The Don Valley was, in sections, parkland, where the woods were tamed and beautified, and walkways ran between beds of cultivated flowers. But there were other areas that were just left alone. The pathway would stop abruptly, and the forest would loom dark and dense.

This was my best shot at adventure, I figured, so I led Jay and Kitchen down into the valley, and we cycled with gleeful fury through the manicured woodlands. And then the path stopped, abruptly, and we leapt off our bicycles and stared ahead to where a forested slope descended to the river. I could spot another body of water, too, small and round. Part of the river had been diverted and formed a stagnant pond. And although no boy on television had ever encountered adventure at a stagnant pond, I said, "We're going down there."

"I don't want to," said Jay.

"I know you don't want to. But you have to. Besides," I said, "it'll be fun!"

The pond had been created by chance, the edge of the river running into a berm, water sloughing off into a depression, a small regular bowl. I'm guessing out in the middle it would have been perhaps three or four feet deep. Around the edges it was only a few inches, and it was easy enough for us to remove our shoes and socks and (seeing as we were already wearing our Cub shorts) go wading into the muck.

"Why are we doing this?" demanded Kitchen, who soon had a leech on his shin. I judged that the kind of thing he'd rather not know.

"We're looking for stuff," I told him.

"Like what?"

"The tadpoles are turning into frogs. They look really weird. They got tails but they're growing legs. They're like little monsters."

"So?"

"So, Kitchen . . . whoever finds the weirdest one wins."

"Wins what?"

"I don't know. They get to keep the little monster tadpole, I guess."

"I win," announced Jay quietly. The sleeve of his Cub shirt was wet with muck up past the elbow and he had his huge hand wrapped around something; he held it up to his eye and peered into the hole made by his thumb and fingers.

Kitchen and I slopped over. "Let's see." Jay brought up his other hand, cupped the two together and then fanned them apart slightly so that we could see the creature caught in the fold. It was not quite frog, and therefore horrible looking, saddled with a long tail that was spotted and decaying. This thing also had a huge bump on its head, a cancerous growth or something.

We stared at this *rara avis* for a long moment, and then we heard a voice. "Hey, kid. What've you got there?"

Two boys stood by the side of the stagnant pond. Both were tall, sprouted violently by adolescence. Although they shared certain clothing and characteristics—jean jackets, jeans, black running shoes, height and build—they were very dissimilar. One was fair— actually, fair is putting it mildly, he approached albinism. The kid didn't have pink eyes or anything, but the blue of his irises was so light that it was virtually invisible. These eyes, these white eyes, the boy kept popped open in apparent surprise, although one would think that the sunlight would rush right through and sear his brain. So he gave the impression of blindness, although it was this boy who had demanded, "Hey, kid. What've you got there?" His hair retained a dazzling whiteness even after maybe half a tube of Brylcreem, and about half a tube is what it would require to create the particular creation he wore. The sides were combed up and the hair met in the middle, actually high above the middle, of the boy's head. Some of this wave rushed back to form an intricate design, what was commonly called a duck's ass, while the rest of the wave pushed forward with increasing volume until it exploded in front of his forehead, by which point it had achieved the firm roundness of a breast or buttock.

The other boy's hair was rather less ambitious. The boy himself wasn't, I mean, he had obviously upswept and teased and Brylcreemed and moulded, but the hair itself just wasn't up to it. The hair was sandy and tired and would have been happier on the head of a bank manager. It lay on top of his head like tangled bedsheets, and no doubt contributed heavily to his air of bitterness. Which was obvious. His face was twisted with it, unfortunately, given that his face was none too pleasant to begin with. To top things off—to jack up the bitterness levels—he had acne, quite severely. It looked as though pimples were battling whiteheads for possession of his very soul.

His role in life was immediately apparent—he accompanied the blond, better-looking boy wherever he went, echoing his words and emulating his actions. "Yeah," he said now, "what've you got there?"

"What have I got where?" asked Jay quietly.

The blond boy took a step forward. "There. In your hands."

I answered, "Just a tadpole."

"It's almost a frog," said Jay, "except it has a tail. And it has a bump on its head."

"No kidding. Let me see."

"I was just about to let him go."

"*Him?*" said the blond boy. "How do you know it's a *him?*"

"He doesn't know," I said.

"Did I ask you?" snapped the blond boy, and all of a sudden I understood that I had found a little more adventure than I had bargained for.

He addressed himself to my brother once again. "Does it have a little dick or something?"

"No. Maybe it's a girl."

"Bring it here," demanded the boy. "Let me see it."

"Yeah," said his companion. "Let's see it."

"I was just about to let it go," Jay insisted.

"Come on, little buddy. Let me see that thing."

Norman Kitchen spoke now, and he spoke at a normal volume. I realized that he was petrified. "Show it to them, Jay."

"*J?* Is that your name, *J?*"

"Yeah, it's his name. Jay," I answered.

The blond boy shook his head with mock puzzlement. "But it's only one letter long. Hey, Terry."

"What, Ted?"

"What kind of name is only one letter long?"

Don't think it was lost upon me that they'd used each other's names. This signalled a reckless disregard—at least it always did on television, the cannier criminals wincing when their foolish henchman identified them. That neither of these kids winced had a double implication: 1) they were both kind of stupid and 2) they would probably have to kill us.

Ted looked us over, Norman and me. "What's you guys' names? Hey, you. What's your name?"

"My name is Norman!"

"That's a nice name. And you, with the glasses?"

"Phil."

"Jay, Norman and Phil." Ted drew ever closer, so close that the toes of his black running shoes stuck into the pond's watery muck. He extended his hand toward my brother. "So let me see the froggy thing, Jay."

Jay thought about this for a moment and then started toward the shore. "Look at it and let it go," he said quietly. Jay put the creature into Ted's extended hand and backed away.

Ted was, for a moment, startled by the sight of the little monster, possibly even terrified. But he managed to squelch this emotion; I suppose, given adult retrospection, that this was how Ted dealt with all of his emotions. He squelched them, and let them fester and infect somewhere down deep. "This thing," said Ted gravely, "is a freak. This thing should never have been born."

Terry picked up the cue. "Put it out of its misery."

"Good idea," nodded Ted. "I'm going to put it out of its misery." Ted curled his hand into a fist and tightened. We heard little bubbly sounds and a long kind of whistle, like a teakettle or something. Ted threw the remains over his shoulder and wiped his hand off on the backside of his blue jeans.

My brother said, "That was a bad thing to do."

"That?" Ted gestured with his head toward where he'd thrown the little corpse. "That was *nothing*."

Our bicycles lay a few feet away. Ted now wandered toward them, pointing a finger. "These your bikes, huh?" He saw the saddlebag behind my seat, noticed the bulging and asked, "What's in there?"

"Just some Cub stuff," I answered. "Nothing interesting."

Ted looked at me with those strange eyes. "Nothing interesting, huh?"

"Cub stuff," I repeated.

"Why don't you go away and leave us alone?" asked Jay, somewhat brazenly, I thought.

"But we're not *doing* anything," explained Ted with exaggerated patience. "We're just asking questions. We're being friendly."

"We're not *doing* anything," seconded Terry, although he couldn't contain a certain measure of malice.

"Let me see the Cub stuff," said Ted, bending over and unbuckling the saddlebag. He pulled out a piece of rope, about four feet long. "What's this for?"

None of us said anything. Ted found Norman Kitchen with his milky eyes. "Norman, I asked a question. What's this for?"

"It's for tying knots!"

"No kidding. Come here and show me how to tie a knot."

"I didn't get my badge yet!"

Ted turned his head toward me. "I bet you know how to tie knots, don't you, Phil?"

"He's good at it," said Jay. "He's the best in the whole pack." I'm not sure if he said this out of fraternal pride or if he was hoping that my mastery of knot-tying would somehow impress and alarm these guys and make them go away.

"Hey, Phil," said Terry. "Come here and tie a knot."

My mind was frantically trying to come up with some sort of plan, and in desperation it latched onto one.

"Okay," I agreed, "I'll tie a knot." I made a motion with my shoulder and waded up onto the bank. I turned around and saw that my shoulder-motion had been to no avail. "Guys," I said to my brother and Norman Kitchen, "let me show you this new one I've been working on."

They hesitated. I knew I could afford only so much encouragement, so I ventured one more sentence, evenly modulated and filled with enough big words to confuse Ted and Terry. "I'm going to do an ornamental knot, called the Four-Strand Sinnet."

"Okay!" Norman waddled out of the pond in a very ducklike fashion. I think he truly wanted to see me tie a Four-Strand Sinnet. Jay followed reluctantly. That kid should have watched more television.

"Okay," I said as they clustered near me. "Now, to do a Four-Strand Sinnet, I need four strands." I had plenty of rope in my saddlebag. I pulled out three more lengths and handed one to Jay, one to Norman. "You hold this one, you hold this one, I've got these two, right?"

"Right!"

"Right," agreed my brother.

"Now watch closely what I do." This was the hard part. Ted and Terry were standing some feet distant, so I turned to them and, quelling the urge to barf, said, "I thought you guys wanted to see this."

Terry came forward first, used to doing what he was told. Ted hung back momentarily, trying to size up the situation, but I think I'd befuddled him with that word "ornamental." He moved, and I immediately put my plan into action, because if I had waited even a moment I would have chickened out. As Ted came at me, I brought the rope up and gave it a snap. I had timed things perfectly; the end of the rope licked a welt across his cheek. It was painful enough that Ted covered his face with both hands and doubled over, and he howled as though mourning many deaths. Jay snapped his rope, too—we'd acquired the knack after bath times, using towels to cover each other with welts—but it didn't quite catch Terry. Terry grabbed Jay's sleeve, but luckily I was able to flick Terry on the ear, and he shrieked and let loose his grip and busied himself with self-inspection, reassuring himself that I hadn't flicked his ear clean off.

Norman Kitchen appeared to be still waiting for me to tie a Four-Strand Sinnet.

"Run!" I screamed, and we bolted for the pathway up above. But I should have known that pain, even intense pain, would incapacitate Ted and Terry for only the shortest of whiles. They were used to it, after all. They'd probably lived with it every day of their miserable lives.

They got Norman first, of course, and then they got Jay, and even though I had just about made it to the pathway, I had no choice but to turn around and go suffer with my brother.

"Okay," Ted said, staring at the three of us huddled together like tremulous sheep. Terry had acquired, almost magically, a stick perfectly shaped to serve as a truncheon, its only imperfection being a set of sharp nodes that increased its potency for rendering pain. He had not yet used this to strike any of us, but he let us know he was eager to, swinging the thing near us with such force that the air whistled.

"Okay," said Ted, "here's what's going to happen. Philly Four-Eyes is going to tie up Jay to that tree right there."

We stood in a small circular clearing, surrounded by trees. Ted had chosen one at random, but its selection seemed to please him. He went over and caressed the bark almost lovingly. "*This* tree."

Terry poked me in the stomach with his club. "Go, Four-Eyes."

"Our father is up there waiting for us," I lied desperately.

"That's not how it goes," said Ted. "It goes, *Our father who art in heaven*. Now, tie Jay to that tree or so help me I'll—"

"Norman," I whispered.

"What?"

"I'll tie Norman to that tree."

Ted considered this briefly. "Okay."

"No, tie me to the tree," said Jay, but no one seemed to hear him. Terry was already shepherding Norman to the chosen tree, digging the stick into the small of his back. Ted looked on with a half-smile upon his pale lips.

Norman immediately embraced the tree, an act that looked like cowardice and made both Ted and Terry snicker cruelly.

"No," said Ted, "move the Piggy around to the other side." Terry prodded Norman unnecessarily, as he was moving willingly, hugging the tree as though it were a lover, or mother. "Okay, Philly Four-Eyes, tie him up."

I took the length of rope and wrapped it around Norman's wrists. I looked at Norman with significance, and I remember noticing—with far more clarity than I remember anything else about the scene—that although his cheeks were red, his eyes were rimmed with tears and snot poured out of his nose, his beautiful golden hair was unaffected by the ordeal. "I'm going to tie an Irish Sheepshank," I said quietly. Because I'd already done so, I trusted that Ted and Terry would think that announcing the name of the knot was an intrinsic part of the process.

Norman Kitchen looked at me sadly. "I didn't get my badge yet," he whispered.

"An Irish Sheepshank," I repeated, and I executed the knot, throwing in a series of slipknots for the sake of appearance.

"Good," judged Ted. "Now Jay."

"No," I said, but Ted ignored me. He selected another tree. "There."

Terry lifted his cudgel to strike Jay and I said, "Okay, okay."

Jay put his arms around the tree, and I tied his hands together, and when Jay whispered, "What kind of knot?" I gave no answer.

"What kind of knot?" he whispered again. "Is it an Irish Sheepshank?"

"Hey, Terry," shouted Ted when I was done. "We better check that knot. Philly Four-Eyes is a tricky little bastard."

Terry took hold of the ropes and tugged at them with such force that Jay's wrists reddened and the skin ripped a little. "Seems good," he judged.

"Now what we want to do is tie Philly up to that tree there," announced Ted. His selection was based on triangulation. As Terry wrapped rope around my hand, and fortuitously managed a sound connection, I saw that if I moved my head to the right (the tree's bark tearing skin off that cheek) I could see Norman's tree; if I moved my head to the left, I could see Jay's.

Ted was breathing quietly but heavily, each inhalation ballooning his bony chest. "Okay. Let's see who's got the cutest bum."

Terry threw away his cudgel with evident irritation.

"Try Philly Four-Eyes first," Ted said, perhaps because of the alliterative quality of the sentence, perhaps because he knew I wouldn't have. I think Ted knew right from the get-go who had the cutest bum, but he wasn't about to let either me or my brother off the hook.

Terry came up behind me and yanked down my Cub shorts and my underwear in one motion. This was because I was a stocky lad, and my shorts were too tight, and when they popped away from my belly, my gotchies got caught by the suction. Terry caressed one of my cheeks, fleetingly, and said, "Philly Four-Eyes has an ugly butt."

And then he flicked the spectacles away from my face. Because they were held on by idiot hooks (curved half-bracelets of wire that wrapped around the back of the ear) this hurt quite a bit, and I hardly noticed as Ted came forward to do his own inspection.

"Yeah, you're right," said Ted. "That's a fucking ugly butt. Try the little guy."

Without my glasses, the world washed together. It looked like the mess in the big kindergarten sink after a spirited session of fingerpainting. I can only imagine: Jay's shorts fell to his ankles with just a slight tug from Terry; his underwear remained clinging to his waist the way a mountaineer clings to a rock face; and with another slight tug it joined the pile around his feet. I could hear Ted and Terry speak, mostly because they spoke loudly enough to ensure that I could.

"This one's not bad," said Ted.

"Not too bad."

"A little too bony, maybe."

"Yeah, yeah. A little too bony."

"Let's try Norman."

I can't imagine them pulling Norman's pants down. I mean, I'm incapable of it. I've used my imagination to fill in all the blank spots in the narrative so far, the holes in my memory drilled by time or corroded by alcohol. But this one is as black as pitch, although sometimes, late at night, I can hear Norman softly wailing.

Then Ted and Terry disappeared, wordlessly.

I listened as Norman's whimpering died away.

"Norman? Are you all right?"

He didn't answer, not until I'd called out his name two more times.

"What?"

"You can push your hands together, Norman. Push your hands together and grab the ropes. You can pull them off."

"Hey!" Norman shouted. "That's a good knot!" Then, very quietly, he said again: "I didn't get my badge yet."

———

"Hello?"

"Is this Norman Kitchen?"

"Yes?"

"Norman Kitchen?"

"Is this, um, Philip?"

"Yes! Yes, it's Phil. Philly Four-Eyes! How the fuck are you?"

"Well, I'm fine. I get the impression I'm decidedly better than you, Philip. You seem to be intoxicated. I am merely sleep-muzzied, because I was sleeping."

"I am not intoxicated. I have been working. Working on my novel."

"Mmm."

"But I need to know, I need to know, Norman, what did they *do* to you?"

"Yes. I know that's what you need to know, Philip. And I really wish I could help. You are not at peace."

"Well, fuck. I got a lot of problems, man. Ronnie, that's my wife, has thrown me out of the house, and I miss my kids, although I'm getting them tomorrow for the next three days, which will be great . . . Where was I?"

"Enumerating your problems."

"Right. And you probably heard about Edward Milligan, the star of *Padre*."

"I read about it in the newspapers."

"I was the executive producer of that show. I wrote that episode, that was my script . . ."

"It is a great loss. He was a very attractive man."

"I'm not saying you can save my life, I don't want to put that kind of pressure on you, Norm, but it would really help me—I'm pretty sure it would help me—if I just knew what the hell they did to you."

"I understand. But, Philip, we've been through this. I do not know."

"Like, your memory is a blank? You blacked out, kind of thing?"

"No. That is not what I mean. What I mean is—and I'd ask you kindly to remember this in future—I am not *that* Norman Kitchen."

"What?"

"You should make an annotation in your telephone directory. 'Not the right Norman.' Something along those lines."

"You mean, your name is Norman Kitchen, but you're not really Norman Kitchen?"

"That is exactly what I mean."

"Are you *related* to Norman Kitchen?"

"Look, Philip. It's three-thirty in the morning. You told me that your children are coming to stay with you tomorrow. Wouldn't it be wise to get a little sleep?"

"It sure would be, Norman. I have to pick them up at seven-thirty."

"So then."

"Okay. You're probably right."

"Probably."

"You . . . you're a nice guy, Norman Kitchen."

"So you say. Every time you telephone."

"Good night."

"Good night, Philip. Sweet dreams."

2 | THE MEMORY

YOU KNOW, THE MEMORY IS A FUNNY THING. I KNOW THAT'S A FAIRLY glib statement, but it's four o'clock in the morning, and if one can't be glib in the dead of night, when exactly can one? So I'll persist in my ruminations re the memory and its funniness. Here's how funny it is: I didn't really remember the incident down in the ravine until I was in my mid-twenties.

One night away back when, my brother and I met for a drink. Jay was having trouble with his first wife, Leora. (He has had two since.) The trouble he was having was that he suspected her of infidelity, even though she was to my mind incapable of such a thing. (Jay had the same problem with his subsequent wives, although they were both more capable.) Leora was utterly devoted to Jay and greeted even my most innocent, imbecilic grins as unwanted advances. I know what you're thinking, maybe she found other men more attractive, but I will tell you exactly what I told Jay . . .

"You're nuts. You're fucking *nuts*."

"But she goes out of the house all the time."

"Jay, Leora is a professional cellist, remember?"

Jay surrounded a beer glass with his hand and lifted it to his mouth. He made the beer disappear. Then he lit a cigarette, and blasted a simoon of smoke into my face.

"And you are a pianist." At this point, Jay still had thoughts of a career in concert and recital halls. "You both have to practise. Now, it is easier for Leora to move her cello than for you to move your piano. *Ergo,* she leaves the house."

"*Ergo* fuck yourself."

I should touch on the subject of failure here, as it is near to my heart.

Jay still had thoughts of a career in concert and recital halls, although, at the same time, he was as intent on scuppering that career as Captain Ahab was on nailing the great white fucker. Jay was either late or a total no-show at the smaller venues—church basements and school auditoria—leaving scores of blue-haired women pissed off. (I imagine these dowagers owing to a remark he once made. As a lad of seventeen, he won a competition playing Edward Elgar's own transcription of his *Enigma Variations.* The prize was a trip to London, England, to perform before the Elgar Society. Jay actually appeared, in that instance, although from all reports he was shit-faced. Anyway, upon his return, he said, "There are two kinds of women who belong to the Elgar Society. Women who knew Sir Edward, and women who look like him.") When he did get slightly bigger chances—performing the Ravel piano concerto with the Kitchener-Waterloo Symphony, say—he showed up, and even comported himself well. He may have had a drink or three too many before stepping onto the stage, and once he stumbled and lurched into the concertmaster, knocking the toupée from that man's head. Remarkably, Jay still managed to achieve a level of success and was offered both a recording contract and the opportunity to play at Roy Thomson Hall with the Toronto Symphony. Again, the piece was to be the Ravel, which I often hear as the soundtrack to our sorry lives. I hear the frantic third movement as I imagine bicycling down the decline into the ravine. Anyway, before any of that could happen, Jay got drunk and—once more damning Leora for her infidelity—smashed his fist into a wall, breaking his right ring finger in the process.

After that, it was piano bars.

"But Leora, she just wouldn't, there's no way on god's green earth . . . ," I said.

"The thing with you, Phil, is you just can't see how *bad* people are."

"I know they're bad but, geez, when you consider some of things *I* do . . ."

"But think about it. Think about those two guys down in the ravine."

You don't need to open the door all the way to know you don't want to see what's lurking inside the closet. So I slammed it shut and demanded, "Proof? Do you have any physical evidence?"

"If I had physical evidence, I wouldn't be sitting here getting drunk with you."

Oh, I thought, this is going to work. He's going to forget he ever mentioned any two fucking guys down in any fucking ravine.

"You can't just accuse a lovely, caring—"

"Their names," said Jay, "were Ted and Terry."

"Their names were Tom and Tony."

And the monster ripped out from behind the curtain and shook its ass in my face.

Jay and I spent the rest of that night piecing the story together. The rendition I gave above is more his than mine. My contributions were, for the most part, odd details. I remembered, vividly, how Norman's hair, his lovely blond curls, remained unaltered during the ordeal.

Some of the story my brother and I decided might never be known.

"What did they do, exactly," we both asked aloud, "to Norman Kitchen?"

"Fuck off."

"How did you know it was me?"

"Fuck off."

"Look, there is no reason we can't have a conversation like two adult human beings."

"Hmm, perhaps you're right—no you're not, fuck off."

"But if you would only tell me why you're so mad at me."

"Fuck off."

"It seems to have something to do with my marriage breaking up, but that can't be right, I mean, you've managed to ruin *three* marriages . . ."

"Fuck off."

"Did it ever occur to you that I might need like a friend, a confidant, a shoulder to cry on, a *brother*, right now?"

"Fuck off."

" *You* fuck off."

"All right. Bye-bye."

3 | THE TELEVISION

IN A SENSE, THIS BOOK IS BEING WRITTEN BY A BOY WHO WATCHED TOO much television. That is the most salient point about me, I think, that for some astounding length of accumulated time—ten of my nearly fifty years, maybe, a fifth of my life—I have sat in front of a television set, my face bombarded by electrons, my mouth hanging slightly agape. Mind you, I have managed to become well-read and my friends consider me quite a film fanatic. This all goes to show how little of my life I have actually spent having anything resembling human contact.

So then, the television. Here's how it all began.

I remember the front door yawing open and my Uncle Johnny backing through. He was a large, square man and seemed to not comfortably fit through the opening. The impression of squareness was exacerbated by the black overcoat he wore, which was huge at the shoulders and draped like a tombstone. Uncle Johnny craned his head around, both to locate the little riser that led from the mud room to the kitchen and to herald, in a booming voice, his gift. "Who ordered one deluxe television set?"

My mother and I were in the kitchen. Here's how the two of us prepared dinner: my mother smoked a long cigarette (her lipstick staining the last quarter-inch of the filter) and drank a tall drink (little half-kisses adorned the rim) and read a novel (she'd broken the spine, even though it was a library book) that lay on the kitchen counter. There was a pot on the element, boiling merrily, and there were macaroni noodles in that pot, and it was my job to spear one occasionally and test its toothiness. I would eat a noodle, count thirty steamboats and eat another. I was at about twenty-three steamboats when Uncle Johnny backed in.

"Who ordered one deluxe television set?"

"Hmm," went my mother, and she pressed her cigarette out in a standing ashtray she kept always by her side, as though it were life-support. "I suppose that would be us."

I extracted a piece of macaroni and shoved it into my mouth. I was diligent back then, and almost always hungry. It was eight o'clock at night, far past the hour when normal families ate dinner.

Uncle Johnny kept backing up the little flight of stairs, and I saw that he hugged to his chest a burnished wooden box that held a dark glass eye. I had, of course, seen television sets before (all of the neighbours owned one) but never, I don't know, held aloft or something. The image of this television, obscured as it was by my uncle's broad back, burned itself into my eyes. Even now I can see the dial and read the numbers; I can remember wondering why there was no "1."

Having achieved the kitchen, Uncle Johnny turned left and headed for the living room. That's all there was to the ground floor of my childhood home, a kitchen and a living room. As the television turned, I saw that Uncle Johnny's assistant in the moving process was my Aunt Jane, a tiny woman who was surprisingly strong.

My mother moved forward and, although I'm certain she only meant to assist her sister-in-law, what she did in fact was shoulder Aunt Jane into the wall, quickly grabbing the back end of the television set before it plummeted to the ground.

I fished out another piece of macaroni. The noodles were ready, so I turned off the heat and moved the pot aside. I knew that by the time cheese arrived (my mother was distracted enough without there being an actual distraction) the noodles would be mush. Unless I drained the noodles right then, in which case they would be cold. Either way, it was going to be another typical family meal, inedible to everyone but a stout little lad such as myself.

"Hi, Philip," said Aunt Jane.

My Aunt Jane made me nervous. It was almost as though I knew that in five years she was going to be the first woman I ever saw naked. (I barged into the washroom at their home on Christmas Day; Aunt Jane was staring at her denuded self in the full-length mirror. I'll never know why she was naked in the afternoon with a turkey roasting in the oven, but it was a fine gift to give a thirteen-year-old boy.) I stirred uneasily and said, "Hi," but I am not certain that any sound came out.

"We've brought you a television set," said Aunt Jane, which was the kind of declarative statement she favoured. She had tiny features that were clustered together near the centre of her face.

"Not just any television set," shouted Uncle Johnny from the living room, "but a goddam *deluxe* television set!"

Through the service bay, I could see that my mother and her brother had placed the set in the farthest corner, beside the sliding glass doors that opened onto the backyard. My mother took a step back and held her hand to her chin; something, clearly, was not right. Uncle Johnny held the electrical cord in one hand and was searching for some place to plug it in.

It occurred to my mother what was amiss, and she returned to the kitchen for her free-standing ashtray. She saw that the pot's boiling had been quieted, so she took a moment to hurl the noodles into the waiting colander.

A cold meal, then. *Fine*.

My uncle had spied a power source deep in the room's corner, and his wide keister was occupying much of the shadow over there as, on hands and knees, he poked around with the plug and tried to make a connection. I don't know why our living room was so gloomy, especially since almost all of one wall was made up of the sliding glass doors. It's not as though outside there were towering buildings, or even other modest houses, plunging our home into shadow. Past our backyard was a ditch and a field that spread out in all directions. To the left there was the schoolhouse, to the right the church, but they were both hundreds of yards distant. Why sunlight never managed to light our pale green carpeting is something of a mystery.

Uncle Johnny straightened up laboriously (he'd been a football star in high school, but this hardly rendered him limber in his adulthood; his body was possessed by cramps and creaks) and turned a knob. After a crisp click, a tiny dot of light, about the size of a dime, appeared on the dark oval of glass. I held my breath and waited. Then I exhaled and held my breath again. Then let it out. The tiny dot of light seemed to have little intention of becoming anything larger.

Uncle Johnny brought the heel of his hand down upon the cherrywood housing and the dot blossomed, its soft black edges pushing outward to the rim of the glass. Inside the oval of light there was a figure, indistinct and wavering. The man (even though the television screen was absolutely grey, there was darkness enough to suggest a black suit) spoke in a voice cluttered with static, but I heard, and I remember, what he said. "You are entering another dimension of time and space . . ."

"Hey," said my mother, "this thing works better than I thought it would."

"Hold on," said Uncle Johnny, and he reached into the pocket of his overcoat and removed a pair of rabbit ears. I guess it says something about my uncle and his dimensions that he could produce one of these portable antennae in this surprising and wizardly manner. He placed the plastic base on top of the console and went behind the set to do the wiring. I peeked around to see what he was up to. I don't remember leaving the kitchen for the living room—I guess I'd moved forward in a sort of trance.

My uncle was removing two screws from a little brass plate at the back with his thumbnail, huge and chipped and stained yellow by the cigarettes he smoked hoodlum-style. Then he positioned the metal u's at the end of the antenna's wiring and drove the screws back in.

The image of the man suddenly hove into focus. He was weedy and sallow and had dark shellacked hair. Despite his elegant black suit, he, like my uncle, smoked his cigarette hoodlum-style, squeezed between thumb and index finger, the ember pointed palmward.

"Submitted for your approval," said this man, "'Time Enough at Last.'"

All right, there are a number of ways to proceed here, at least three different areas that must be covered, and while a better writer might be able to continue forward in a linear manner, juggling them all, I'm just not up to it.

So in a blocky and unimaginative form, here are the three things you should hear about.

The television show was *The Twilight Zone*, a continuing series of one-offs (excuse the argot), strange and twisted fictions largely written by the man in the black suit, Rod Serling. I think Serling is one of the great dramatists of the twentieth century—at least, I have made this claim at various industry seminars, and I have supported the claim by belligerently (usually drunkenly) refusing to brook any argument. But there is something to it. Even ignoring some of his wonderful long-form stuff (*Requiem for a Heavyweight*, for example), many of the episodes of *The Twilight Zone* have made lasting impressions. Ask anyone over a certain age to name their favourite, and it will be quickly forthcoming. Rainie van der Glick was always very partial to an episode entitled "The Eye of the Beholder," which featured a woman whose entire face was swathed in post-plastic-surgery bandaging. Doctors surround the woman (we see them only from the back, or hidden by shadow) and, as they cut away the gauze, they wonder and hope aloud about the success of the operation. The bandages are removed to reveal a woman of stunning beauty; the doctors and nurses are then shown to be hideously deformed. And, of course, the medical people are repulsed, because beauty is in . . .

"Time Enough at Last" is likewise a famous episode, starring Burgess Meredith, who plays Henry Bemis, a meek bank teller and bibliophile. Reading constitutes the whole of this man's life and passion. He resents even the most innocent demands on his time, and can't wait for lunchtime, when he can escape to the huge vault with his bagged lunch. (Henry is also burdened with a shrewish wife, something I am a little hesitant to bring up, for reasons that may make themselves clear.) Anyway, Henry is in the vault one afternoon when suddenly he is rendered unconscious by shock waves. When he comes around, he discovers that the world has been destroyed by a hydrogen bomb (and such was the temper of those times that this little plot point struck no one in our living room as particularly unlikely). Bemis stumbles around in the debris, mournful and despairing. Suddenly, though, his face lights up—he spots a library and realizes that finally he has "time enough at last," i.e., nothing to do but read, read, read.

Serling, of course, is a master of the plot-twist, so the story is not quite over. Before I relate the dramatic irony—the ghost of Rod Serling would not want me to spill the beans too quickly—I want to write about how my Uncle Johnny enhanced the reception by using his wife as a human antenna. He spun the little dial on the front of the rabbit ears and pulled the metal rods in various directions, but found that it was awkward to both do this and judge the results—whenever he let go of the rods the picture would revert to its bleak snowiness. He therefore told Aunt Jane to hold onto the antennae, and he instructed her on how to move them. When the reception was as good as it could get, he snapped, "Stay there! Don't move." My aunt was beside and slightly behind the television set, her trunk twisted awkwardly. She couldn't see the show, and would regularly ask, "What's going on now?" We took turns answering her, although none of us was very helpful. My uncle grunted, my mother was always waiting for additional information and I was pretty much engrossed.

Through this oval piece of glass was another world, I discovered. It was indistinct and it was in black and white, but it was a magical place. I was also drawn by one specific aspect of this episode of *The Twilight Zone*, namely, that the Burgess Meredith character was burdened by thick spectacles—as I had been since the age of three. When those fuckwits in the ravine called me "Philly Four-Eyes" they were coming as close as they could to a kind of forbearance, even mercy, because my corrective lenses, which were as thick as pucks and housed in what looked like welder's goggles, made me look distinctly freakish. I thought it was intriguing that the man on the television wore cumbersome glasses. And herein lies Rod Serling's little narrative trick. When Henry Bemis, who has arranged hundreds of books on the bombed-out library steps, bends over to pick one up, the spectacles slip from the bridge of his nose and smash on the ground below. Suddenly the post-apocalyptic world is nothing but a blur.

"Son of a bitch," muttered my uncle.

"What's going on?" asked Aunt Jane.

"Well, that's no good," said my mother, lighting one cigarette from another and grinding out the spent butt in the ashtray.

"What's no good?" asked Aunt Jane.

"*That.*" My mother gestured as the credits rolled. "The story was just about to get interesting."

"What do you mean?" asked my uncle.

"Well, the way it ends now, it's just about hopelessness. About the death of hope. But there's always hope. Right, Philip?"

I shrugged.

"I'm telling you there is. He could, I don't know, find some pieces of glass and grind some lenses himself. You know what? He could check all the corpses until he found one wearing some glasses that would work."

"Maybe all the glasses got destroyed in the nuclear war," suggested Uncle Johnny.

"What nuclear war?" asked Aunt Jane.

"Maybe, but he'd better go check. Check all the dead bodies for appropriate spectacles."

My mother shrugged and headed back to the kitchen. She took her ashtray with her. Apparently she was done with the television set.

———

"Van der . . . Glick?"

"Ah. McQuidgey."

"One thing I can count on, you never give me grief for waking you up."

"'Cause I don't sleep. Sleep is for the innocent, the pure of heart."

"You and I, Rainie, run on heavy fuels."

"So what's up? To what do I owe the honour of this telephone call?"

"I don't know. Just wanted to say hello, I guess."

"You didn't."

"Huh?"

"You didn't say hello."

"Oh. Hey, I know why I called. Fact-checking. Name your favourite episode of *The Twilight Zone*."

"I know you want me to say the what-the-fuck 'The Eye of the Beholder,' because it was my favourite when I was thirteen and feeling more than a trifle hideous, but you know, I have managed to acquire a small modicum of self-esteem. So, I'm going to think about it for a moment and in the meantime I'm going to ask you, why have you not called me in a year?"

"It hasn't been a year."

"It's been a while, Phil. It's been at least a few months."

"Has it? It never seems like it to me, because I hear you all the time, I mean, I listen to your show."

"I had to read in the newspapers about what happened to Milligan."

"Milligan happened to Milligan."

"Is that your official stance?"

"Hmm?"

"I'm just wondering if that's a position you've taken for reasons of legality, you know, distancing yourself from the event, or if somehow that's what you believe."

"I'm not following. What is what I somehow believe?"

"That you had nothing to do with it."

"Milligan was unstable."

"In the land of the crippled, the one-legged man is king."

"You've been drinking."

"*You've* been drinking."

"Touché."

"It was just so odd. I mean, it was exactly like in that stupid movie, you know. 'The Cross and the Bullet.'"

"'The Bullet and the Cross.'"

"I got goosebumps and could practically hear the spooky Theramin thing, a-woo-oo . . ."

"Could we change the subject?"

"What are you going to do now?"

"I'm finally going to write that novel."

"Oh, yeah. I remember you mentioning that once. You were about *eight*."

"Right."

"About what?"

"What?"

"What's the book about?"

"About . . . me."

"Uh-huh. What about you?"

"Lots of things. My life. You see, something happened when I was a boy . . ."

"Right. You felt me up."

"No, not that, there was this *incident* . . . I felt you up?"

"You were demonstrating wrestling manoeuvres. You were showing me moves by Sweet Daddy Siki and Whipper Billy Watson. You took the opportunity to grab my left tit. At least, that's what you thought. You actually had hold of some foam rubber and a wad of toilet paper, but you popped a boner just the same, and you stopped the wrestling demonstration abruptly."

"I don't remember any of this."

"Well, I suspected it never made the highlight film. So, Phil. When were you going to tell me about your marriage breaking up?"

"Oh, I don't know. In a couple of minutes, I guess. I thought what might happen was that I'd say I'm writing a book, and you'd ask why, and I'd say how I wanted to explain to people—to Currer and Ellis, anyway—who I am. Why I am the way I am. And you'd ask me why I wanted to do that, and then I thought I'd slip in the whole marriage breaking up thing. How did you hear about it?"

"Fuck, are you thick. Ronnie told me, asshole."

"You must not think very highly of me."

"Did you ever notice, Phil, that the more personal, the more *intimate* a conversation becomes, the way you talk gets poncier and poncier?"

"I hadn't noticed, actually."

"There!"

"Okay, you heard about it from Ronnie, therefore—"

"Therefore I want to hear your side of the story."

"Oh."

"Why don't you come over for dinner sometime?"

"Sure. I'm not sure when would be the best night. I have the kids for a couple of days."

"Sunday night?"

"What?"

"Sunday night. We'll have dinner. We'll talk. I'll listen to your side of the story. If you play your cards right, I'll let you have another crack at my left tit. You missed it in its prime, no use denying that, but it's still got a little resiliency left."

"Okay. I mean, okay about the dinner."

"Remember where I live?"

"Yeah."

"Be here at eight o'clock. Bring wine. I'll cook."

"Okay."

"It's what you need."

"What?"

"I just remembered my other favourite *Twilight Zone* episode. 'What You Need.' Remember? The old guy with the matches and the shoelaces and all that shit?"

"Right, right."

"The old guy would look into people's eyes and then he'd give them, you know, spot remover or something. *It's . . . what you need.* And then a little later they'd get mustard on their jacket or something . . ."

"Sure. That actually never happened, I mean, you've conflated some of the story elements."

"You know me. Little Miss Conflation."

"So, I'll see you Sunday."

"Hello, Phil."

"Yeah. Hello."

4 | THE BROTHER

JAY WAS NOT AT HOME WHEN UNCLE JOHNNY AND AUNT JANE DELIVERED the television set. I'm not certain where he was. I guess it is unreasonable to assert that a six-year-old boy was simply "out," but my brother was away from the house far more than he was inside it. Sometimes, weather and sunlight permitting, he was allowed to roam free. Other times neighbours had custody of him. Jay had adopted the Plums, a huge and highly dysfunctional clan, as a kind of parallel family. Ostensibly this was because of his fast friendship with the stuttering little Polly Plum, but I knew that Jay could barely tolerate her. He liked instead to be in the company of Ray Plum, a vicious, predatory preteen. Jay even preferred the companionship of the astoundingly elderly Mr. Fenton, who was as near death as one can come and still retain a little heat. But history has informed us that what Jay truly enjoyed about the Plum household was the presence of the hulking upright piano standing in the corner of the living room. The first time he struck a key was probably mere whim, perhaps even an accident, but the next time Jay drifted near the instrument he hit two, first sequentially and then simultaneously, and noted the relationship. And from that moment on he was hooked—music was the whistling monkey on his back. So Polly Plum shared her lessons; the vicious Ray taught him some show-offy knucklebusters, because Ray was musical despite himself; and the ancient Mr. Fenton introduced Jay to the music of the masters, especially the French school that included Satie, Ravel and Debussy.

At any rate, when Jay returned my mother rushed him upstairs and stuck him into a bath and then into bed. Jay was always begrimed and besmirched and my mother could bathe him in a trice, managing a cigarette, drink and novel all at the same time.

Then Jay was put into the top bunk (I wouldn't sleep up there, fearful that I might topple out) and, after a moment of silence, I told him about the show I'd seen.

"*The Trilight Zone?*" he repeated.

"Not *trilight*, *twilight*." Trilights were a recent innovation back then, you know, a single light bulb that with three successive turns of the switch goes from dim to very bright. That is why Jay thought the show might be called *The Trilight Zone*, but it doesn't explain why, forty years later, he still believes that to be the case.

Then I told him the plot of "Time Enough at Last," and he agreed it was a good story, although I could tell the point was lost on him. He couldn't read, and had no notion that the activity was worthwhile in any way.

Jay didn't get around to the television set until the next afternoon. But when I woke up, as soon as I was done eating cereal, I went into the living room and twisted the little knob, cracking open the ball of light. I waited many long moments for it to explode across the screen; when it failed to do that, I imitated my Uncle Johnny, rapping the top of the console with the heel of my hand. "Out of the western sky . . .," sang a voice. Those of you of a certain age may remember *Sky King*. That show made me desperately want to be a pilot, to own a little plane so that I could fly out of the western sky. Next there was *Fury*, which was

about a horse and the boys who owned it. That show made me desperately want to own a horse, to live on a small ranch, to dress in white
and wear a cowboy hat. I changed my desire with each successive
show—what didn't change was the degree of desperation involved.

There were more shows, but I believe I've mentioned the soggi-
ness of my memory. Besides, from that point forward I watched
thousands of hours of television programming. It filled me up as rain
fills a barrel, my point being, there is no possibility of, or usefulness
in, trying to distinguish the individual drops. It is worth noting, I
think, that my favourite show was *The Twilight Zone*, which invited
me week after week to enter another dimension of time and space,
something I was ever willing to do.

That first morning drifted into afternoon—television screws around
with time in a big way, spreading moments over hours, compressing
months and years into foggy little clumps—and then Jay entered the
living room. I was lying on my belly, my hands cupping my chin, my
head heavy with the first batch of television-wrought mush. Jay
placed a foot on my back in order to cross to the set, but he was so
slight I only grunted. He reached out and twisted the dial, sending
the television through its frequencies. He didn't pause long enough
on any station to see what it was broadcasting, merely spun the dial
and watched the light spark and sputter. But then he reversed to
channel four and stepped away from the set.

"Coming up to bat," said a voice, "Mickey Mantle."

"Mickey Mantle," repeated my brother. I should mention that
neither Jay nor I was a baseball fan, but we knew that name. Mantle
was fabled, legendary, one of the gods that ruled in the huge land
across the great lake.

We watched as Mickey Mantle took three ill-timed swipes at
three pitches. He intended to put one out of Yankee Stadium, but

looked as incapable of doing so as, well, me. After the umpire's understated "You're out," Mantle dropped the bat and wandered back to the dugout, his head hung in shame.

Jay reached forward and switched off the television. He walked through the sliding doors and disappeared into the world. I waited quite a few minutes before turning the set back on.

I was willing to forgive the television; for me it was still the messenger of magic. But to Jay it was the great destroyer of same. I'm fairly certain that he never watched television again. I'm only "fairly certain" because it seems an almost absurd assertion to make, doesn't it, in this day and age? One would have to be a locust-consuming hermit to have nothing to do with television. But I can't recall Jay ever sitting beside me to watch the thing, even when I implored him to. Although sometimes, as we lay in our bunk beds at night, he would encourage me to tell him the story of some of the shows I had consumed during the day. I suspect that in a way this helped me later on, professionally. I acquired at a very early age a sound narrative sense; I knew when my audience's (audient's) attention was flagging, I learned how to milk tension. ("Then what happened?" Jay would demand from the bunk above. I would wait a few moments before speaking, and then my voice would issue forth dramatically. "You want to know what happened? I'll tell you what happened . . .") I know that Jay, as an adult, has never owned a set. Mind you, he is and ever was materially impoverished. But I have money, more than I know what to do with, really—I have offered to purchase him a television on more than one occasion. "Fuck off" is his usual response.

"Why not?" I countered, the last time the exchange was had.

"Well," said my younger brother, "just look at what television has done to you."

"Fuck off."

"I figured it out. You're mad because I got involved in the television industry. You fucking snob. You snoot. Just because you play the *grawnd* piano, you think that anyone involved with a popular, a popul*ist* medium, is beneath your contempt. If you knew anything at all, anything about *anything* except the fucking piano, you'd know that the great artists, Shakespeare and Beethoven, wrote for the common man and woman, using what were, for the time, the mass media. Well, screw you, baby. *Screw you*."

"That's not why I'm mad."

"Oh."

"Fuck off."

5 | BIRDS OF A FEATHER

I HAVE A FRIEND WHO IS A NOVELIST—PERHAPS YOU HAVE HEARD OF him, John Hooper. He has just published a new novel, *Baxter*. I know this because I received an invitation to the book launch, which you couldn't pay me to attend. When I say "friend" I mean that we hate each other pretty much, but are bound together by history. We met in university and were both involved in the theatre there. It was through John Hooper that I met Veronica Lear. I place this fact high on the list of reasons why I hate him. (I'm joking, if badly. I loved, I love, Ronnie. But on nights like this one—it is three-fifteen a.m., the little computer is overheated, my wineglass has left ghostly rings on the tabletop—it is hard to remember that my marriage was ever a good thing.)

So I'll transcribe, with all the fidelity I can muster, the conversation I had with him last night, and see if you don't hate him, too. If you don't mind, I'll do it in a style I am more at home with, or as John would put it, placing his hand over his face (his impulse is to adjust his spectacles, even though he doesn't wear any), in a style with which I am more at home.

INT. LOUNGE—NIGHT

McQUIGGE sits with HOOPER at a little table. The
place is nearly empty. A few pallid drinkers. A couple
in the corner, arguing about the circumstances under
which they met. The WAITRESS is young, sexy. She
brings drinks over to their table, two tumblers
of whiskey.

In the room's darkest corner, a man plays the piano.
He plays very beautifully.

              McQUIGGE
    So? What did you think?

              HOOPER
    It's good.

              McQUIGGE
    Is it really?

              HOOPER
    No.

McQUIGGE drinks his drink.

            HOOPER (cont'd)
    It starts well enough. I liked
    the ruffian stuff, the rape.
    Gripping. Not too badly written.
    Then, suddenly, there's pages

and pages about a television
set.

McQUIGGE

I never said Kitchen was raped.

HOOPER

Well, what happened to him?

McQUIGGE

I don't know. *Something*.

HOOPER

Ah. The famous McQuigge story-
sense.

McQUIGGE

I couldn't see. My glasses had
been knocked off my face.

HOOPER

You lose quite a bit of narrative momentum if your mate
wasn't actually raped.

McQUIGGE

My "mate"? Why do you say
things like that, Hooper?
You're not English.

                    HOOPER
Don't go on the attack, Philip.
I'm trying to help you with
your book.

                    McQUIGGE
And anyway, those pages and
pages aren't *just* about the
television set.

                    HOOPER
They absolutely are.

                    McQUIGGE
I wanted to write about the
other people in my family. My
mother. My brother.

                    HOOPER
Ah, yes. Your weird little
brother.

                    McQUIGGE
That's him over there, you
know.

                    HOOPER
Where?

                    McQUIGGE
Playing the piano.

HOOPER swings around in his seat. He watches the
piano player for a little while and then focuses his
attention on the WAITRESS, who is young, sexy.

> HOOPER
>
> He's pretty good.

> McQUIGGE
>
> He's great.

> HOOPER
>
> What's that song he's playing?
> It sounds familiar.

> McQUIGGE
>
> Hmm . . . "Waltzing Matilda."

> HOOPER
>
> It is?

HOOPER listens briefly, without taking his attention
away from the WAITRESS, who is young, sexy.

> HOOPER (cont'd)
>
> No it's not.

> McQUIGGE
>
> Sure it is.
> (singing along)

Once a jolly swagman sat beside
the whatever it was . . .

The WAITRESS, quite rightly, frowns at HOOPER. He
redirects his attention to the PIANO PLAYER.

                    HOOPER
        Is he, is your brother crying?

                    McQUIGGE
        Yes.

                    HOOPER
        Why?

                    McQUIGGE
        I think because the song is too
        beautiful.

                    HOOPER
        You didn't say hello to him or
        anything when we came in here.

                    McQUIGGE
        He's not talking to me. He's
        mad at me.

                    HOOPER
        Why?

                    McQUIGGE
        I think because I fucked up my

life. Can we talk about my
novel?

                    HOOPER
It's not a novel. There's no
kind of thematic unity. I mean,
there's kids getting terror-
ized, then you start going on
about the television set.

                    McQUIGGE
The television was important,
well, significant in my life.

                    HOOPER
You know, I think the novel,
the *form*, is sacred. *Sacred*.

HOOPER repeats this word too loudly, in hopes that
the WAITRESS will be somehow impressed that he is
speaking about sacred things. And, in fact, the
WAITRESS is, which is yet another reason why
McQUIGGE hates HOOPER.

                    HOOPER (cont'd)
You were seduced by the novel's
sexier—and less bright—sisters.
By the theatre. By television.
So why you now think that you're
capable of writing one is, well,
I feel that it's unreasonable.

                    McQUIGGE
          Okay. I'll take out some of the
          stuff about the television.

                    HOOPER
          Your brother's mad at you for
          fucking up things with Ronnie,
          do you mean?

                    McQUIGGE
          I think so.

                    HOOPER
          There is no man alive who could *not*
          have fucked things up with Ronnie.
          You made it, what, twelve?—

                    McQUIGGE
          Thirteen.

                    HOOPER (cont'd)
          —years, which is a testament
          to your patience and fortitude.
          Oh, hi, what is it, Amy?

HOOPER reads the name tag on the WAITRESS's shirt
correctly.

                    WAITRESS
          You don't often hear that word
          "sacred" in this place.

McQUIGGE

He says that the novel is a
sacred form and that I am violating it.

WAITRESS

Are you?

McQUIGGE

Probably.

WAITRESS

You should stop, then.

McQUIGGE

But it's all I have. All I have
left in my life is this idea, this
notion, that I can write a book.
About my life, and how I lost it.

WAITRESS

You should keep at it, then.

HOOPER

There's a lot in his book about
a television.

McQUIGGE

But the television is important, because I ended up working in television.

                    WAITRESS
        You work in television?

                    McQUIGGE
        I used to.

                    WAITRESS
        What show?

                    McQUIGGE
        Padre.

The WAITRESS reacts.

                    WAITRESS
        That guy, what's his name . . . ?

                    McQUIGGE
        Edward Milligan.

                    WAITRESS
        He was cute.

All right, enough. Although we stayed for more drinks, very little got said after that. Hooper left fairly early, claiming he had a rendezvous with, I forget what, a diplomat or a runway model or something, some international woman of intrigue, possibly even a secret agent.

I stayed on in the lounge until the bitter end. By that point my brother had given up any pretense of playing popular tunes; he'd moved on to the French composers he so adores, Satie, Fauré and Poulenc. Ravel's *Pavane for a Dead Princess* was a crowd pleaser—

Jay became completely undone. It was not so much that he wept, because he'd been weeping, on and off but mostly on, all evening. But the *Pavane* caused his hands to tremble (although he missed or flubbed no notes) and his chest to heave. His head jerked convulsively; sometimes its sheer weight made it plummet, and once or twice he came within an inch of knocking himself unconscious on the keyboard.

Then, with a quick little flourish full of mordents and pralltrillers, *Good evening, friends!!,* he was done.

There was a smattering of applause, but Jay rose without acknowledging it and disappeared into the shadows. I know that he backed through a small doorway and mounted a flight of stairs to a little apartment above the lounge. There he lay down on a small bed. He rested his heavy head upon a thin pillow and waited for sleep to come.

Myself, I went home and dreamt of Milligan.

In my dream, Milligan is dressed in his Westernized garb, a beaded buckskin jacket over his soutane, a large white stetson over the golden curls. His boots are made from snakeskin, his blue jeans flared slightly to fit over them. Otherwise, his denims are so tight that he seems to have been vacuum-packed into them.

It is not all that odd that I dreamt Milligan this way, because 1) I was dreaming, after all, and 2) he dressed in wardrobe a lot, even when he wasn't due on set for hours, even when he was nowhere near the studio. On occasion he even went out to the bars dressed that way. He'd check his belt and holster, assuring the bouncers that the guns were merely replicas, although that wasn't *always* true. Edward Milligan had a vast collection, revolvers of a mostly historical significance, from the Old West circa 1880. In my dream, Milligan and I are down in his rumpus room, and it is a very strange place. Mounted vintage revolvers cover three of the walls, the fourth wall is a huge plasma television screen. The broadcast image is of a group of naked women going at each other with huge strap-on dildos. They have smaller dildos, too, which they use to penetrate smaller orifices. The rumpus room contains a well-stocked bar, well-stocked to the extent that it contains things like *árbol de los brujos*, or sorcerer's tree, and various exotic fungi. All of the horizontal surfaces—the bar top, a coffee table, a few shelves—are mirrored, the better for their employ as conveyors of cocaine.

Now, I want to admit to you, this isn't *all* dreamt up. Indeed, it is a fairly accurate depiction of Milligan's rumpus room, which I had occasion to visit a couple of times. The only thing that may be a little fanciful is that I don't think his bar actually had any *árbol de los brujos*, because that particular hallucinogenic concoction is a little hard to come by. (The only reason I've even heard of it is that Milligan often bemoaned the fact that it was extremely rare and oh-so-illegal.)

Okay, so there we are in the rumpus room and Milligan has taken some guns from the wall, and he is demonstrating his quick-draw and gun-spinning techniques. This is something of a lost art, you know. We often saw it as youngsters, sitting in the gloomy plush of the Galaxy Odeon (you shall hear more of the Galaxy Odeon, indeed, it's coming right up). Cowboy heroes, even though their lives were on the line, would often take a few nanoseconds to orbit their revolvers around their trigger fingers, first this way, then that, before popping off a lethal round. Milligan was excellent at this. He is demonstrating his technique, high on *árbol de los brujos*, and I have guns, too, and then (it's a dream) I start shooting. I shoot at the plasma screen, and naked women start to scream and to bleed. I'm not aiming the guns, but every bullet I fire seems to find a perfect trajectory. The bottles behind the bar explode with a stately rhythm, pop-pop-pop!! Milligan doesn't seem to notice that I'm shooting up his rumpus room, as he's concentrating on his gun-twirling. And then, of course, one of my bullets hits Milligan, and explodes his skull, and I wake up and go to get a drink.

6 | THE BULLET AND THE CROSS

HOOPER'S NOT GOING TO LIKE THIS, BUT I THINK IT'S TIME I TOLD YOU about *The Bullet and the Cross*. It explains much. I mean, it's almost embarrassing for me to admit this, but if you know about 1) the "incident" in the ravine, 2) my addiction to television and 3) the movie I'm about to recall, you'll understand pretty much everything about me. You'll understand my current situation, which I'm gearing up to describe in some detail. Hey, you'll even understand certain details in the pages of what you've already read—for example, why I thought that distraction-by-knot-tying might be an effective escape strategy.

The Galaxy Odeon lay on the outskirts of our survey, surrounded by high-rise apartment buildings. Rainie and her mother lived in one of these buildings, so on Saturday afternoons my brother and I would go into the lobby and press the button beside the name "Van der Glick." Then we would wait. There was never any staticky communication from above, never an inquiry as to our identity or an admonition to wait patiently, so we would just sit there in silence and in a few minutes the elevator doors would open in the lobby and out would step Rainie.

One time, I remember, I buzzed and there came a curious clicking sound, repetitive and insistent. (I was calling on Rainie alone, which was rare but not unprecedented. Jay was sometimes elsewhere, and no one knew where that "elsewhere" might be.) I understood that someone upstairs was releasing the lock on the big glass door that separated the vestibule from the lobby, and without thinking I pulled it open and entered. The elevator waited and I stepped inside and pressed the button numbered "14." Rainie and her mother actually lived on the thirteenth floor, but the designers and architects were unwilling to acknowledge that fact. I rode up—I recall that a very thin man dressed in pyjamas got on at the fourth floor and ascended to the fifth—and then I wandered the hallway until I came to 1412. I knocked lightly at the door and almost instantly it was opened, but not all the way. The security chain was still attached, allowing a crack of perhaps five inches. That afforded me my only impression of Rainie's apartment, namely: it was very dark inside, full of shadows, and what light there was flickered, as though produced by candles. There was a painting on the wall opposite the door, and I could see some of it, an aggressively geometric abstract. And then Mrs. van der Glick's face filled the opening, gaunt and heavily made up. She wore only a nightdress. "What do *you* want?" she demanded.

"Is Rainie in?"

"Leave her alone," said Mrs. van der Glick, closing the door and throwing a deadbolt.

But what usually happened was that Jay and I would wait in the lobby, Rainie would appear and the three of us would head toward the Galaxy Odeon Theatre for the Saturday matinee. We would pay our fifty cents, regardless of the fare, and the fare was wide-ranging. There were war movies, although they were occasional, as they tended to overexcite the children. There were films about pirates and knights, and these were Rainie's favourites, although she complained constantly about historical inaccuracies. She also disliked the overtly romantic moments—the kisses and tearful farewells—which caused her to squirm in her seat. Having typed these last sentences, I realize it's hard to credit that period dramas were Rainie's favourites, but they were. As soon as she saw a foreign land—a Saharan desert or a tempest-tossed coastline—she would smile and, for a while, cease to be the tightly twisted little ranker she was.

Yes, Rainie was a ranker, and I can call her that because I was a ranker, too. The term may be particular to the Norman Ingram Memorial Grammar School, but the concept is universal. As any sociologist will tell you, there is a definite pecking order in any system—this is especially true of grade schools—and when we use the term "ranker," we are speaking of those at the very bottom.

I was included in the number largely because of my spectacles. They were massive and cumbersome, so much so that the temples ended in wire hooks to prevent gravity from hauling the things from my face, which gravity was always threatening to do. I had to wander around with my hand plastered across my brow, as though thinking great thoughts or wanting to vomit. Either activity was bound to garner ranker points.

Mind you, I shouldn't attribute my status solely to my spectacles. I earned a lot of points from the fact that I was related to the very bizarre Jay McQuigge. Jay's strange behaviour was well-known throughout the school. On his first day of kindergarten he refused, tearfully, to nap during naptime. He called his teacher "Mommy" (and continued to do so for months). I had done this myself once or twice—it is a fairly common gaffe for a little kid to make—but in Jay's case it created a problem because his teacher was a man, Mr. Raleigh. That Mr. Raleigh was undeniably effeminate did not cause the stigma to fade in any way.

But what really got me the huge tallies was the fact that my best friend at school was not only a ranker, she was a girl. She was a scrawny girl with a strange name, Rainie van der Glick. The name alone would have consigned her forever to rankerdom. The first name was ripe for punning, and the three components that followed made her an outcast in the public school system, forever unable to line up in alphabetical order. And Rainie was the only person at Norman Ingram Memorial with vision-ware anything close to mine. I cannot recall meeting her for the first time, but I'm sure it was this that drew us together, two little kids wearing their weakness, their weirdness, right on their faces for all the world to see. Rainie had rhinestone-encrusted wingtips, fancy and fashionable, which only made the distorted fish-eyes swimming in the lenses all the more rank.

And for a few bonus points: my mother often wandered across the ancient cow pasture that separated our little house from Norman Ingram. She typically came at morning recess, moving slowly, a cigarette in one hand and a drink in the other. The drink was usually coffee, but on one or two occasions she clutched a glass tumbler. My mother would come within fifty feet of the school, stop and watch. She was searching out neither Jay nor me, because when we presented ourselves she merely waved, and vaguely at that, as though she could not quite remember who we were. After a few minutes she would turn and saunter back to the house.

The issue here was not so much that my mother's behaviour was odd, it was that her behaviour was conspicuous. Rankers shared this characteristic, mothers who were notable. It would be impossible, really, for a kid to be a ranker all on his or her own, no matter how weird and damaged he or she might be. You needed to be sponsored, in a sense, by your mother.

—

Rainie van der Glick's mother was an extreme example; she was about as crazy as a rat in a coffee can. She came to the school on a daily basis to confront the administration, with such fury that she might as well have been toting a battering ram and bazooka. Her complaint, at least originally, was that Rainie was a bona fide genius and that the school was not serving her special needs. No one disputed this, but the principal, Mr. Bowman, explained that there were no provisions made for genius, and Rainie was obligated by law to sit in the classroom all day. Somewhere along the line it got personal; Mr. Bowman said something that stepped on all the twigs in Mrs. van der Glick's mind. After that, she simply came to do battle. The police were called more than once. For a time Mrs. van der Glick was legally enjoined from stepping onto school property, although this was quashed during one of the many trials held to settle all the suits and countersuits. There were two rumours that captured the imagination of all the schoolchildren. When Mr. Bowman appeared with his foot in a cast, it soon became common knowledge that the damage had been done by a thug, at Mrs. van der Glick's behest. We would brook no other explanation—although one was delivered over the PA system, concerning a gardening mishap. And the other rumour was that someone—and the identity of this kid changed with each telling—went to the office on an errand, and saw Mr. Bowman lying across his desk. Mrs. van der Glick had her skirts hiked and was sitting astride, pumping merrily.

Mr. van der Glick committed suicide around when Rainie was born, although I doubt if he hanged himself *as* she was being born, which is what Rainie believes.

Myself, what I liked at the Galaxy Odeon were the westerns.

Indeed, I was a pretty big fan of the genre in general. Some of my favourite programs on television were westerns, *Gunsmoke* and *Have Gun Will Travel*. You know, it's an interesting thing about that latter show, and something not commonly known, but the story of Paladin, the jaded and educated gun-for-hire, was actually developed by the playwright Clifford Odets. The author of *Awake and Sing!* and *Waiting for Lefty*, the great young hope of the American theatre, ended his life in Hollywoodland, drinking too much, dabbling with various illicit substances, robotically screwing young starlets and writing for the boob tube.

I'd kindly ask you to remember this as I write down the details of my life.

I also *really* liked, I want to mention, those episodes of *The Twilight Zone* that were of the western genre. They were not infrequent, although apparently Rod Serling insisted these episodes be shot in Death Valley, where the actors and crew suffered from dehydration and even delirium. (That's my kind of show-runner!) The most memorable was "Mr. Denton on Doomsday." It was about this schoolteacher who finds a Colt .45, which keeps misfiring when he holds it. He accidentally kills a rattlesnake at fifty yards, and shoots the revolver out of the hands of a notorious gunslinger. So Mr. Denton is accorded a fearsome reputation, even though he is, in reality, a quiet little man. Serling seemed to understand that we are not always responsible for our actions, although that does raise the question *Who, exactly, is?*

But of all the westerns I have seen, the most significant is certainly *The Bullet and the Cross*.

Like all of my important memories, it has a potency that has influenced the pocket of time that holds it, so I can remember that particular Saturday afternoon, even though in many ways it was no different from any other. I can remember, for example, what van der Glick was wearing as she stepped out of the elevator, which was a dress covered with clownish polka dots. Rainie would make these heartbreaking stabs at femininity; indeed, she still does. It's not that she doesn't possess a woman's body now, and didn't possess a girl's body then. But clothes never seemed to fit her correctly, and the more girlish they were, the worse they would hang. So on this day she wore a dress, and knee socks although her legs were too thin to support them and they gathered in folds around her ankles. She'd also done something odd to her spectacles. The lenses were darkened, so that her eyes were obscured.

"Are those new glasses?" I asked, although I knew they weren't, since I recognized the rhinestone-encrusted wingtips.

"Yes," she lied.

"We're going to the movies!" said Jay. "Wanna come?"

Jay asked Rainie every week if she wanted to come to the movies, even though we never did anything else. Rainie's answer was likewise invariable.

"Might as well." She shrugged. "There's fuck-all else to do."

Oh, she had a mouth on her. Still does. Rainie hosts a radio talk show these days, and her speech is peppered with beeps and whistles. She has had a series of careers, proceeding from straight journalism (she spent a few years in Russia as an official correspondent for one of Toronto's dailies) to somewhat bizarre magazine reportage (when the female press were finally allowed inside the Maple Leafs' locker room, for example, Rainie took it a step further, actually showering with the lads) to this radio show where she is paid, handsomely, to be cantankerous.

The Bullet and the Cross was made in 1960 and the director's name was given as Alan Smithee. What this means is that the real person (or persons) responsible for it were so embarrassed by the results that they chose this default accreditation. Any film bearing the name "Alan Smithee" is by definition bad, just so you can be on the lookout. Perhaps you knew this, but I'll bet you're surprised to discover that the practice dates back to the 1960s. I know I was, when I did this research a few years back. I think it's possible that *The Bullet and the Cross* was the very first Alan Smithee movie.

The writer of the screenplay didn't hide behind a pseudonym. His identity is announced with some boldness, given that it contains even a middle name: Peter Paul Mendicott. Moreover, it is repeated on another title card: *Based Upon the Novel by Peter Paul Mendicott.* I have to tell you that I don't remember this from that viewing so long ago, I know this because I have watched the movie a few times subsequently. I sought out and purchased what seems to be the only extant print of the film. I have screened it in private, renting whole movie theatres, which can be surprisingly affordable, especially if you want to watch something in the dead of night. Edward Milligan watched it with me one time. He fell asleep in the middle, but I should mention that we were both very stoned and drunk.

Not that the film isn't tedious. The story mostly concerns a lawman named Johnny Mungo, portrayed with mind-numbing inertia by someone named Mark Goode, who was semi-famous as a stock car driver. It may be baffling to you, the kind of productorial thinking that went into designing a vehicle for a stock car driver (I know, I'm sorry about that), but I have been in the business long enough to know the kind of twisted logic that exists. All it takes is someone half-crazy with a little bit of money, and bingo, you got a movie.

The story is basically this: the town is bad, because of the evil and pervasive presence of a fellow named Black Chester Nipes. (He is not a black man, but owns that sobriquet because a gun backfired and the gunpowder stained his face. A nice touch, wholly preposterous.) Mungo comes to town, clears away all of the henchmen and riff-raff and finally confronts Nipes himself. Mungo emerges victorious, soupy music fades up and that's the end.

Pretty unimaginative stuff, for the most part. By far the most interesting thing about the story, at least for me, is the secondary character Father White. He is a young, good-looking clergyman, singularly uncowed by Black Chester Nipes. As soon as he stepped onto the screen, I knew I wanted to be this man. It had something to do with the way he looked, because he had a raffish quality and, although I remain a little uncertain as to what that actually is, I've always wanted to possess it.

About an hour into the story, there is a big fight in the town tavern (which is far nicer than the one Nipes hangs out in) and, through various plot machinations on the part of Mr. Mendicott, Father White is there. At one point during the brouhaha, a brace of henchmen approach the clergyman, obviously with mayhem on their minds. Rather than appearing afraid, Father White takes up his Bible and begins reading with intense concentration, concentration that is rewarded by the blossoming of a blissful smile. The henchmen are so intrigued with this that they lean in to see the passage in question, leaving their weapons hanging at their sides. Father White lashes out with the Good Book, snapping it shut on one of the thug's nose. Then he grabs a whiskey bottle and rather impassively cold-cocks the other guy, dropping him like a sack of wet bricks. The man with the sore nose hightails it out of the barroom, a story contrivance I should have made more note of. I mean, even given the questionable logic and reality that permeated the Galaxy Odeon every week, there was nothing preventing the guy from simply lofting his side arm and drilling Father White a third eye. But I was too taken up with the laughter that sounded in the theatre to reflect on this. My, how the children laughed. Even Rainie van der Glick laughed.

And then, at the end of the movie, when Black Chester Nipes and Johnny Mungo meet on the street for the traditional shootout, Nipes has Father White as a hostage. Nipes presses the barrel of his six-shooter into the clergyman's temple and says, "Take another step, Mungo, and I'll shoot the padre." (A script editor might have found that dialogue unnecessary, but *The Bullet and the Cross* is full of such on-the-nose stuff.)

What can Johnny Mungo do? Nothing. And indeed he does nothing. Mungo stands there and stares forward with a doltish expression on his face, which is how the actor Mark Goode portrayed most emotions.

It is Father White who acts, reaching up, taking hold of Black Chester's hand and squeezing. There is no attempt at screen realism here, no exploding skull or blood, but we children, all of us, gasped with terrible shock as the padre slumped to the ground. And then we began to weep.

Not everybody in the theatre, but the three of us certainly, we erupted into blubbery tears. I knew we were not weeping for the clergyman's huge self-sacrifice, not exclusively. We were weeping because this selfless act on his part (this bit of cheap melodrama, when you get right down to it, after which Mungo summarily shot Chester Nipes through the heart) allowed us to. We were weeping, finally, for our own rankerdom.

In some strange way, I saw suddenly the trajectory of a man's life, of *my* life; how, lacking the courage to do anything remotely close to what Father White had just done, I would end up wallowing in besotted loneliness.

And here I am.

———

"Hello?"

"McQuigge here."

"Phil?"

"Yeah, *but* do not call me *Phil*, because this is not a social call. How are you, anyway?"

"First-rate."

"Okay, great, but never mind about that right now. I want to take issue with the phrase *rose above the mediocrity of the material*."

"I'm not with you, Phil."

"In the obituary. Ed Milligan's obituary."

"Ah. Wrote that, did I?"

"I think you even said *consistently. Consistently rose above the mediocrity of the material*."

"I see. And you've been brooding about it for all these months."

"No. Yes."

"And which aspect of the phrase in particular are you taking issue with, Phil? Milligan's rising above or the mediocrity of the material?"

"What do *you* think?"

"For starters, I think you're drunk. And I think your relationship with Milligan was complicated, that you resented his stardom. And lastly, I think you know that *Padre* was a mediocre program."

"Really."

"Don't feel badly. Almost everything on television is mediocre."

"And what, precisely, is so mediocre about *Padre?*"

"I'll tell you what's mediocre about it, Philip. Here's the thing. The writing is actually quite good. Sometimes, especially when *you're* writing it, there's very good dialogue. Clever stuff. And I appreciate the plot twists, don't think I don't. Often I'm reminded of your man Serling."

"Oh, you and I have discussed Rod Serling?"

"Philip. We came to blows in Banff whilst discussing Rod Serling. At least, you did."

"Ah, yes. Now I remember."

"No, you don't."

"Carry on. You like a lot about *Padre*, despite which, it remains, in your view, mediocre."

"Here's the thing. Sometimes the show seems like it was created and written by a prepubescent boy. And it's not just that the women are either virtuous or slatternly. Although there is that. But the show exhibits a very immature, a very unexamined, world view. It's a black-hat white-hat show, Philip. And you're far more intelligent than that. Now, I know what you're going to say, that it is mere entertainment. But that would be disingenuous on your part. The show purports to be dealing with questions of good and evil, and its failure to do so consigns it to the bin marked *mediocre*. Milligan—who was neither wholly good nor wholly bad, but managed, as we know, to be both in grand measure—at least shaded things slightly. Lent the proceedings some ambiguity. And in doing so rose above the mediocrity of the material."

"Oh. I see."

"Are you working on anything now, Philip? I could mention it in my column."

"Thanks, man, but I'm out of the television business."

7 | THE SITUATION

I LIVE IN A BASEMENT APARTMENT, COMPRISING A KITCHENETTE, A bedroomette and a sittingroomette. I could afford more spacious lodgings; I did, after all, labour long in the fields of television, which my colleague William Beckett once described as a "river of money into which we must jump." (Beckett was my Hermes into the land of television. He took great glee in, and I quote faithfully, "turning a promising young dramatist into a hack." He didn't know, because I never told him, that it was a land into which I'd always wanted to travel, having been seduced, at a very young age, when I heard those words, "You are entering another dimension of time and space.") But my prospects of future income are very dim, so I rent this basement apartment, from a man who was once my employee. Michelangelo Barker was a junior writer on *Padre*. Every script Barker submitted I performed a page-one rewrite on, not that they were all that bad, and likely because they were much too good. Barker didn't accept this well, and often, when I passed him in the hallway, he bristled with artistic indignation. "Stout lad," I always thought.

Michelangelo is an imposing figure, six foot seven or something. Much of his size is concentrated in his legs and feet; he seems always to be shot from a low angle. His head is small, encircled by a nap of golden hair, for he wears his hair buzzed short and has cultivated a moustacheless chinstrap for adornment. He wears tiny glasses, the lenses smaller than the glaring eyeballs they serve. Michelangelo lacks shoulders—God just forgot about them. He has a narrow chest, a belly created by a bad diet and endless video rentals, then those legs blast onto the scene, massive thighs, inhuman shins and monumental feet. So he was a hard man to sneak past, as he stood there sipping tea in the hallway outside the kitchen. He was in that position far more often than he was inside the closet I'd assigned him as an office.

So I'd nod at him and he'd bristle, and sometimes I'd stop and say, "That was a great script. There were just a few little problems."

"Like what?" Michelangelo's voice is very high-pitched and seems to come from someplace other than his mouth.

"Well," I say, "Padre knows that O'Grady is really the cattle thief because he compares the *typewritten* letters. But they didn't have typewriters in 1880."

"Yes, they did."

"They did?"

"Certainly. Although they had not standardized the keyboard. Many preferred the Dvorak arrangement. Indeed, Mark Twain invested heavily in the Dvorak, and lost much. Ironically, the man who possesses the title of world's fastest typist—and yes, it is a man, a soldier in point of fact—employs a Dvorak keyboard. Hmm." He always adds those little *hmms* at the end of his sentences, impressed with whatever he's just said.

"Okay, fine, maybe they had typewriters in 1880, but they had like *two*, and it is just not an effective narrative device."

"I see. Fine." Michelangelo Barker, like everyone else on staff, is paid, and paid well, to be deferential.

Despite my past treatment of him, he is a very kind landlord. He is respectful of my privacy down there in his basement, although I suppose I send up enough sozzled ululations that he'd be a fool not to be. He often effects home improvements on his own initiative, trying to make my life a little more comfy. Michelangelo can't stand erect in the basement and is constantly bumping his head on the ceiling, which makes his handyman stuff all the more endearing.

Barker is the only person, other than my children, who has ever been down in my basement. So it's time to introduce the girls, even though you've missed them, I've dropped them off at their schools this morning, kissed them goodbye, and it will be a week or so before I see them again.

Currer is twelve and Ellis is seven.

I maintain that it is simply a linguistic anomaly that Currer is not a teenager, that there is no logical reason why we say "twelve" and not "two-teen." Because she certainly acts like a teenager; she is withdrawn and a bit sullen (except with her friends) and takes an enormous amount of time to perform even the simplest task. Currer is not without sweetness; if there is trouble or sadness she is quick with a comforting hug and a whispered "I love you." But left to her own devices, she would rather drift around the planet with earphones plugged in, dexterously manipulating the buttons on her portable music player, getting the machine to repeat favourite tracks and to avoid ones that fail to meet her standards. Her music of choice is, quite frankly, dreck, but this is an age-old generational battle, and needn't be gotten into here. Currer does, I will say in her defence, adore the music of her Uncle Jay. We have gone to see Jay play on a few occasions, mostly when the owners of Birds of a Feather have ordered him to do matinees. Currer has sat stone-still for the entire performance, nursing a Coca-Cola, a look of rapture on her face.

Ellis has been to those same matinees, of course. She is not enthralled by her uncle's music, although on the few occasions when she knows the tune—"Over the Rainbow," for example—she will sing along with ear-splitting enthusiasm. Curiously, seeing as many of the people in my family are musical—my mother had her grade eight piano and a lovely voice—Ellis appears to be singing-impaired. She hollers out notes at random, or with a profound attraction to quarter-tones. She is quite good, though, on the more showbizzy aspects of singing, twisting her body with rhythmic abandon and occasionally calling out, "Everybody!" When she does this, of course, everybody obediently joins in.

Currer has a lovely voice, although she is loath to use it. Currer will sing—with Ellis's encouragement—at bedtime, when our custom is to belt out a rousing version of "The Window." I know, because I used to overhear it (standing outside the doorway with my heart banging inside my ribcage), that their mother sings them actual lullabies, quiet serenades, even the occasional hymn. So the girls are used to music after they've scurried under the sheets, although "The Window" is hardly a peaceful air. I take up the banjo from its position in a shadowy corner and thrum out a few introductory changes. I don't know how it is that I can play the banjo, but somewhere along the line I acquired a few chords and a rudimentary strumming technique. "The Window" is not that complicated a song, at any rate, and is boisterous enough to forgive all sorts of mispickings. I learned "The Window" from a record by a group named Troutfishing in America. It is a long song wherein a number of well-known nursery rhymes are recited, except that at the end of each there is the same sharp, stinging departure, which has to do with violent defenestration:

> *Georgy Porgy, pudding'n'pie,*
> *Kissed the girls and made them cry.*
> *And when the boys came out to play,*
> *They threw him out the window.*

(everybody now)
The window, the window, they threw him out the window . . .
When the boys came out to play,
They threw him out the window.

Old Mother Hubbard went to the cupboard,
To get her poor doggy a bone,
But when she bent over, the doggy took over,
And threw her out the window.
(everybody now)
The window, the window, he threw her out the
window . . . etc.

Currer sings with the tranquil intensity of a chorister; Ellis hollers like a drunken lumberjack in the advanced throes of cabin fever. She is so unmusical that I would suspect Ronnie of infidelity, except that Ellis is clearly my child; the tips of her little fingers are bent inward and her eyes are brown and very weak, so that she, too, is saddled with spectacles. Besides which, I don't believe Ronnie was ever unfaithful during our marriage, so it's unfair to raise the accusation even in jest. (Don't think it has escaped my attention that Veronica has popped up twice in the past couple of paragraphs. She is certainly banging on the door of this narrative.) So I attribute Ellis's lack of musicality to some genetic throwback. I will say this, though—Ellis can dance. She takes all sorts of lessons—ballet, jazz, tap and Scottish—competing in those disciplines that allow it (Scottish dancing is a highly competitive affair), performing whenever she gets the chance. She is a sturdily made little beast, with legs that would look more at home on a steroid-riddled sprinter. She inherited this tendency toward muscularity from her mother, Veronica, and I guess I can put this off no longer.

I'm going to write about Ronnie.

———

"Do you want me to talk sexy, baby, or do you want to talk sexy to me?"

"You know, I just got through repeating my Visa number about forty times. My mouth is incapable of sexiness."

"You want *me* to talk dirty, then."

"Dirty, or sexy? I mean, I could probably talk dirty. Like I say, I just got through saying my Visa number over and over again."

"Okay, so go. Tell me what you like."

"Uh . . ."

"Like tell me what you'd want me to do if I was there. What kind of thing? Do you like to have your cock sucked? 'Cause I would *love* to suck your cock."

"Well, yes, I mean, that can be very pleasant."

"I could lick your asshole."

"Uh-huh. Um . . . sure."

"What would you do to me if I were there?"

"If you were here? Hmm. I'd probably be incapable of actual physical intimacy."

"Oooh, baby."

"What?"

"Sorry, that was just kind of a habit kind of a thing."

"I suppose I could feel your breasts. I could try to do that very tenderly. You might enjoy it. *I* would *really* enjoy it, think what you will of me."

"I'd like it if you felt my titties."

"I suppose it's kind of adolescent of me."

"Do you always analyze all this shit?"

"I think so."

"So you're gonna feel my titties, 'the twins,' I like to call them, and I should tell you, they are awesome."

"Awesome. I would fall down before them on trembling knees."

"And what else?"

"Well. Good question. I guess I could, um . . ."

"Lick my pussy?"

"Just so."

"Tell me how you'd lick it."

"How much variance is there?"

"You know what, you have to just take a deep breath and give yourself *over* to this."

"Huh?"

"There are as many ways of licking pussy as there are tongues and pussies. An infinite array of motion and sensation. No other tongue has ever felt like yours, nor will any tongue feel like yours again."

"Uh-huh. I'm falling asleep, aren't I? I'm drifting off."

"And the contact cannot help but be intimate. We will connect physically. It will be both fleeting and eternal."

"I am most definitely passed out here."

"Hang up the phone, darling, or this is going to cost you a fortune."

"All right. All right. Good night."

8 | THE EX

I FIRST LAID EYES UPON HER WHEN I WAS THIRTY-ONE YEARS OLD. I WAS a young playwright who had met with some success, although in any other career this success would translate as dismal failure. My plays earned me very little money, and given the time I spent working on the things, my actual hourly wage likely didn't top a buck. But my life was thoroughly enjoyable, because the theatre is a world that allows, even encourages, transitory, superficial relationships, the kind I liked best. And these relationships were typically with actresses, pretty and shapely and deeply insecure. It was hard not to hurt these women, sometimes it seemed avoiding it was impossible, so I had acquired a reputation as a rake and a cad, a reputation that gave me some small satisfaction.

I was also reputed to be a prolific writer, churning out two or three plays a year, although at this period in my life I seemed to have dried up. Really, though, I hadn't dried up, I had rather become all too sodden, liquor-logged. I would rise around noon, read newspapers and magazines until around six (a torpid activity to which I gave the name "research"), and then around six o'clock I would go out to eat, although I almost always headed directly for the Pig's Snout, a pseudo-English pub that offered only pickled eggs and potato chips as comestibles. There I would find a table full of my cronies. Gig

Withers, for example, an actor. Gig was a kindly man, burdened with such a malevolent aspect that he portrayed only serial killers, axe murderers and ghouls risen from the dead. He worked a lot and his face was well-known, although this only served to get him arrested once or twice a week, overly zealous cops leaping upon him as he strolled down the street. And there was Joanne Wenders, a poet, although she now lives in Mississauga and raises children and bull terriers. She had a bull terrier back then, a mangy brute named Kingsley who was allowed his own seat at the table. I was very attracted to Joanne, but never had a physical relationship with her, largely because Kingsley hated me. He glared at me and let it be known that he would be pleased to bite off my balls.

Then there was Bob Hamel, the most boring man in the universe. I don't mean that as an insult. Bob Hamel would agree that he was the most boring man in the universe, it was almost a point of pride to him. Bob Hamel worked for one of the big insurance companies, in some capacity that none of us could begin to fathom. He wore blue three-piece suits and hauled around an enormous briefcase everywhere he went.

Bob Hamel would sit at our table and grin at everything anybody said. He would laugh obediently when he thought something was supposed to be funny. Hamel himself would never state any thoughts or observations, knowing full well how dull he was, but he was vastly appreciative of our collective wit and wisdom. Oh, now that I think of it, Hamel did occasionally have something to offer: knowledge. Whenever our conversation ran aground on the rocks of ignorance (which was frequently), Bob Hamel would save the day by actually knowing something. For example, Hooper and I almost came to blows one evening while discussing the existence or non-existence of God. Bob Hamel interrupted with an apposite point (that Charles Darwin was ignorant of Gregor Mendel's experiments in genetics, even though they were performed during Darwin's lifetime) and then proceeded to give us a concise overview of the theory of evolution and its implications re theology. Of course it was dull, but I still remember much of what he said.

Bob Hamel was a handsome enough fellow, in that his features were regular and everything was about the right size. It was said that he had a huge penis. I have no personal knowledge of this, but Rainie van der Glick told me it was so. Rainie would show up at the Pig's Snout every now and again, ostensibly to see me, although she would hardly speak to me. She would say that I looked like shit and then she would proceed to insult the other people at the table. She did this with no particular relish, but much of what we said was pretentious tripe of the first water, and Rainie was ever incapable of holding her tongue. On one occasion she hooked up with Bob Hamel, although I can't remember whether this was after one of his displays of erudition or after an evening Hamel spent grinning like an idiot, toting his briefcase with him when he went to the malodorous head. Rainie referred to herself back then as Our Lady of Perpetual Mercy Fucks, and I suppose either one of these situations might have summoned forth that tarnished angel.

The most regular of the Pig's Snout regulars was the young novelist John Hooper, although at the time he had written no novel. He had written only titles. Oh, John implied that in his squalid bedsit there were reams of paper spackled with deathless prose, but we saw no evidence. We only heard that work was progressing well on, say, *They Both Were Naked,* or *Puke.* Hooper was conflicted as to what kind of titler he was, one given to poetry or to effrontery. A very good example of this would be the period during which he was labouring on something that he named both *Lissome Is the Naiad* and *Hellhag!* (He added the exclamation mark, not me.) I often wondered, aloud, how something could have both titles (Hooper seemed legitimately to be working that time; he would show up bleary-eyed, his long fingers spotted with ink), but I gained some insight when he began to show up with this woman, this Veronica Lear, by his side.

There now, you see, I've done it already, I've written something catty. I had promised myself that I wouldn't, that I would try to be fair-minded in my presentation of my estranged wife. After all, it wasn't Ronnie who scuppered the marriage, it was me, acting with mind-boggling confusion, my enormous ego and smallish dick getting me into all sorts of trouble. So I will begin afresh; I will detail my first laying eyes upon her, when all was new and possibilities curled through the air like smoke from exotic cigarettes.

I was late getting to the Snout because I had stopped by to visit one of my girlfriends. That woman, Frieda, had advised me that I was an unfeeling scoundrel. She had actually employed that word, "scoundrel." Mind you, Frieda was with the company at Stratford, so her word choice could be a bit Shakespearean. "Phil, you're an arrant scapegrace." I had answered in kind, or at least I will report that I did. "My conscience hath a thousand several tongues," I told her, "and every tongue brings in a several tale, and every tale condemns me for a villain."

I arrived at the pub tardy but cleansed. I was well into my first pint of ale when I noticed that there was a stranger sitting beside Hooper. Writers are supposed to be gifted with observational skills, but you can see that I have my limitations—the fact that the most beautiful woman in the world was nearby escaped my attention for a few long moments.

Her hair was an unsettling collection of hues, everything from ebony to strawberry blonde. Her hair was also wild, flying off in all directions. This was not entirely natural; she was at the time acting the role of Ophelia—not in *Hamlet*, exactly, but in some Bizarro World version of the classic. I went to see the play the next evening, so I can report that it was vaguely Hamlet-like, although the male lead gave none of the famous soliloquies, replacing them with arrhythmic grunts and monkey-hoots. He also spent much of his time naked. Veronica Lear wore more clothes, but not a lot more. Her costume was an elaborate tenting of diaphanous fabric, and as she flitted about, the material would flounce, revealing glimpses of naked flesh. And so, while I am bolting ahead chronologically, at least in terms of what I was entitled to know, I will describe her breasts as perfect. Likewise her backside, which was so muscled that one could imagine that she had spent her childhood gambolling through the grasslands. But none of this was as breathtaking as her face, which was framed by the unruly and mottled locks. The thing to know about Ronnie is that her family history is cosmopolitan and complicated. Her father was Scottish and her mother Malaysian, but even those bloodlines were not quite pure, and there are evidences of everything from North American Indian to Nordic. So while her hair was enhanced in order to portray the Bizarro Ophelia, when the colouring was washed out the effect was not eradicated, merely muted.

Her eyes seemed like a painter's palette; from a distance they were a startling blue-grey, but on close inspection (and I spent hours inspecting them closely) they were flecked with almost every tint. Ronnie's eyes were large, and she had inherited from her mother epicanthal folds, which somehow made her seem ever on the verge of laughing or weeping. Her nose was ever so slightly flattened, just enough that one could imagine (or so I imagined, the first time I laid eyes upon her) that in the throes of passion the nostrils would flare and possibly even shoot out licks of flame. Then there was her mouth; Veronica Lear had perfect teeth, dazzlingly white, and she had a nervous habit of bringing down the top set upon her lower lip, just for a moment but with conviction, and when she lifted them away the lip would blush with blood.

At that particular moment I would have rated my chances of dating this woman as maybe a thousand to one, so with typical male defensiveness I made a point of ignoring her. She didn't seem to mind, mostly because she had yet to notice me. Hooper was in the middle of a story—I'd entered in the middle of a Hooper story, and he had made no great progress through the morass that was the middle—and Ronnie was listening, or half-listening, to him. She smoked and looked around the pub, and every so often something Hooper said would make her smile, but I could never detect any causal relationship. It was as though she were smiling at some mispronunciation or speech impediment. I couldn't see how these smiles, slight but stunning, were related to whatever John was saying, which turned out, ultimately, to be a joke of the shaggy-dog variety. I was astounded that Hooper had been so reduced. Where were the fearless contentions that Shakespeare was a hack, that Samuel Beckett was twice the dramatist old Will could ever hope to be? Where were the stories about Mexican cantinas and toothless dogs, tales where even Death got drunk and Fate was feckless? This could only mean that John Hooper was in love.

At the conclusion of Hooper's joke, Ronnie laughed with condescending politeness, but it was a glorious laugh nonetheless and I decided to tell a joke myself. Some of you may be noticing the ease with which I elected to betray my friend Hooper. You're wondering if I lack a conscience. My response is that I do indeed have a conscience, I just like to make sure it's got plenty to do.

So I decided to tell a joke. After all, I had nothing to lose. Not only had this woman not returned any of my dark-lidded smouldering glances, she had yet to even look at me, to register my existence on the planet. I slammed my empty pint mug down as a cheap attention-getting device and launched into the old "chee-chee" chestnut.

You know it, of course you do. Three missionaries are taken captive by a tribe in some deep, dark jungle. The chief imperiously announces, "You have two choices. Death or chee-chee." The first missionary, being a moral coward, elects "chee-chee." He is taken away and all manner of sexual atrocities are performed upon him, leaving him badly damaged but still breathing. So the second missionary, when given the choice, likewise chooses "chee-chee." He is subjected to brutal depravity, and then his body is tossed away, ruined but still functional. The third missionary, though, declares that he will have none of this. "I choose death."

"You are a brave man," says the chief. "So be it. Death. But first . . . *chee-chee*."

I believe I told the joke well. I was vague enough about the setting that I could lend to the chief's voice a creamy yet acidic resonance without giving ethnic offence. (A crime for which Joanne Wenders would have been all over me, and Kingsley would have eagerly torn out my windpipe.) I was tactful yet graphic in detailing the treatment the missionaries received. And my delivery of the punchline, timing-wise, was perfect.

I guess Veronica Lear had never heard the joke. At any rate, she laughed with all of her being, and for good or for ill, our fates were sealed.

———

"It's me."

"Of course it's you. It's always *you*."

"Subtext?"

"It's *me*."

"What am I missing here?"

"Everything."

"Let's start again."

"Not on your life."

"I mean this conversation."

"Who said we were going to have a conversation?"

"Well, jesus, we have to converse. I mean, we're co-parents and everything."

"We're co-parents and that's *it*."

"You seem a little bit angry with me."

"What insight. What empathy."

"Are you going to be mad at me for the rest of your life?"

"I doubt it. I expect you will predecease me by quite a few years."

"Christ, Ronnie."

"I'm sorry. How about if we don't talk now? Why don't I call you when . . . I don't know. Sometime."

"I wrote about how you and I met."

"Right. You told some stupid joke. I went home with Hooper and we fucked like crazed banshees."

"Really?"

"Okay, I suppose it was an all-right joke."

"Did you and Hooper really . . . ?"

"Yes, Phil, that's what's important now. Let's get into that, who fucked who all those years ago. Then we can talked about who fucked who more *recently*."

"There's another reason I hate Hooper."

"What?"

"It's kind of a sub-theme in my novel."

"You're drunk."

"What insight. What empathy."

"I'll call you back. Sometime."

"Yeah, okay. Whatever. I just wanted to say, um, I love you."

"You know what, Phil? *Don't*. Just don't."

PART TWO
THEATRE AND TELEVISION

9 | ACT TWO, SCENE ONE

INT. LOUNGE—NIGHT

CLOSE ON: WILLIAM BECKETT, television producer.
Beckett is a man in his forties, handsome
despite hair that is similar to Einstein's,
only messy.

> BECKETT
> (reacting to music)
> Ah! A Neapolitan sixth, that
> chord so beloved of Wagner, the
> great anti-Semite.

> McQUIGGE
> He was a great anti-Semite?

> BECKETT
> A miselocution. He was a great
> man, despite his abhorrent
> anti-Semitism.

The waitress, AMY, drifts near the table. You remember
her, don't you? Sure you do. She is young, sexy.

> AMY
>
> How're you guys doing over
> here?

> BECKETT
>
> All the better for your asking,
> my lovely.

> McQUIGGE
>
> More beer. More beer, and
> another one of these, um,
> double Laphroaigs.

> BECKETT
>
> I myself am fine. Perhaps a
> glass of water.

> AMY
>
> Sure.

The waitress leaves. McQUIGGE stares after her.

> McQUIGGE
>
> She's good-looking.

BECKETT

*Then come kiss me, sweet and
twenty. Youth's a stuff will
not endure.*

McQUIGGE

So . . . how are things in
teevee land?

BECKETT

A bit quiet since your abrupt
departure. Our greatest source
of gossip has dried up. There
are fuck-ups aplenty, but none
with your panache. I miss you.
And you tell me you've been
holed up in your squalid bedsit, composing deathless prose?

McQUIGGE

I'm trying to write a novel.

BECKETT

About . . . ?

McQUIGGE

About, um, me.

BECKETT

Ah! Then I shall read it with
great interest.

                    McQUIGGE

I always wanted to be an
author. I don't know what happened. I started writing for
the theatre, probably because
there were girls involved, and
then *you* came along . . .

                    BECKETT

Yesssss! Notice the manner in
which I hiss, very like a
serpent.

                    McQUIGGE

It wasn't your fault.

                    BECKETT

No, indeed. No harm, no foul.
The leper has no control over
his contagion.

                    McQUIGGE

I guess not.

                    AMY

Okay. One water, one draft, one
of those double Laphroaigs. For
thems as want to get drunk as
quick as possible.

McQUIGGE

Hmm?

AMY

Hey, are you still violating
the sacred form of the novel?

McQUIGGE

Yep.

AMY

Good on you.

BECKETT

At least there's no issue with
violation in the land of the
big eye. It's hard to violate
television.

McQUIGGE

There is that.

BECKETT

That strange young man playing
the piano . . .

McQUIGGE

What?

BECKETT

He seems to be playing a fugue,

improvising upon the melody of,
if my ears don't betray me, "A
Foggy Day in London Town."

                AMY
He's good, huh?

                McQUIGGE
He's my brother.

                AMY
No kidding?

                BECKETT
I didn't know there were other
McQuigge offspring.

                AMY
How come he never talks to you?

                McQUIGGE
He's mad at me. He's mad
because I, well, I've made certain poor life choices.

                AMY
Such as?

                McQUIGGE
They are innumerable.

AMY

Give me a for-instance.

McQUIGGE

Well, I, I kind of, um, you
see, I was married . . . still
am, technically . . . and I got
involved with . . . say, I need
another double Laphroaig.

BECKETT

Currently Phil is attempting to
kick his own arse-end for getting into the television bidna.

AMY

That's your name, *Phil?* My
name's Amy.

McQUIGGE

Yes, I know. It says so on
your, um, name tag.

AMY

Right. Well, I'll get you more
hooch.

McQUIGGE

No, that's all right. I'm okay
for now. Thanks.

                    AMY
Any time, Phil. That's what
we're here for.

AMY leaves. McQUIGGE stares after her.

                  BECKETT
You are imagining Amy naked
with such intensity that I find
myself blushing on her behalf.

                  McQUIGGE
Actually, I wasn't imagining
her naked. I was imagining her
with clothes on. Not many. And
somewhat diaphanous.

                  BECKETT
I shall imagine this with you.
I was always very taken with
the force and power of your
imagination. I cite as an example your script for Episode 215
of *Sneaks*.

                  McQUIGGE
Hmmm.

                  BECKETT
Mind you, the episode itself
was unmitigated shite. But not

your fault. Say. That strange
young man—your brother—appears
to be shedding tears.

                McQUIGGE
You know what? I'm working on
this novel—

                BECKETT
Yes! I shall read it at the
first available opportunity.
When it hits the bookstores, I
shall say, *Give me the master-*
work of Philly McQ. I shall
hold it in my hands and my
bosom shall fair burst with
pride.

                McQUIGGE
There's this thing I want to
write about—this incident—but
I get a little sidetracked from
time to time, and I write down
other memories. And you know
what occurred to me? *Padre*
wasn't my idea. I've always
known that, of course, but was
never really willing to admit
it to myself.

BECKETT

I shall thumb through the
pages, looking for references
to myself. And if I find any,
I'll sue your ass off.

McQUIGGE

Huh?

BECKETT

My pride shall be diminished
not a whit.

McQUIGGE

Why would you want to sue me?

BECKETT

Want to? Not a bit of it. But I
would sue you, if only to prove
the point that people, human
beings, are not mere fodder for
your pages. Say what you will
about hour-long television
drama, it's got this going for
it, it is made up. It's inven-
tion. Besides, it's clear how
you intend to paint me in your
novel.

McQUIGGE

"Television is a river of

money, into which we must
jump."

          BECKETT
I may have said that television
is a river of money. I never
said you had to jump into it.
Why would I? You would end up
like me.

          McQUIGGE
What about "I take great pride
in turning one of Canada's most
promising dramatists into a
hack"?

          BECKETT
I've said that, yes. I've said
that to entertainment journal-
ists. And when were they ever
given, when did they ever
expect, the truth?

          McQUIGGE
Hmmm. This novelizing is not
the liberating lark I had
hitherto imagined.

          BECKETT
Ah! There! You've proven my

point. You've begun to speak
like me.

McQUIGGE

Everyone seems to be mad at me.

BECKETT

I suppose you have to question
your motivation, then.

McQUIGGE

I just want to tell the truth.

BECKETT

Then why choose a vehicle
designed to transport lies and
fabrication? More to the point,
what makes you think you know
the truth?

McQUIGGE

Hmmm. It's true, I'm discover-
ing that my memory is not all
it could be.

BECKETT

Come back into the light of the
big eye, Phil. Come and write
for *Mr. Eldritch*. It's an
anthology show, not unlike *The
Twilight Zone*. I thought Rod

Serling was your hero.

McQUIGGE

No. No, I don't think so.

BECKETT

I'll give you co-pro.

McQUIGGE

You see? You are the Great
Seducer.

BECKETT

I don't mean to be cruel,
Philip, but it's not as though
you are a vestal virgin. One
doesn't seduce trollops; one
sets out terms.

McQUIGGE

Thanks very much.

BECKETT

Besides—and I really don't care
to mention this, but I suppose I
must—I'm the only one in the
industry who would even consider
hiring you, given what happened.

McQUIGGE

If I ever decide to get back

into the industry, Mr. Beckett,
you're my man.

BECKETT
Promise me you won't put me in
your novel.

McQUIGGE
I promise.

10 | VAN DER GLICK

PEOPLE ARE NOT MERE FODDER FOR MY PAGES.

Rainie van der Glick, racing around her kitchen, said, "Hey, I don't mind. You want fodder, feel free."

I nodded and said, "Thanks," but I wasn't sure what particular beast in the barnyard of my memory could use the stuffing. It's not that Rainie hasn't been important in my life, but she has been a constant, and there were few significant incidents. At least, that was the case until Sunday evening, a version of which I am now setting down on paper.

I will start by describing Rainie, who had made yet another of what I have called her heartbreaking stabs at femininity. She wore a tight red skirt that fell well below her knees and forced her to wheel about the kitchen with hobbled wobbles. Her blouse was white and sheer, and beneath it she wore a black brassiere. Her hair was piled up and pinned, although tufts and sprigs exploded everywhere. She had lightened it; she had gone from very blonde, as a youngster, to dirty blonde, and now she was back to very blonde, except that her eyebrows had darkened over the years and the combination gave her a vaguely sinister mien. She had forsaken her spectacles for contact lenses, although the optometrists could not make them strong enough, and her eyes were usually watery and pressed together in a squint.

"So did you have any trouble getting here?"

"No. Just took the subway to Eglinton, walked over."

"Subway? How the mighty have fallen."

I do not drive, something I have, perhaps unconsciously, been keeping from you. I know that earlier in these pages I used the phrase "dropped them [the girls] off at their schools," and you likely pictured me rolling up in front in some sort of SUV or sleek Volvo tank, which is what all the parents drive. But I walked with the kids, toting both their schoolbags because I am not good at negotiation. When we got to the grammar school (grades one through six) I kissed Ellis and sent her inside. Currer attends middle school a couple of blocks away, and she said she would walk there herself, and I nodded and said, *Fine*. Currer turned away, plugging in her headphones, proceeding at an excruciating slow pace, her footsteps as small as a geisha's. I ran after her, explaining that I wanted to buy a Sunday *New York Times* and some little cigars, purchases I could effect at a store on the same block as her school. I sometimes have to think hard to come up with chores that take me to the vicinity of Currer's school. There is a fine wine shop nearby, and that comes in handy, although not as handy as you might think, because the owners know a wino when they see one. I ask all sorts of questions about vintages and vineyards, but usually my eyes are red and my breath is stale and wailing, and I know the proprietors want to hand me a bottle of Four Aces and tell me never to return.

"Hey!" Something occurred to me as I sat at Rainie's dining-room table, which is surprising because my mind was occupied with trying to determine just how much wine I should pour into my empty glass. Rainie had filled me up shortly after my arrival, but that was long gone. I had refilled modestly, drained it, and now I was looking at the bottle and wondering how much I could and should claim. I didn't want the ullage to exceed half, because Rainie hadn't had a glass yet, but then again, I craved more than another mere mouthful.

"Drink up," said Rainie. "I bought two bottles, plus you brought one."

"Okay."

"We might as well get lit to the tits," said Rainie van der Glick.

"I was wondering," I mused, giving my glass-filling an aura of civility, "about your spectacles. What did you use to do to them?"

"Huh?"

"Sometimes the lenses would be black—"

"Oh, right. I used to hold them in a candle-flame to blacken the lenses. I wanted sunglasses, right, but Mother would never buy me prescription sunglasses, because, well, I was a homely girl and such vanity did not suit me. Quote unquote."

"Parents don't understand the burden of spectacles."

"Quite so, Philip." Rainie had come over to the table to pour herself a glass of wine, so she too was affecting culture. There is nothing so refined as the language of two boozehounds in the early stages of wine-consumption.

Rainie returned to the kitchen and, watching her go, I noticed that her stabs at femininity weren't half as heartbreaking as they had once been. "So," she called over her shoulder, "what's happening with you and Veronica?"

"What's happening? What's happening is that Ronnie hates me."

"I'm sure she's angry with you," acknowledged Rainie, which is much like acknowledging that water is wet. "I'm also sure she doesn't hate you."

I shrugged, because I wasn't really interested in discussing Ronnie's emotions. I wasn't *capable* of it, to tell the truth, although that may not have been my fault entirely. Veronica's heart is like the sun; it may be comprised of various gases in various combinations, but the big point is, it's way too hot to go anywhere near, or to look at directly.

Rainie and Ronnie were friends, of a kind; they dined together two or three times a year and went on annual shopping campaigns, a couple of which I witnessed in my capacity as sherpa. These campaigns were mounted post-Christmas, when the witless shopkeepers lowered the prices in an effort to clear stock. Ronnie and Rainie would hit each store with the intensity and coordination of bank robbers, Rainie booting open the door, Ronnie making for, not the nearest sales table, rather the one farthest to the rear. Ronnie would throw the merchandise in the air, judging quality and aesthetic appeal through slitted eyes. Rainie would work on the closest tables, winnowing out articles that might have worth and merit, which she would show to Veronica as that woman made a patrol of the perimeter, circling as a hawk circles, ever ready to pounce. Ronnie would dismiss the stuff in Rainie's hands, and Rainie would toss it back onto tables, never the table whence it originated. It was as though the women were punishing the shopkeepers for selling such shoddy merchandise.

So I suppose Rainie might have had insight into my wife, but I didn't draw her out on the subject. There is a large element of shame-faced reserve here, because although I'd told Rainie the headlines—MCQUIGGE HAS AFFAIR WITH MAKEUP, IS THROWN OUT OF THE HOUSE—I'd managed to avoid spilling most of the actual beans.

"What happened," asked Rainie, setting before me a plate of pasta with pesto, "*exactly?*"

"Hello?"
  "Hello, is Phil there? Philly Four-Eyes?"
  "Who is this, please?"
  "This is Bill Nystrom. From the Valleyway United Church?"

"... Yes?"

"Well, I'm returning your call!"

"There's been some misunderstanding."

"That goes without saying, Phil."

"Hmmm?"

"A joke!"

"Mr. Nystrom—"

"Please. *Bill.*"

"Bill, look, I was just, you know, resting. You know. With my eyes closed. Isn't it some ungodly hour of the morning?"

"Nine-thirty! Hardly ungodly."

"Uh-huh."

"Besides which, there's really no hour of the day that's *ungodly,* is there, Phil?"

"You called me *Philly Four-Eyes.*"

"Correct. Well, that's what you called yourself on the message machine."

"Oh! I left a message!"

"Yes, last evening. Don't you remember?"

"Well . . . no. Not exactly."

"You asked if we could *check the books,* that's what you said, *check the books,* and see if we could dig out any information on a *Norman Kitchen.*"

"Uh-huh."

"You understand, Phil, that we don't really keep those kinds of books."

"No. No, I guess not."

"I don't even know what kind of books those might be! Might I ask what this is all about?"

"You see, Norman Kitchen and I both attended Wolf Cubs at the church, in the early sixties."

"Indeed? Well, I really should be able to help you then."

"Why? Were you a Cub, too?"

"I was the scoutmaster for many years."

"You were the guy who held Akela? The guy with the really bony knees?"

"Yes. Yes, that's me. Not *too* bony."

"No, no. Not at all. I just remember they were a little bony. It's Phil. Little Philip McQuigge. Don't you remember me?"

"Oh, gosh, I'm sorry, Phil. There were just so many young lads over the years."

"I wore glasses. Really, really thick ones."

"There were several boys who wore spectacles."

"I was stocky. *Husky* was the word they used back then. My mom bought all my clothes from the Boy's *Husky* section at Eaton's."

"Mmmm . . . I'm so sorry."

"I had a brother named Jay."

"Oh, yes! I remember Jay."

"Really?"

"Oh, yes, Jay. He would play the piano in the rectory. He would come over often, to the church, and he would play the piano. Once or twice we even let him have a go at the organ, mind you, back then we couldn't afford a real pipe organ, still can't, although we have mounted a campaign, a drive, perhaps you might care to donate a few dollars?"

"Jay would go over to the church?"

"Yes. *McQuigge*, that's right, it's coming back to me now. A strange name. Jay McQuigge. You boys didn't have a father."

"Well, we were rankers. Rankers don't really have fathers."

"Er, ah, beg your pardon?"

"Sorry. I just meant, yes, we had no father."

"Was your mother a divorcée?"

"No, a widow. My father died. In a car accident. He sailed a blood-red Edsel into an abutment of the Diamond Bridge. Remember the Diamond Bridge?"

"Yes indeed. How old were you when this happened?"

"Oh, I was young. Four. Nobody really knows much about it. There was no evidence of steering failure, the weather was good, and back then there was no such thing as blood-alcohol levels, so there's no way of knowing what happened. I have to admit, Bill, that I have entertained the notion that he suicided. I entertain the notion especially late at night, especially these days."

"Especially these days?"

"It is not insignificant to me that my father died while crossing the Don River. My father died going through the ravine."

"Ah. The ravine can be a very dangerous place."

"Who are you, Bill?"

"Who am I in what sense, Phil?"

"Well, you tell me you were the scoutmaster, and I remember a tall man with a tallow complexion, clutching the broomstick that held the plastic wolf's head. I remember your knuckles would blanch, that's how seriously you undertook that task. You were a kindly man, but you didn't say much."

"I see. Yes. That sounds like me, all right."

"You showed me how to tie knots. And I was good at it, the best in the whole troop."

"Pack."

"Yes, the best in the whole pack. That's probably the thing I'm best at in life, tying knots."

"What is it you do for a living, Phil?"

"Oh . . . I'm in the television business. I was. Writer slash producer."

"Anything I might know?"

"Did you ever watch *Padre?*"

"Yes, indeed. In fact, that show is the only reason my grandchildren find me in the least bit *with it.*"

"You actually cradled the phone under your chin and made those little quote marks when you said that, didn't you?"

"Now that you mention it, I did!"

"So, what are you talking about, anyway? Why did my show alter your grandchildren's perception of you?"

"Well, you know. Because I too am a man of the cloth."

"Yipes!!"

"Hmm?"

"You're a priest?"

"We don't have priests in the United Church of Canada, Phil. You know that, don't you?"

"And all the time you were holding that wolf's head—Akela, dib dib dib—you were a priest?"

"A minister. Retired now, but they can't seem to clear me out of the place. I attend to the clerical work, I answer the telephones, check the messages . . . so what is the deal here, Phil? You and this Kitchen boy were close friends and now you want to reconnect?"

"Something like that. We were never all that connected."

"Google him!"

"I don't have access to the Internet, Father. Don't have it, don't need it. I'm more comfortable with ancient technology, like this telephone. I prefer real human contact."

"Are you making a joke, Phil?"

"No. I don't think so. I guess I am."

"If you want real human contact, come by the church sometime."

"I'd love to. But I'm somewhat busy these days. Working on a book, kind of a memoir. Only I'm calling it a novel because my memory is so fuzzy. Right now I'm writing about my dinner with Rainie van der Glick. I really should be getting back to that."

"Well, I'm here. Anytime you want to talk. But I wouldn't leave it too long, Phil."

"You mean, I should attend to matters of the spirit whilst I may. Seek my salvation before it's too late."

"That, and the fact that I'm eighty-seven years old."

"Got it. Nice talking to you, Bill."

"God bless."

11 | WHAT HAPPENED, INEXACTLY

TRUTH-TELLING IS EASY. AT LEAST, IT CAN BE. THAT IS THE OBSERVATION I am delivering, although you should know that it is, what, two o'clock in the morning. I am hovering over the laptop. Beside me is a bottle of wine, three-quarters full. But you know what? That's not the bottle I'm drinking from, ha ha, fooled everybody. No, in the kitchenette there is a soldier an inch away from being dead, that's the baby I've been sucking on. There are also a few beer cans retired to the recycling, enabling me to forget that I ever drank them, that they ever existed.

You wonder what I've been doing all these hours? When Reverend Nystrom woke me up this morning, I implied that I was going to buckle down and get to work right away. And that truly was my intention, but somehow I've managed to fritter the day away. I had errands to run, which is how I refer to the act of walking to the liquor store and buying booze. They've opened a new LCBO a few blocks away, a huge one with an extensive Vintages section, which is where they really gouge you for the plonk. Still, I tend to select from the Vintages section, hoping to give the impression I'm some sort of connoisseur. Then I take my purchase to the cash desks and select the queue I will stand in. My selection is not based on length of line, rather on which clerk is working the till, and how many days it's been since he or she has seen me. I've got them on a four-day rotation. Anyway, I bought some wine, then on the way home I impulsively ducked into the public library. All right, all right, I admit it, I pulled *Baxter* down from its perch in the "New and Notable" shelf, I leafed through briefly and determined that it was much like Hooper's other books, dense and impenetrable. And then I waited for a very long time for one of the computers to free up. There were four terminals, but young Asian men occupied them all, each intent on, I don't know, proving Fermat's Theorem or something. They clouded the screens with symbols I couldn't fathom, strings of numbers that seemed to stretch into infinity, squared and cubed and squared again. Finally one of them was successful at whatever he was doing and he signed off and I jumped into the wooden chair and called up the Google screen. Then I entered the name "Norman Kitchen," and was surprised to find no fewer than forty-eight of them spread across the North American continent. Forty-eight men with elaborate hairdos and fat, blubbery lips. Forty-eight men who'd had something terrible done to them before they were able to discover that life held beauty and wonder. I lost my stomach for the search, wandered out of the library and went for a long walk, which ended when I passed through the doors of Jilly's, a strip club. I sat there and looked at naked women and wondered if I would ever feel anything again. I wondered if I had ever felt anything. I came home, drank one of the bottles of wine—a very tasty Pinot Noir—slept it off, got up, and even though it seems like about an hour and a half's worth of activity, it's taken me until now . . . two o'clock in the morning.

So where was I, right, talking about truth-telling. What I'm getting at is that it is sometimes easy to tell the truth, as long as you are operating within a certain circle of humanity. Of humanness. Here's my metaphor. The truth, the ugly truth, I represent as a hammertoe. Know what one is? John Hooper has one, his little toe seems to come from someone else's body, it is tiny and lacks a nail of any significance and plays no part in the day-to-day operation of Hooper's foot. When he removes his right shoe and sock, this little appendage waves happily, hovering almost a full inch from the floor. And sometimes, at parties, Hooper will denude his foot and demonstrate his odd toe, and everyone is vaguely repulsed for a moment, and then someone, usually a woman, will want to touch the thing, and Hooper will end up in bed with yet another beauty. I've mentioned that I hate the man, correct? He slept with Veronica, you know that, despite which, his novel *Baxter* is receiving excellent reviews. Soon they are going to announce the short list for the Giller book prize, and I'll be surprised if *Baxter* isn't there. I'll be surprised if it isn't there and I'll kill myself if it is—anyway, the truth is like Hooper's hammertoe, and it is easy enough to reveal. But me, you know, I have no little hammertoe of a deformity, instead I am like the Elephant Man, shrouded from top to bottom with filthy rags. Any small parting of the cloth and people bolt, howling with fear. *I am not an animal*, I shriek at their disappearing backsides, although as the sound of the footsteps fades away, I fall silent and think, *Oh, who am I trying to kid?*

But Rainie van der Glick was with me as I donned the rags, wasn't she? As blemishes, boils and deformities manifested themselves, there was always a bit of time before I covered them up, a few days when they were exposed. There is no mirror for the soul, after all, one can only judge by the look of revulsion in the eyes of the citizenry. My belaboured point is, Rainie knew all about my failings. And didn't really seem to mind, kept nodding and shovelling pasta into her mouth, pausing three times during the meal to light cigarettes, smearing the filter-ends with bright red lipstick.

"Phil, Phil, Phil," she said, "what a mess you've made." She touched my hand, not especially tenderly—she prodded it almost as though testing for life, pressing down and releasing, seeing if blood would return to the clammy flesh.

"We're out of wine," I pointed out.

"I have some, um . . ." Rainie moved her mouth to one side to aid in taking mental inventory, but she quickly released it. "I got booze."

"Good."

"Don't drink too much, though," she said, rising from the table. "Don't forget, I am Our Lady of Perpetual Mercy Fucks."

I bet you want to know what happened, don't you? Not with Rainie van der Glick, although you no doubt want to know what happened on that front, too, but I bet you want to know what, precisely, my confession entailed, what I did to end up where I am today.

Seven years ago, I created a television series called *Padre*. You may very well have seen it, especially if you're Canadian, because the series was on the air for a grand total of one hundred and fifty-six hours. You may also have seen the show if you live in either Germany or Japan, where it is something of a hit. It has always struck me as odd that the show is appreciated in those countries, because, as a postwar baby, I tend to view those nations as the Enemy. I have attended a fan-fest in Japan (they hold them annually) where I was confronted by an auditorium full of people, most of them men, most of them dressed in clerical garb and wearing white ten-gallon hats. If you live in the United States of America, it is not likely that you have seen the show, where it ran for a grand total of two episodes on UPN. The second episode actually made the Guinness Book of Records: lowest ratings for a network television show. And I wrote it!

The premise of *Padre* is simple, compelling and totally stolen from *The Bullet and the Cross*. I have never been called on it, because

a) more people saw the second episode in the U.S. than saw *The Bullet and the Cross* and b) I lifted my premise from the B story, that of Father White, the virile clergyman. In *Padre*, Edward Milligan portrays Gabe Quinton, a pastor sent westward by the higher-ups in some church, a Christian denomination characterized largely by the apparency that their ministers have very little actual ministering to do, and therefore have lots of time left over to duke it out with blackguards and ne'er-do-wells. Father Quinton does give the occasional sermon, but they are almost always interrupted by gun-toting desperadoes. If I lived in the fictional Boone City, I wouldn't attend one of Father Quinton's gatherings for anything, but in the world I created the little church is always filled to the rafters with wholesome people, fresh-faced farmers and their progeny, chaste-looking women with large breasts.

The show was popular (at least in the unlikely axis of Canada, Germany and Japan) largely because of Edward Milligan. Milligan was a stupefyingly handsome man, and his perfect features were laid out in such a manner as to suggest a purity no amount of evil could sully. I point to his features because he surely lacked the acting ability to portray this innocence, which was in violent opposition to his true nature.

The last credit in the title sequence read: CREATED BY PHILIP MCQUIGGE. The card immediately preceding this one identified me as the Executive Producer. Those of you unfamiliar with the television industry may wonder what, exactly, that position entails, so by way of explanation, I will describe a typical day. Actually, if I describe a day that occurred in the last six months of the show's production, you may get a pretty good idea of what went wrong.

I enter the production facilities at about nine-thirty in the morning; shooting doesn't start until two-thirty, because it has been pushed an hour. Production went late the night before, and the unions are very strict about turnarounds, so although the boards announce a call-time of eight o'clock for six consecutive days, we are now starting in the afternoon. And, I'll point out, one doesn't get to this point without spending thousands of extra dollars on overtime, so I enter the building with a dour expression pasted firmly on my face.

I choose the door that is closest to my office, but that still forces me to walk down thirty-five yards of corridor. I have considered having a door built so that I could enter my office directly, but there is no money for anything like that; the budget barely covers production costs, and there are always overages, particularly when Jimmy Yu is directing, which is the case on this day.

So I walk the thirty-five yards, and people descend upon me. "Phil!" "Phil!"

Willy Props comes at me toting a cumbersome machine, a typewriter so antiquated that it looks almost postmodern, the keys ovular, the striking pegs thin and bent like spider's legs. "Check it out," commands Willy, who is perpetually drug-addled. "For 607." I have to stop to think: we are filming 605, this is the last day of pre-production for 606, so this is for, um, right, Barker's script, which is in pre-pre. I vaguely remember the plot twist that necessitated an ancient typewriting machine, but I thought I told him to deep-six it.

"Look," says Willy, "this baby is a hundred and sixteen years old."

"Where did you get it?"

Willy Props has to think about that. He remembers. "Oh, yeah. There's a typewriter museum in, what, like, Canton, Ohio. We're renting this baby."

"For . . . ?"

"Two thou. American."

"Too steep. Send it back."

"But—"

"See, the thing is, Willy, there is *magic* in television. But no one around here ever trusts the stuff. We don't need to get an actual hundred-and-sixteen-year-old typewriter. We could shoot a dishwasher and just *say* it's a hundred-and-sixteen-year-old typewriter, and everyone—everyone except Ernst Kibble—would believe us. Send it back."

Ernst Kibble, in case you are wondering, is a man who lives in, I don't know, a rabbit warren in Northern Ontario. He watches *Padre* faithfully, but has no interest in the show other than the spotting and reporting of historical inaccuracies. He's the supreme bullet-counter. You know what I mean, right? For example, in the crowd at the Galaxy Odeon there were at least four kids who, upon commencement of any gunfight in the Old West, would start counting aloud the bullets fired. If there was ever a seventh bullet discharged from a six-shooter these little creatures would howl derisively. Bullet-counters grow up to be accountants, for the most part, although Ernst Kibble has the syndrome too profoundly to function in society. He once pointed out to us—via an email, a godsend to the insane—that the stars in the night sky were in an alignment that belied our stated time of year. "That is simply not a November vistage!"

At any rate, Willy turns around dolefully. I make a short bolt toward my office, but I am confronted by Dirk Mayhew, the production manager. "He's insane!"

"I know he's insane. He's also a genius." No, we're not discussing Mr. Kibble, rather Jimmy Yu, the director.

"Fire him!"

"I can't fire him," I sigh wearily, "there's only two days left in the shoot."

"You have to fire him . . ." I don't have to record all of this conversation, which actually went on for close to ten minutes, these sentences and minor variations deftly lobbed back and forth. It ends when something explodes inside Dirk Mayhew's jacket. He pulls out a walkie-talkie and barks into it. A huge gust of static is returned. I can hear nothing that even resembles the human voice, but apparently Dirk can, because he wheels about and charges away. There are only about ten yards to the door to my office (at least, the door to the productorial bullpen) and my sanctuary.

I launch down the narrow hallway. Michelangelo Barker stands there, a mug of tea in his hand. Michelangelo is so large that his finger can't fit through the cup's handle; he pinches it tightly between thumb and index. All colour has drained away from the skin. Given how pale Barker is anyway, this means that his digits virtually glow. It is my intention to ignore him—I'll throw him a nod, flicker the edges of my mouth briefly—but he bristles as I pass by. He bristles so forcefully that I am tossed into the opposite wall.

"Is there a problem, Mr. Barker?"

"Ah, no, no. *Yes.*"

"And that would be . . . ?"

"You have taken out Padre's dialogue with the dying old woman."

"Dialogue? It was a *speech.* The old woman says nothing."

"She is too weak to enunciate. But human intercourse doesn't always rely on words. Hmmm."

"It does on the wonderbox, Michelangelo."

"All right. I'll ignore science and give the old woman some lines, even though her lungs are clogged and useless."

"Okay, but that's not really the problem. The problem is with what Padre says, this *You were always like a mother to me.*"

"What's wrong with that?"

"Well, he hardly knew the woman. She's only in this episode. She's a fucking plot device, Michelangelo."

"Yes, but we know that Padre's mother was killed by despera-does, therefore this shadow taints his relationship with women."

"Who says Padre's mother was killed by desperadoes?"

Michelangelo's eyebrows knit momentarily with confusion. "You did. It's in the Bible. He was a baby in a bodega . . ."

"On television," I interrupt, "relationships can't be *tainted*. The audience can't understand a tainted relationship. The medium is not designed to convey *taints*."

"Hmm. Really." It is all there in Barker's attitude, in the slight stirring of his body. He looks down upon me; his eyebrows ripple across the top of his tiny spectacles. And he might as well speak it aloud: *It is not the medium that can't convey taints—subtleties—it's you.*

"Besides," I barge on, "the scene went on too long. It went on for three pages. Too much. Get to the action. Always remember that. *Character is action.*" I often offer up little dicta of this nature, to emphasize the fact that I am experienced, crafty and, more to the point, his boss. Barker backs away into his office, the former broom closet. I run at the door that says EXECUTIVE PRODUCERS and hurl myself through.

"Good fucking morning." Dora Worsley is looming over Cassie's desk, a sheaf of contracts in her hands. Dora is the Producer. In the land of television, there are various sorts and levels of produc-ers, and you may not care who's who and what's what, but just in case you do, here's how things break down. I am the Executive Producer, having created the show. There is also a Supervising Producer. In the case of *Padre*, it is an earnest young man named Stevie Medjuck. There is also a Co-Producer, who often (and in this case) is simply a writer with a good agent. And there's a plain old producer Producer, who does all the work. And that is Dora Worsley, a woman who always looks as though—if she doesn't get something to eat damn soon—she's going to die.

There is something in Dora's tone that suggests all is not as it should be. (The expletive inserted between *good* and *morning* means nothing, Dora's speech is peppered with obscenities. Dora was abandoned as an infant in a truck stop, subsequently raised to adulthood by the drivers and waitresses. At least, that's my theory.) But I am in no mood to deal with problems. I never am, for one thing, but also there is work to do, so I simply nod a greeting at Worsley and extend my hand toward Cassie Elliot, who stuffs it with slips of paper, my telephone messages. At last I achieve my own office, and I slam the door shut behind me.

I have eleven messages; seven are from Carla Dowbiggin, who is the network executive assigned to our show. One is from my brother, Jay, because, on the day I am describing, he is still willing to talk to me. However, I am not talking to him, exactly; I crumple up the piece of paper with his name on it, toss it into the wastebasket. What else do I have here? A message from Ian George. Who the hell is Ian George? Into the trash with that one. There is a request to call from Pamela Anderson, no, not that one, this Pamela Anderson is a journalist from *Canada Screen*, an industry organ. The industry, as you may know, is dead, and the writers from *Canada Screen* are desperate for copy, so I often have a message from one of them, usually Pamela Anderson. Occasionally I call her back, but . . . not today. Into the bin. And the final message is from Ronnie, but there is nothing noted in the little box marked TIME. I don't know if this message is fresh or stale. She may have left it yesterday, after I'd left for the day. Or she may have left it this morning, in which case there is likely some small bit of kid-related logistics to work out, which Ronnie will discuss with frosty hauteur. She is angry with me, although she has no reason to be.

Let me restate that. I mean that there is no discernible trigger for Veronica's anger, no misdeed or hurtful incident. I don't suppose that's the same as having no reason for anger. Although last evening I executed my duties successfully—I took Ellis to her Scottish dancing lesson, I drove Currer to the mall and helped her buy a slide rule (did you know we still used slide rules or did you, like me, think that we'd abandoned the mysterious things as ancient technology?) and then I picked up Ellis and delivered everybody home—I did all this in a state of muted annoyance. Ronnie asked, "Everything okay at work?" and I shrugged. That wasn't fair, in retrospect; it's one thing to give a surly non-verbal response, it's another to give one that doesn't convey *anything*. Ronnie then tried to detail her day, which was informed by activity for the sake of activity, at least, that's the dismissive view I took of it, because why didn't Ronnie care about the hellish day *I'd* had?

You're beginning to get a dim notion of the dynamics between my wife and me. Not very healthy, oh no. We really should have been in counselling for a long time, probably since, I don't know, right after she laughed at the chee-chee joke. But after a few years our relationship was so twisted and gnarled that it gave the illusion of functionality; at least we both knew how each day would proceed, so we lied to ourselves and believed that everything was all right.

But, as you may gather from the vigour with which I crush the message slip, such is not the case.

I take a deep breath of air and stab in the numbers that connect me with Carla Dowbiggin. Carla is a housewife and mother of four from Aurora, Ontario, who, through some twist of fate, is in charge of fully one-half of the network's production slate. She's a nice enough woman, I guess, but she has no grasp of dramatic structure, no feel for characterization or dialogue, despite which, these are the things she criticizes on a daily basis. I am phoning for the non-stop note-giving, in which Carla addresses what she calls "network concerns." Some of these concerns are grandly pitched—"The network is concerned that Padre's decision is ethically fishy"—and some are aimed low—"The network is concerned about the usage of the word *crap*."

"But Padre's just stepped in some."

"Some what?"

"Crap."

"Oh . . ." I hear the riffling of paper as Carla checks her script. "Oh. Yes, he's just stepped in some, I see, but maybe it could just be a take. You know. See his expression. He needn't say *crap*."

"Okay, let me just make a note of that. Doesn't . . . need . . . to . . . say . . ." I, of course, am making no note. I never do. For the most part I merely allow Carla to ramble on, mumbling haltingly to give the impression that it is all being recorded. Occasionally I'll argue, and quite vociferously, just to keep her happy. "Carla, I can't change that!"

"Phil, the network is very concerned—"

"It's integral to the script. I can't, I *won't*, change it."

At this point I may not have any idea what it is I won't change, but if I don't put my foot down every now and again it becomes difficult to do so when it's absolutely necessary. Because sometimes Carla will convey a network concern of such numbing stupidity that it takes me a long moment to react.

"*What?*"

"It gives the impression that she's actually sleeping with this man."

"But but but . . . she's a prostitute."

"She's a *dance-hall queen*. That's the name of the episode, after all."

"But *dance-hall queen* is not her *job*, Carla. Of course she's a prostitute, and she has to be, I mean, that's why the people of Boone City want to throw her out of town."

"Couldn't she be, um, you know, a strong-minded independent woman who has more than one steady boyfriend?"

"I suppose so. As long as she has sex with them and charges them money."

This practice of moronic note-giving has been part of the industry since the very beginning. A story that I sometimes tell at workshops and seminars (I *was* a gun in Canadian television, which, I'll grant you, would be a gun of very low calibre, maybe even just an air pistol) has to do with a wonderful episode of *The Twilight Zone* called "The Last Night of a Jockey," starring Mickey Rooney, the great (I think perhaps the greatest) American actor. In it, the Mick plays a disgraced jockey who, drunk and alone in his seedy hotel room, wishes only that he were a "big man." He wakes up and discovers his head hits the ceiling—he's eight feet tall, way too tall to sit on a horse. Anyway, Serling employed the word "dwarf" when scripting one of the jockey's drunken, self-pitying diatribes. Carla Dowbiggin—at least, her spiritual forebear—insisted that he use a less offensive term, like (and I quote) "shrimp" or "half-pint."

After I get Carla off the phone, I power up my computer and get to work. I have to put out the pinks of 606. In the television business, successive drafts change colour, pink to blue to green, etc. It is possible to run through all the available hues and end up with a script printed on white paper, although, in the logic-defying parlance of the industry, this is referred to as "double white."

And as I do so, I imagine myself in a garret somewhere, writing a big novel bulging with thematic concerns, a tome that is problematic structurally, but so vast in scope that it must be thus. That was the plan, wasn't it? I was going to write a novel. My mother could take it to the sofa, recline, press her cheek against folded knuckles and read the day away.

Instead I am writing an hour-long television show and talking on the telephone to people who are all, to one degree or another, angry with me.

It is with this thought in my mind that, two hours later, I dash out to the makeup trailer.

Edward Milligan is in there, two hours before his first scheduled appearance before the camera. People often imagine that television stars lead fabulously glamorous lives, pausing only occasionally to work, to smile and emote on the sound stage, but Milligan has no other existence, really. He sometimes shows up at shopping malls or charity events, but only to get his photograph taken. And there is some weird corner of the night that Milligan inhabits from time to time (in the bars and down in the decadent rumpus room) which is informed by drug use and jaded sexual acts, as in, *I'm going to suspend you from the ceiling and lash you with licorice twists, not because it turns me on but because I've never done it before and it might for a few moments dull my boredom.* I know this because, as Executive Producer, I have received some letters:

Dear Mr. McQuig,

It may interest you to know that Ed Milligan, your fucking priest on your show, is really a asshole, because he hung me from a ceiling and whipped me with licorice twists, and not even real black licorice but that red stuff which isn't even licorice, anyway, I was humiliated and I have talked to a lawyer and he says that I deserve some money . . .

But for the most part Edward Milligan is on-set, where all of his basic needs can be met. There is food there, for example, and a jesus-big trailer equipped with a state-of-the-art entertainment system and a bed. Milligan can also sate his most basic need on-set, that for adoration. The crew stop short of actually kowtowing, but they exhibit a more muted sign of veneration, lifting their hands at his approach, palms outward, the universal sign of meekness and surrender in the face of power. The studio also supplies a steady stream of bedmates, and although I have occasionally tried to intervene ("You know, sleeping with Milligan might not be the best move, career-wise"), these affairs are usually over days, sometimes only hours, after their onset.

Milligan also spends hours in the makeup trailer, fine-tuning his appearance. He is the Aryan ideal to such an extent that I think Hitler himself would have balked—"Oh, come on, let's not get carried away!" Milligan's looks are so perfect that they don't really require any attention, but Edward likes to sit in the chair and have Bellamy work on them, dividing his attention between the mirror in front of him and the stack of magazines on his lap, which he flips through like an automaton, his eyes scanning for images of himself.

When I enter on this day, Milligan says, "This week's script sucks."

"Mm-hmm," I hum as I climb into the chair next to him, after passing a hand lightly across Bellamy's backside.

"I liked it well enough," says Bellamy, whose diction can be a little odd. She comes from a small town in Manitoba, and I sometimes imagine a tiny hamlet inhabited by chinstrapped farmers and weeds-wearing women, the people hailing each other with phrases like "How goeth it with thou?"

"Padre is being too passive."

This *passivity* thing is Milligan's constant bugbear, something he must have picked up at, say, the Banff Television Festival. (He would have been dragged, sleepless and buzzing with pharmaceuticals, into an onstage panel, the area of discussion something like *The Arc:*

Narrative in Long Form. He would have spent his time gazing at the audience, searching for likely fuck-friends. But someone, a writer or producer or someone, must have addressed passivity, at which point Milligan's ears would have sharpened like a Doberman's. He has many physical skills that he feels are underutilized. Besides the gun-handling artistry that I told you about, he can also do some fancy lariat twirling and work a bullwhip. He resents the fact that he too rarely gets to demonstrate these things, that Padre spends a lot of time simply standing in front of the congregation.)

"How about," says Milligan, "when that guy, the bad fuck, comes into the church, here's what I was thinking, I stop the sermon about the good samma-ritten and I jump, you know, leap, you know, dive, across people, which I can do, we won't need a stunt double, and I take him down, grab his gun, you know, do a little flashy spin and then stick the barrel down his throat and say, um, *Now laugh, asshole.* Or whatever they said for *asshole* in the olden days."

There are many things wrong with this idea, but I should tell you that Padre's clearly psychopathic behaviour is not at the top of the list. Gabe Quinton does this sort of thing quite a bit. In season one, he was studious, more sedate, but over the years—in part due to Milligan's campaigning, in part due to the network's interventions—he has become alarmingly vigorous. More to the point, none of Milligan's suggestions would serve the story, only the moment. This is a truth about actors, I think; they are doglike in terms of their conception of time—they exist only in the here and now. But none of this can I explain to Edward Milligan, so, being petulant and argumentative, I demand, "What the hell is a *samma-ritten?*"

"Someone from St. Moritz?" suggests Bellamy, who has quite a good sense of humour, although I only allow myself to appreciate it in the dark belly of the night.

"I don't know," says Milligan. "It's in the fucking script."

I reach into my pocket and pull out the sides, unfold them. The actual text for the day's shooting is at the back of a little booklet detailing the military logistics. It is set in very tiny type, demonstrating just how much weight it carries. I search for Padre's sermon and locate the source of confusion. "Oh. Samaritan."

"Whatever," says Milligan. "Samma-ritten."

"No, Ed . . ." (I call him *Ed* when I want to press a point.) "You have to say *Samaritan*."

"What the fuck is a *Samaritan?*"

"Someone from Samaria."

"And Samaria is exactly where?"

"Well, uh, I don't think it exists any more."

"So who the fuck cares? I'll say what I want. It's not like we'll get letters from insulted samma-rittens."

"But if you say *samma-ritten,* no one will know what you're talking about."

Bellamy has opened one of the drawers beneath the makeup mirror, is bending over and rooting about for some unguent. I stare at her ass, which is one of the things I like most about her, the perfect, unblemished rear end.

"No one's going to know what I'm talking about anyway. No one's ever heard of a Samaritan."

"Wrong-o, Edward. It's a famous story. The reason you haven't heard of it is, it's in the Bible."

"Oh, fuck. Not that again. Bible this, Bible that. Why is Padre always going on about stuff in the fucking Bible?"

You see what I have (what I had) to deal with?

"You do know, don't you, what the Bible is?"

"Yes, I know what the Bible is, there's no reason to get all, all . . ." Milligan is at a loss for words, which is understandable; I estimate his expressive vocabulary at about eight hundred words.

"*Shirty?*" suggests Bellamy.

"Yeah. No reason to get all shirty." Milligan doesn't know the expression, but is willing to defer to Bellamy. He trusts her, perhaps more than he trusts any other human being; she does, after all, tend to his appearance.

People tend to trust Bellamy, anyway. I guess I should describe her, being as she is the woman with whom I had an affair. You probably picked that up, I sure hope you did, I wouldn't want you to think that I grope and leer at every woman who happens across my path. I suppose there was some leering done at Amy, the waitress at Birds of a Feather, and, to be truthful, there has been a little gropage here and there, which I discount as largely the result of overdrinking.

Bellamy is a small woman but substantial, nowhere near fat but, well, there is some meat on her bones. In the imaginary Manitoban town there were dairies and immense cattle farms, and Bellamy was raised on a diet of healthy but fatty foods. Her skin radiates wholesomeness, even though Bellamy has been citified to the extent that her clothes are often tight-fitting and revealing. Her hair is light brown and rambunctious, and she contains it with a variety of twists, sticks, pins, even the occasional bow. She has grass-green eyes and blindingly white teeth and she is young, there's no getting around that. She is only twenty-eight years of age, and I will be fifty in two years (or—another way of putting that, given the pace at which I'm composing—sometime near the end of this book). She is cute, rather than beautiful. (Veronica is beautiful.) She is almost always smiling, and only isn't when listening to another's problems, when offering solace. Many people turn to Bellamy with their trials and tribulations; she possesses good sense abounding, and receiving a hug from her is a great treat. In bed she is athletic and playful, and that last adjective is important, at least in terms of understanding my infidelity.

I should make it clear here and now that I don't mean to excuse my behaviour. But neither do I mean to simply kick my ass around the block, which would be every bit as tiresome, wouldn't it, as a litany of lame justifications. I guess the thing is that the past is the past, as hard and permanent as stone. So I did what I did. I must therefore have had my reasons, although at the time I could not have stated with any clarity what they were. I still can't, although I am getting some clues. Like this playfulness thing. Every time Bellamy stripped off and leapt upon the mattress it was as though it were the first time. Not that she was virginal, more that she'd forgotten that there were standard procedures and practices. Bellamy would invent the act anew, which may be a little hard to comprehend without you having been there. I want to avoid unseemly details, but I'll cite, as an example, the occasion in which Bellamy backed up into me with such determination that I half-heard an insistent *beep-beep-beep*.

The matrimonial bed was a little stern. A bit grim, if you want to know the truth. I'm not alluding to any frigidity on Ronnie's part; she was game enough (if only occasionally so) but rather single-minded in her quest for release, which sometimes placed me on the sidelines, like a coach, even a cheerleader. That's fine, you know, every man for himself, but problems started popping up—actually, I've made a little joke without anyone, you or me, realizing it, because problems *didn't* pop up. Ah-hah. The spirit was indeed willing, but the flesh was weak.

I discussed this with my doctor, and he prescribed some drugs that worked, the only problem being that the drugs had to be ingested an hour before lovemaking. Ronnie liked spontaneity, and I was deprived forever of this luxury. I took oodles of pills on the off chance that the night held promise, but too often she drifted off to sleep and I lay beside her, lightheaded, all my blood rerouted to an aching, wailing penis. And many times Ronnie caught me unprepared. I would do what I could, but this was too often not good enough, so, like any sensible couple, we simply ceased discussing any of this. We certainly didn't seek counsel, which maybe should be the motto of our civilization, emblazoned on the entranceways to subway stations and shopping malls: SEEK COUNSEL.

When I did go visit Bellamy at her apartment, once every three weeks or so, I was already fired up when I knocked upon the door. So inside the tiny one-bedroom (which she shared with a number of stuffed animals and a live turtle, although it was barely more animate than its roommates) I became a fully functioning lover, although I gather I fell short of noteworthy studliness. "That was swell," was something Bellamy tended to say, or "Nice!"

Okay now, I'm bailing out. These things shall be addressed again, as well as all the aspects I'm avoiding: how the affair was discovered, Ronnie's reaction (!), things like that. In terms of novelizing, I see I have a couple of story-points to cover (in the argot of the television industry, I have beats to hit) before moving on to the next section.

One takes place in the makeup trailer, where I am achieving emotional equilibrium by bickering with Milligan on one hand, and basking in the subdued light of Bellamy's affection on the other. And I challenge Milligan, I say, "Why don't you read the Bible? I mean, you're the one who prides himself on the research you do for your roles, did it ever occur to you to pick up a copy of the Big Book and have a little peek inside?"

Milligan actually prides himself on being someone known as someone who prides himself on his research. I don't believe he ever did a lick of the stuff, but he plucks up my challenge. "Okay, smartass," he snaps. Milligan looks at himself in the mirror, adjudges himself perfect and leaps from the chair. "I'm going to do that."

When he leaves the trailer, Bellamy and I kiss, I fondle her breast, everything is quite pleasant for a few minutes. Then I return to my office, although you should know that, halfway to the main building, something inside me bellows and then deadens. I stumble and go down onto my knees. A grip comes out of the Craft Services truck and lifts his eyebrows. "What's the matter?"

I don't have the wherewithal to create a response, the question being so dismal and massive.

And the next beat: given the proclivities of (what my mother called) the little man, how did I fare when Our Lady of Perpetual Mercy Fucks decided I required her blandishments and blessings? Well, um, I did okay. It was largely a case of Rainie van der Glick not taking no for an answer; after all, she had come to perform a little miracle and she was determined to do so.

I got up, slipped on my clothes in the darkness. Not knowing what to say, but wanting to say something, I offered a lame "Thanks."

"*It's*," said Rainie van der Glick dramatically, "what you need."

———

"Hi. It's you."

"What?"

"See, it's not me. It's not all about *me*. It's *you*."

"Ah! A highly amusing canard."

"Have you been sleeping with Willie Beckett?"

"Excuse me?"

"Oh, you know. It's a joke. Only not funny."

"Phil, Phil, Phil. Don't make me shoot for sole custody. The girls couldn't stand it, and neither could I, but when you act like this—"

"Like what?"

"You're lit to the tits."

"Why do you say that? Who have you been talking to?"

"Oh man, I can tell when you're drunk. I used to believe I could tell how much you'd had as soon as you walked through the front door. Or stumbled into the bedroom, whatever. I'd take a look and say, um, *Four pints and a shot of single malt. Three vodka martinis. A bottle of wine, not a particularly good one.* I can't do that any more, Phil. You're off the scale."

"No, it's just a funny expression to use, *lit to the tits*."

"Because you don't technically have tits?"

"I really don't like discussing tits with you."

"We're not discussing tits."

"I miss yours."

"What about your little whatever-her-name-is, Bellamy? She's got tits, doesn't she?"

"She's not *mine*. I'm not with her."

"You have no right to miss my tits."

"I can't help it."

"Listen, it's good you called."

"It is?"

"Because I need to discuss something with you. I want to go on a little trip, you know, get out of the country and this foul weather for a week or so."

"Oh. Sure, you deserve a holiday."

"So I'm going to Mexico."

"Mexico? Mexico is *dangerous*."

"Don't worry. I'm going with Kerwin."

"Kerwin?"

"My friend Kerwin."

"Oh. Fine. Fine. Just one thing, won't Kerwin miss too much school?"

"No, not really. He can trade off his teaching assignments—"

"He'll fall too far behind with his homework."

"Oh. Very funny."

"When would this expedition take place?"

"In three weeks. We leave on November 15."

"Wait, wait, wait. I thought you said you wanted to discuss this with me. What kind of discussion is *We leave on November 15?*"

"Fine, it's not a discussion. Mark it on your calendar."

"And who's paying for this trip?"

"Kerwin."

"Really? How long has he been saving up his allowance?"

"Give it a rest, Phil."

"He didn't have to break open his piggy bank, did he?"

"Hey. Kerwin is older than fucking Bellamy."

"Yeah, yeah, yeah, but I'm not going to Mexico with Bellamy."

"Well, get a life, Phil. You wanted another life, you certainly didn't like your life with me, so go get another. I did. And I *like* it."

"See, that's just it. I never wanted another life."

"That's what you say. That's what you may think. But it obviously didn't mean anything to you, our life together, because you were willing to risk it. And now it's gone, Phil. It is *so* gone."

"Maybe we should see, you know, a marriage counsellor."

"Oh, come off it. That'd be like taking a car that was totalled to a mechanic. This is beyond fixing, Phil."

"But I can change, I can change. Like didn't I say, *It's not me, it's you?*"

"You can't change, Phil, because you don't know who you are. You have no concept of the things you do, or why you do them. You're a mystery, an enigma. A fucking black hole. And you're just not capable of change. You may be capable of learning little tricks— *It's not me, it's you*—but notice that it is *still* you, I tell you about my trip to Mexico and your reaction is to get your dick all twisted, you have the emotional intelligence of a thirteen-year-old. A mature human being would tell me to have a great time."

"That's pushing it. I'm supposed to say, *Have a great time with your boy lover. Have a great time bouncing from bed to bed in some resort, snorting pina coladas to replenish energy and fluids?*"

"The girls say you never have anything good to eat over there."

"Whoa. What happened to that conversation we were having?"

"It ended."

"You could have at least made some half-hearted segue. *Speaking of replenishment, the girls say*, and what do you mean? I have all sorts of good things to eat."

"Pickled eggs?"

"Yeah, I got pickled eggs."

"I know you have pickled eggs. That's *all* you have, a jar of pickled eggs. And the girls loathe them, in fact, I don't know a single person who likes pickled eggs. I don't even think *you* like pickled eggs."

"No, I hate 'em. I thought the girls liked them."

"If you want, I'll help you do the shopping for when I'm away."

"Oh, fuck."

"What?"

"I don't know, the whole notion is just sickening, that's all."

"The notion of me going away with Kerwin?"

"Yeah, and the notion of you helping me shop for while you're away, while you're flipping from bed to bed with Kermit. I think I have to go throw up, now."

"You're off the scale, Phil. You have to do something. I worry about you."

"Like shit, you do. Bye-bye."

"Okay, we'll talk in a few da—"

12 | KÜNSTLERROMAN

I PRINT OUT ALL THE TIME, EVERY FIVE PAGES OR SO, THE PRINTER spitting papers into the gloomy sittingroomette. From there I ferry them into the kitchenette, where I do my proofing at the little table. You may find it hard to credit, but I take pains. I adjust adjectives and adverbs, I tinker with syntax and there is often wholesale excising that must be done. I am, these past few days, driven to do this not so much out of artistic pride as out of bitter pettiness, because Hooper's novel *Baxter* was indeed nominated for the Giller Prize. His novel was also placed on the short list for the Governor General's Literary Award. What irks about this is not the sudden fame Hooper has gained (there is an arts magazine show on CBC television that now features him weekly), nor is it the money he's made (the rumour is that the sale to the American publishers was for half a million bucks), but rather the fact that Hooper has, against all odds, lived his life with determination and dignity. He has spent years grinding out novels, fat and dense and often unreadable. Hooper has existed in penury and squalor. His situation has, from time to time in the past, been ameliorated by the acquisition of a rich girlfriend, but Hooper has resisted any and all civilizing attempts, and these women have vanished. And instead of dying penniless and obscure, he has become rich and famous. Is there no justice?

The true target of my anger is, of course, myself. I chose not to live in penury and squalor, my present situation notwithstanding. Instead I went to work in teevee land, I jumped into Beckett's fabulous river of money, and you have probably gathered that all my claims of seduction and coercion are groundless.

Any ambition I may have had to be a novelist was abandoned early on, when I decided that my talents were more suited to the theatre. I don't feel guilty about *that* choice; playwrighting is an honourable profession that offers more than ample opportunity to die penniless and obscure. I even lived happily enough in destitution, banging out my plays on an old typewriter, the kind that might have been toted behind enemy lines by a hardened, alcoholic war correspondent. And I resisted civilizing every bit as categorically as Hooper; there was a sizable percentage of Toronto's female population who thought me one of the great assholes of all time. So what went wrong?

Well, I met Ronnie Lear, and tumbled into love. I consider it love at first sight, although I've described how I initially spent many minutes staring at her, wary and vaguely nauseous. But when she laughed, I was doomed; I set about winning her.

She was with Hooper, which I didn't really consider too great an obstacle. True, he was much better looking than I. (In fact, a recent newspaper profile granted him "movie-star good looks," a phrase that sent me scuttling for the toilet.) Hooper was also much more charming, erudite and amusing than I, at least he usually was. But I saw with delight that in the company of Miss Lear he *wasn't being himself*. His Shavian wit quit him; he quipped in a desperate, scattergun manner, hoping that *something* would hit the target. (The target being Veronica's delectable funny bone.) His more serious, learned comments didn't fare any better. He would quote philosophers, refer to ancient texts, summarize Victorian novels in an offhand manner. It got him nowhere. Sometimes Veronica would gaze upon him as though he were a blithering idiot, and when that happened, Hooper invariably became one.

"But but but," he'd stammer, "you've read *Daniel Deronda*, haven't you?"

"Naw-uh. What did he write?"

"No, no. He's a book. I mean, *it's* a book. It has a man's name, but it's a book. That is what we call an eponymous, um, did you want another drink?"

Myself, I had nothing to lose and, when sitting at a crowded table in the Pig's Snout, would patiently await my chances. When they came, I would get off a good one, amusing the table and invariably delighting Ms. Lear. One has one's moments, you know. And although it shames me to admit it now (at the time, of course, I had no shame), I would often bring a young woman with me. I would lavish attention and affection upon my date, which was usually reciprocated; this helped nurture the illusion that I was desirable.

Mind you, I knew that I couldn't attempt a direct romantic onslaught. I was bound by the Male Code of Honour, a vague canon of conduct that some of us had hammered out in the belly of the night while pissed as newts. John Hooper was one of its most influential authors, the one who had decided that there must be consequences, punishment for transgressions. Therefore, when a young theatrical director named George Gordon treated his girlfriend with what even we could see was contemptible contempt, Gordon was forced to apologize publicly and to offer an engagement ring as a token of atonement. (The woman in question, thank god, declined; I have enough weighing on my conscience without that.) Some of the chastisements were harder to bring into effect. So, for example, if I obviously tried to bird-dog Hooper's girlfriend, a drunken tribunal would be convened, and it would rule, oh, that I should join the Foreign Legion. Or the priesthood. Or that I should be doomed to stumble along the sidewalks forever, half-drunk and maudlin, my heart destroyed not by romance but by my own despicable betrayal. Who needs that?

What I did instead was write a play. I would guess that it took me about a month, but that is not the way I remember the act of creation. It seems to me that I sat down behind my old typer one night, armed with cigarettes and whiskey, began banging away and did not stand up until my crippled fingers had beaten out the words "Lights down." From there I staggered into the Pig's Snout, and threw the thing onto the table. "You might want to give this a read, Ronnie," I said. "There's a good part there for someone like you."

Someone like you. I believe I really said that, so fundamentally crafty am I. The part could *only* have been played by her, that was the whole point. I might as well have written:

```
Enter HESTER, a young woman of
incredible beauty. We get the
impression that her father is
Scottish and her mother
Malaysian.
```

The play in question is entitled *The Hawaiian*, which is, in my fictive world, the name of a particularly seedy little tavern. (Almost all of my plays took place in bars—*Write what you know,* said Hemingway, although I bet he regrets that now.) Hester is the waitress. There are four regulars, witty young writers who discuss high-minded subjects like literature and philosophy. Into this scene walks Oscar, who has just murdered his parents and still clutches the smoking gun. As police surround the Hawaiian, Oscar takes the people hostage. Things get thenceforth pretty tense. The police exhort from outside, the people within plead urgently, tearfully, but Oscar is obdurate and deranged. It all culminates in the young man taking Hester as a human shield, throwing open the door to the Hawaiian with her neck caught in the crook of his arm, the gun barrel pressed up against her beautiful temple. (I know it's hard for temples to be beautiful, but hey, we're talking about Ronnie Lear here.) No solution seems possible, until Hester reaches up and squeezes Oscar's trigger finger, sacrificing her own life for the greater good.

You may think me an idiot—go ahead, be my guest—but the paucity of my ideas, the meagreness of my creativity, hasn't really registered until just now. Until just this afternoon, anyway, which is when I wrote that last paragraph. I immediately reeled out of the basement apartment in search of stuporifics. I went first to the Pig's Snout, but it was no longer there. In its place there was a small health club. Behind plate-glass windows, a group of women in leotards moved in sweaty synchronicity to music I could not hear. I stared at the edifice wistfully, until a policeman came and instructed me to move along. My avowals of innocent nostalgia fell upon deaf ears. It occurred to me that I *was* pretty much a lecherous voyeur, which didn't improve my self-esteem. I searched out the nearest bar, the Reno, a place that survived on the welfare cheques of diurnal drinkers. There were six of these creatures represented as I slipped through the front door. I fell into conversation with an older man named Christos, who was so embittered by women and the vagaries of fate that I acquired a sheen of innocence through proximity and comparison. I was the one dealing out hopeful maxims: "Things are never as bad as they seem," I said, not giving voice to the codicil, *as long as you are blind, stinking drunk*. I tried to discuss my own problems, but Christos couldn't really see that anything was amiss. I had acted appropriately manly in fucking a young woman, and if my wife couldn't accept that, I was well shed of her. My wife was, at any rate, certain to grow fat and disgusting. And if I'd managed to forge a career by filching from a bag of stolen ideas, more power to me. Or as Christos put it, "So *fuck*." This little phrase was very versatile when spat through Christos's moustache, which was huge and seemed to have a life of its own. Indeed, it sometimes seemed I was conversing with the moustache. "So *fuck*" could be freighted with despair, optimism or meek acceptance. So *fuck*.

When night came, Christos and his fellows disappeared, fearful perhaps of having their blood drained by vampires, especially now that it was forty-proof. I toddled off to Birds of a Feather.

Jay wasn't talking to me, which you know, which you've heard, so *fuck*. I conversed instead with Amy, during those moments when she was ferrying me drinks. This was a tricky business, because I was tempted to order lots, not just to satisfy my wet tooth but to hold her near the table. Mind you, I wanted to present myself as other than a sot, so I staggered the beer and whiskey requests. This didn't irritate her as it would many a waitperson, and it even seemed as though she came to empty the ashtray more often than was absolutely necessary. She asked how the novel was going and I lied and claimed it was going very well, although I admitted to a certain amount of inky grappling with the great unruly beast. Amy, it turns out, is a doctoral student in English, and has achieved All But Dissertation status. Her thesis has something to do with Anthony Trollope. Man, I wish I'd read some Anthony Trollope books; indeed, it has truly long been my ambition to do so. After all, Trollope is admirable on many counts; foremost in my mind is his modest industry. He spent a quiet life in London producing huge, weighty tomes. Dickens lived just around the corner, I believe, and Trollope maintained a friendship with Chuck, even though Dickens was rich and famous and had an actress for a mistress. The point is, I don't believe there ever was an occasion when Tony Trollope threw down his pen in artistic despair and scrambled off to drink with a moustache named Christos. Anyway, my small victory was that I didn't lie about my ignorance. I was tempted to do so;

Hooper had bandied the name about years ago, in the Pig's Snout, and I could have probably voiced a few of his observations and complaints re Trollope and claimed them as my own. But I didn't. Instead I said simply, "You know what? I've never read any of Trollope's novels."

"You," said Amy, "don't know what you're missing."

At last call Jay began to improvise his jeremiad, variations on an air of sadness. That's when I stumbled out of the bar, overtipping Amy and leaving her with a promise to read *Barchester Towers*, which I keep, believe it or not, on my bedside table. Granted, it is there mostly for protection against intruders, but I didn't mention that.

Despite fairly vast amounts of alcohol, I never became drunk, as is evidenced by the fact that I am typing this now.

"Uncle Johnny?"

"Jay?"

"No, it's Phil."

"My boner."

"Why did you think it was Jay?"

"No reason."

"It's just that you kind of jumped all over that. You know? *Jay?*"

"He calls me more often than you do."

"Oh."

"He was over on Thanksgiving. He brought turkey."

"Really?"

"Actually, he brought a bottle of Wild Turkey. We had a few little snorts. What did you do on Thanksgiving?"

"Um . . . I forgot to give thanks."

"Uh-huh. Yeah, Jay told me you were having a few little problems, Phil. Well . . . shit happens."

"You said it."

"That's the way the cookie crumbles."

"Uh-huh."

"That's life."

"Right."

"You need any more clichés?"

"No, I'm good, Uncle Johnny."

"But, you know, you have to give thanks for the good things. And there's a lot of good things in life. When I think back, I remember all sorts of good, good things."

"Uh-huh."

"Jane was a great lay."

"Okay, you know what, Uncle Johnny—"

"She had a great little body. Tight."

"Uncle Johnny—"

"And pepper steaks."

"Huh?"

"Not that shit you get in Chinese restaurants, with green peppers, that's no good. I'm talking about a steak with peppercorns *actually embedded in the meat*, and that beautiful sauce, I believe they make it with shallots and cognac. *That* . . . is what life is all about. Okay, now you go."

"What?"

"You say something you think is good."

"Well . . . Okay, well, um . . ."

"Is Veronica a good lay?"

"Were you always like this?"

"Like what?"

"You just seem a little bit crude."

"How is Ronnie, anyway?"

"She's—"

"Christ, what a rack on that babe."

"Uncle Johnny—"

"Okay, lay it on me. Give me a good thing."

"That's a tough one for me right now."

"How about this one, kid? *Television.*"

"I don't think so."

"You should see the set-up I got now. I got this plasma screen, thing is like five feet wide. I got stacks of speakers. Woofers, tweeters, bass drivers. *Super-deluxe.*"

"What do you like to watch?"

"Not porn, if that's what you're thinking."

"That's not what I'm thinking."

"Between you and me, it scares me shitless. Twats were never meant to be that big."

"So what do you watch?"

"I don't know. Lots of shit. Hey . . . when are we going to have a new episode of *Padre?*"

"We're not, Uncle Johnny."

"Why not?"

"Edward Milligan is dead."

"Who?"

"The star. Padre."

"Christ! That sucks sewer water."

"Tell me something, Uncle Johnny. You say Jay was over there, and he told you I was experiencing a few little problems?"

"Check."

"But you don't seem to know that I'm separated from Veronica—"

"You're kidding!"

"—and you don't seem to know that I'm experiencing some, um, professional difficulties."

"Yeah, I guess if the guy's dead, that kind of puts the kibosh on *Padre.*"

"What exactly did Jay tell you?"

"Oh. He said that some greaseballs frightened you when you were a kid and now you're emotionally stunted."

"Hmm."

"I said, *Shit happens*. That's life. When I think back—over eighty-five years, kid, eighty-five fucking years—I can't believe the shit that happened. And it all took me by surprise. Jane dying, my sister dying, meeting Claire, having a baby when I was forty-nine years old, Claire taking off with a kid younger than you . . . my god. There's only one thing certain in life, Phil."

"And what's that?"

"Televisions just keep getting bigger and better."

"I'll tell you why I called, Uncle Johnny."

"Oh, I know why you called. Same reason your brother calls. You guys want to talk to your mother, but she's gone. So I'm the next best thing."

"I was looking in the mirror the other day. And I noticed something remarkable. I look just like you."

"Really? You're all wrinkled and bald and your testicles drag on the ground?"

"No, I mean I look just like you used to look. I'm big and boxy. I've got wavy hair with a distinguished streak of grey. Some people consider me handsome. I look just like you."

"Huh."

"Except for my spectacles, of course. So I guess l look like your secret identity."

"Oh yeah, I just remembered something else your brother said about you. He said you've been hitting the juice pretty hard."

"Uh-huh."

"Your mom would be worried about you, Phil."

"You know what, Uncle Johnny? Mom would be right to be worried about me."

13 | CAREER MOVES

THERE WAS CONSIDERABLE EXCITEMENT DURING REHEARSALS OF *The Hawaiian*, none of which I noticed, being far too occupied with the wooing of Ms. Lear. I undertook this wooing with the cerebral detachment of a field marshal. I had plans and tactics, although I was always prepared to make a responsive or impromptu strike. A case in point: as I sat in the theatre watching rehearsals, I saw that the director was making moves upon Ronnie. He was in a strong position— the director/leading lady relationship is very intimate and always on the brink of becoming sexual, assuming that the participants' inclinations run along those lines. I had campaigned to have *The Hawaiian* directed by Penn Goldman, who possessed very fine dramatic sensibilities and was gay as all get-out. But the play's producers thought we needed a more masculine sensibility to deal with the table of regulars, who were all, to one degree or another, great heaving pigs. So George Gordon was brought in. You may remember, he was mentioned a few pages back; he had treated a woman so egregiously that he was hauled before the drunken and howling tribunal. Gordon had a good reputation as a theatre director and a very poor one as a human being. He treated actors shamefully, he fired designers impetuously, he was known to kick technicians in the seat of their pants if they happened to get in his way. He was especially rotten to writers, although—and I wish there were some way around this point—he quite liked me. "You and I, Philly," he used to say, "*understand* each other."

Perhaps. Certainly I had insight into him, and when he sidled up beside Veronica and cooed, "That's not quite on, beauty," I knew what he was doing. (Incidentally, he wasn't British, although that sentence might suggest he was. He was from Sarnia, Ontario, although very few people were in on that little secret.)

"Sorry, beauty, that's not quite what we need."

"How so?"

"This woman, this Hester, I feel she should discover this, this, you know, this *thing*, within her, something she little suspected she had, this rare, rare . . ."

"Rare what?"

"Right, right." I didn't know if George Gordon was being an idiot due to his proximity to Veronica, or simply because he was one. "Her attitude."

"A rare attitude?"

"No, darling, no. Her attitude when she, when *you*, attend the fellows. She seems strong."

I was sitting in the seats, in the shadows, a battered and splotchy copy of the script on my lap. I spent hours so, waiting for someone on the stage to ask for clarification. The most I ever got was Gordon shouting toward the loges, "Dropping that line! Too wordy!"

"I don't think she's all *that* strong, George," Veronica said, which made me wonder whether she'd ever ended a sentence with *my* name; I decided she hadn't, because it surely would have made me faint.

George lowered his voice then; he also lowered his head so that it practically rested upon Ronnie's chest. He spoke, hushed but urgent, causing various reactions on her part. Her brow furrowed, then smoothed with understanding. She bit on her bottom lip, and then she laughed. She stared at the floor and suddenly lifted her eyes until they met Gordon's. She touched him on the shoulder and nodded. I was beside myself with grief.

George Gordon spun around, hollering, "Let's run it from when Hester comes in!"

Hester/Veronica made her entrance, with an arm cocked upwards and her palm flat, because when props got her act together there would be a salver covered with draft glasses there. She stopped by the table of braying regulars, and I saw what change Gordon had effected; Hester was timid now, timorous, to the extent that her free hand floated about her nether regions as though on guard, ready to land and shield her most private self. This lent an interesting tone to her lines; I had crafted them with some wit (I thought), which now served as a huge defence. It struck me that Gordon was gearing Veronica's entire performance toward the final moment; he wanted the audience to think that Hester was perpetually, eternally, a victim, and therefore incapable of the decisive act that was to come. That was how Ronnie played it all that day. I watched the two confer between run-throughs; they had begun to touch each other by way of punctuation, resting fingertips on shoulders, elbows, cheeks(!), and once, as Ronnie turned away, Gordon passed a hand across her perfect backside.

This was danger, big danger. George Gordon was a Lothario, and although he was in some ways an ill-looking fellow (pale and rail-thin, his fingers so nicotine-stained that they glowed orange), I thought Ronnie was falling under his influence.

After rehearsal that day, many people gathered at the Pig's Snout. Veronica sat down beside me, which cheered me momentarily, until I realized that it was the only seat available. Across from us George Gordon held court, drinking too much (in apparent victory) and telling tales of squalor and scandal. Hooper came in, poor lost Hooper, and although he grabbed a chair and tried to ram it in between me and Ronnie, he couldn't (I didn't budge), and eventually he ended up sitting beside Bob Hamel, the most boring man in the universe.

As drinks were consumed, everything became louder, a cloud of confusion descended upon the table, and at some point in the midst of all that, Veronica tilted her body toward mine and said quietly, "What do you think of George?"

What would Rommel or Patton do under the circumstances? They wouldn't pussyfoot around, that's for sure, and neither did I. Screwing up my face with what I intended to pass for considered reflection (but no doubt looked like exactly what it was, a goatish, hormone-addled grimace of sexual longing), I pronounced, "I think he's an asshole."

Ronnie patted my leg, or squeezed my knee, or did some damn thing underneath the table that involved my limb and her hand, flickeringly brief but chubb-producing. "I think you're right," she said quietly. "This Hester business, don't you think it's wrong?"

"I think it couldn't be wronger."

"There's a word for it."

I panicked briefly: a word for what? A word for my expression—*stupefied?* A word for what was happening to me underneath the table—*engorgement?*

"Madonna complex," Ronnie recalled. "That's what George has. It's like women are saints, you know. Hester is this timid little virgin. I want to play her, you know, *bolder*. More real. Like a woman who's done a few things. Laughed, had a drink, fucked. That way it means—jeez, Phil, you've gone really pale."

"You're right."

"Sorry?"

"Muwahhh . . ." (Which was me sucking in air, my lungs popping apart with an audible shudder.) "You're absolutely right. Gordon doesn't really understand women." Please don't ask if I do, please don't ask if I do, let this pass as the truth. How could Gordon understand women, how could any of us?

"What are you two prattling on about?" Because George's ears stood at right angles to his skull, they were very powerful.

"Just stuff," said Veronica. "Just, you know, man/woman stuff."

"Oh, really?"

John Hooper stood up from his seat and pretended to yawn. Actually, as he had been sitting beside Bob Hamel, the yawn may have been genuine, but it certainly didn't look that way. It looked as if an alien, perhaps an invader from the Dog Star, Sirius, had occupied Hooper's body and was controlling motion with some crude internal block and pulley. "Come on, Ron," he said. "Let's go."

"You go on, Johnny," said Ronnie. She said these words in a very friendly fashion. Too damn friendly, so friendly that the Hooper/ Lear relationship was instantly defined as one of camaraderie. They were done as a couple, and Hooper stumbled out of the bar in utter despair. And although there has been a certain consistency in John's attitude toward Veronica since then (you may recall his remark beginning "There is no man alive . . . ."), I know that really he has never gotten over her. But I had no time, then, to reflect on this victory, because my potential happiness was being besieged by George Gordon. "The playwright and the leading lady," he said authoritatively, as though quoting Sir John Gielgud or somebody, "shouldn't be talking to each other."

"But I enjoy talking to the playwright," said Ronnie.

"I'm sure you do, beauty," George Gordon said with a knowing smile. I will say this—he was right, the playwright and the leading lady probably shouldn't have been talking. They certainly shouldn't have been discussing an interpretation of the role that was at odds with the director's vision. But we continued to do so over the course of the rehearsals. We were crafty—Ronnie's Hester continued to be cowed and subservient. Occasionally, though, she would signal to me as I sat in the tiers—subtly, a small shrug or a short glance—and the more assertive Hester would make an appearance. George Gordon would stop the proceedings immediately. "Beauty, darling, what the *fuck* was that?" But I would smile, and the corners of Ronnie's mouth would flicker. There is nothing like collusion to bring two people together. Why do you think the milieu of the French Resistance is romantic, why do we imagine ourselves wearing scarves and berets and rutting like bush-babies as the storm troopers patrol the streets?

Opening night was a triumph. Indeed, it was probably the best evening of my life, and I would claim it as such unreservedly if I had not spent a certain portion of it wanting to throw up. I wanted to throw up for several pre-curtain hours, although when Ronnie/Hester wheeled on, carrying a tray of draft and looking as though she'd lived a full and *very* active life, the butterflies landed. And when the curtain descended, the audience members sprang to their feet and roared. Backstage there was pandemonium, much of it created by the irate George Gordon, who wanted to tear a strip off Ronnie's hide. By this point, he knew he was out of the sweetheart stakes, and was legitimately angry over artistic matters, but every time he tried to blast Veronica, someone would stop in front of her and gush. In a few minutes George was beaming, pocketing a few free-floating kudos. They gushed over me as well, friends and strangers alike. I remember a young fellow with wild hair that was already peppered with grey. "My god, that was a fine bit of writing," this man said. "Lambent" was the word he used, over and over again. "Positively lambent." He gave me his card, which I threw on my dresser and never thought about again. Mind you, it had no information embossed upon it, not profession nor address nor phone number, other than the man's name: WILLIAM BECKETT.

The post-play celebration was, where else? at the Pig's Snout, but we didn't stay long. *We didn't stay long*, christ it stings me to type that, to remember that we once operated as a single entity. We didn't stay long, we only had one drink and then we disappeared without any fare-thee-wells. We went back to her place, because we thought mine was a filthy pigsty. (Ronnie had never seen my place, but she's always had good instincts.) We made love.

I will supply no details. It's not that I'm being genteel, but I can't really remember the event. All of my Ronnie-related lovemaking memories tend to blur, although that word has connotations of indistinction, and that's not at all the case. I can remember details, oh brother, can I remember details. I can recall precise shades of coral, I can summon to mind exact constellations of goosebumps. But it is hard for me to remember any individual act.

Excuse me, that's not so. I can remember very clearly the *last* time I made love to my wife.

———

"For what city, please?"

"Ah."

"Ah?"

"Mmm. Ah. What city."

"Yes. What city?"

"*That* . . . is a very good question."

"Ah."

"Ah?"

"A bottle call."

"Sorry?"

"A lot of people, when they have a few drinks, they start making phone calls."

"Really. Well, I can assure you, young lady, that I am very definitely one of those people."

"For what city, please?"

"Let's put our heads together on this, Watson."

"Leslie."

"Leslie. I'm looking for a fellow named Peter Paul Mendicott."

"Two tees?"

"I'm sorry."

"At the end of *Mendicott?* Two tees?"

"Yes! Two tees."

"And what do we know about Mr. Mendicott?"

"He wrote a movie that has had a profound influence on my life."

"If he's in the movie business, shouldn't we try Los Angeles, California?"

"Spot on. Give it a go, Les."

"All right, let me take a look here . . . mmm . . . nope."

"Mind you, this movie was based on a novel he wrote. So, perhaps New York City."

"One should always check New York City. And there I have a, um, a Michael Mendicott. And a J and a G. No Peter Paul."

"I'm not sure what I'm going to say to him, Leslie. I'm afraid I have to confess to what, at least at first blush, looks like plagiarism. But there is a sense in which the movie *happened* to me."

"Do you mean that he stole your life story?"

"No, I don't mean that. You see, I was just a kid when I saw the film, and I was very affected—"

"Excuse me, Mister—?"

"Phil."

"Excuse me, Mr. Phil, but may I ask how old you are now?"

"Yes, you may. Forty-eight."

"I see."

"How old are you, Leslie?"

"I'm twenty-one."

"*Then come kiss me, sweet and twenty. Youth's a stuff will not endure.*"

"But I'm twenty-*one*."

"That was poetic licence, dear."

"Besides, I'm . . . here's what I was thinking, Mr. Phil. It seems as though you saw this film approximately forty years ago."

"Besides, you're what?"

"We are not supposed to get involved in personal discussions."

"Who's going to know?"

"The supervisors listen in every so often. Clandestinely."

"Besides, you're *married?*"

"Oh, no. My gosh, no, Mr. Phil."

"Besides, you're what?"

"Well, the thing is, you know, it happens from time to time that men will, um, *respond* to something in my voice."

"Well, yeah. I would think so. You have a very sexy voice."

"Mm-hmm. And then they find out I'm young, and single . . ."

"Do you field a lot of bottle calls?"

"I get my fair share, Mr. Phil. The telephone traffic is mostly bottle calls after a certain time of night."

"Really."

"Really."

"And so these men, these somewhat pathetic men, fall in love with you . . . ?"

"It has happened."

"Yes. I can see that. I have some insight into pathos. Not to take anything away from the sexiness of your voice. Or your pleasant manner."

"Well, that's just it, isn't it? I mean, all I am is pleasant. Helpful. What kind of dismal existences do these men have that me being pleasant is all it takes for them to fall in love?"

"Good question."

"This Peter Paul Mendicott, he might be a very old man now."

"Not so fast. I need to know, besides you're *what?* Please."

"I'm large."

"Large."

"Very large."

"I see."

"Do you?"

"Don't I?"

"You're likely imagining me now as, well, *plump.* Well-proportioned but oversized. Whereas in reality I am freakish. Sideshow fat, Mr. Phil. I am what they call morbidly obese, which means that my weight will kill me. What do you think of that?"

"I think . . . I think we all have something freakish about us, Leslie. While yours seems harder to bear than most—I'm not trying to demean your suffering—we all have some crooked cross to bear."

"What's yours?"

"Blindness."

"You're blind?"

"Yeah."

"Really?"

"Really."

"Have you been blind from birth?"

"I would have to answer that in the affirmative."

"See now, you must be lying to me. Making fun of me. Because you *saw* this movie when you were a kid."

"Ah. I had corrective lenses."

"Is that a fact?"

"But they got broken. I walked outside—there was all this rubble everywhere—and I realized that finally I was all alone. I could live my life with books. But somehow my spectacles got pitched off my face. They shattered into a million little pieces."

"You'll forgive me if I don't exactly believe you."

"Hey, you know what, Leslie? I don't believe *you*. How's about them apples?"

"You don't believe me?"

"I think you're one of the most beautiful women in the world. Stunning. You're perfect, and that's what makes you feel like a freak. *That's* what I believe, and I'm going to go to bed believing that I made contact with a woman of inconceivable exquisiteness, and my sleep, if it comes at all, will be troubled."

"Carson City, Nevada."

"What?"

"This Peter Paul Mendicott. I realized he would be a very old man, so I checked places where you might find very old people. Arizona, New Mexico. The air is better for them in those places."

"Great! Thank you. Is there some way I can call you back if I find him?"

"Please hold for that number, sir."

. . .

PART THREE

THE TWILIGHT ZONE

14 | THE DATE

I CAN SEE NOW THAT THE MCQUIGGE / VAN DER GLICK RELATIONSHIP IS doomed. At least, it's very ill, and I can't see it living much longer than a few weeks. Rainie and I are rankers, after all, and even our most tender moments possess a sort of spastic desperation. It's not pretty.

Last night, we went on a date. Neither of us called it that, indeed we took some pains to avoid the word. When she called, Rainie suggested a "get-together." I responded by saying (and note that I employ the terminology of a thirteen-year-old), "Sure, let's hack around." She pointed out that there was a play in Toronto that had received stellar notices and heralded the arrival of a fresh new voice in Canadian theatre. "That sounds great," said I, a position of such manifest disingenuousness that the prospect was instantly abandoned. Then we discussed movies; Rainie read titles from the newspaper and gave me a brief précis or some salient point, the name of the star or the director. I had heard of very few of these people, which made me wonder how long, exactly, I had been living underground. Rainie was more knowledgeable. Her gig at the radio station brought her into daily contact with people, and very often the topic of her phone-in show had something to do with popular culture. So even though she never listened to her callers (the show's popularity had much to do with the inventive ways Rainie hung up on these people), she could say to me, "Oh, you know the guy, he was the star of that television show *Island* and he married Grace Juniper and he was in that movie *Hellbent for Heather*."

I knew none of this, of course. And although I kicked myself mentally for never thinking of it, the title *Hellbent for Heather* struck me as so profoundly idiotic that I began to think Rainie and I existed in the Twilight Zone.

Submitted for your consideration: Phil and Rainie, two lonely people who were ejected from the Garden of Eden prematurely, propelled from childhood to adulthood without stepping on the rocky shores of adolescence. Now, they try to reclaim it . . . But their purchase on reality grows weak, and they enter . . .

"Aw, fuck it, Phil," said Rainie. "Let's just eat, get drunk and screw."

The eating portion of the evening didn't really amount to much. Rainie said she'd heard that this particular restaurant was good, so we went there and started to run through the wine list. Our waiter, who'd identified himself as Maurice, drifted by the table regularly, a little notepad in his hand, a pencil licked and poised. Rainie and I would pluck up menus, stare at them blearily. "Need a couple more minutes?" Maurice would ask. We would nod, he would disappear, Rainie and I would dive for our wineglasses. I finally demanded a piece of meat, but when we left, the thing still lay on the plate unmolested. It had a tiny wooden stake driven into it (labelling it as rare), and looked much like a vampire's heart that had been mercifully laid to rest.

"Where to now?" I asked. A cold wind blew, but I didn't button up my overcoat; I enjoyed the fresh and sudden pain.

"Hey, I know," said Rainie, who was working all the fasteners she could, in meek defiance of the October weather, "let's go to that place where your brother plays."

"Birds of a Feather," said I, and off we stumbled. I had had sufficient wine that I never considered whether the excursion was a good or bad idea. It was simply an idea of something to do, of which I had none, so we journeyed forth to do it. But as we entered the establishment, I had misgivings. For one thing, I wasn't sure I wanted to present my intoxicated self before Amy. Plus the fact that I was with a woman, quite a tipsy one, who, as she removed her outerwear, popped almost all the buttons on her blouse and displayed an intricately lacy brassiere. Not that I thought there was anything happening with Amy, who, after all, was quite a bit younger than myself—oh, who am I kidding? I probably nursed some tender hope deep in my soggy heart. But whatever else Amy thought, I hoped she might perceive me as a moderate, thoughtful and basically decent human being rather than a satyriatic souse. But as Rainie and I lurched forward I realized there was little chance of that. Not only did I bump into a table, forcing the occupant to rescue a tumbling martini glass, but Rainie commanded, at a high pitch, "Don't drink too much, Philly. We got some serious fucking to do."

Uh-oh, thought I. Serious fucking. This was trouble. I had hitherto thought van der Glick was only interested in lighthearted, pointless, inconsequential fucking, my old specialty.

Amy didn't seem to find anything untoward. She smiled and greeted me nicely enough, although her question "Have you read *Barchester Towers* yet?" may well have contained a little barb, being as it appeared, at that moment anyway, that I was incapable of reading.

"This is Rainie," I explained. "A childhood friend."

"Vodka martini. A great big fucker," ordered Rainie, who hadn't really had a childhood. "With about seven olives."

"How about you, Phil?" asked Amy.

"Oh, um . . ."

"A pint of bitter and a double Laphroaig?" she suggested.

Spot on, I wanted to say, but instead I shrugged as though the order would never have occurred to me, although I was willing to try this unique combination.

Amy wheeled away and I was forced to consider the other downside of going to Birds of a Feather, my little brother, Jay.

I stole a glance. He was hunkered over the keyboard, his huge head so close that his curly hair brushed across the ivory. He was playing an odd and disjointed piece, his right hand picking out a frangible melody, his left banging out dense lumbering chords. To me it sounded atonal, like Charles Ives or something, Ives on heavy-duty medication, but Rainie began to sing along.

"—you'll come a-waltzing, Matilda, with me. Waltzing Matilda, WALTZING MATILDA . . ." The song becomes quite lively and rousing there, you know; Rainie didn't quite accomplish it, and her attempt was screechingly loud. All of our fellow patrons startled and looked. Even Jay raised his head from the piano, squinting into the shadows.

"Jay-Jay," called Rainie. "It's me. Van der Glick."

"Ah. The fairest of the rankers. Requests?" asked Jay.

"Don't get me started."

Jay lowered his head and concentrated on his music. Amy brought the drinks. Rainie moved her seat so that she could 1) watch Jay directly and 2) bury her hand in my crotch, and although this last was accomplished under cover of the tabletop, that was mere coincidence. I was aghast, but nowhere near as aghast as my dick, which burrowed into my tummy.

"He's not talking to me," I said to Rainie.

"Who's not?"

"Jay."

"How's come?"

"He's mad because I fucked up my life."

"That can't be right, Phil. If that was his attitude there'd be no one left to talk to."

"He's mad because, you know, I broke up with Ronnie."

Rainie tilted her head, considering this. "But if neither one of you guys was happy, then it was the only reasonable course of action. I think Jay would understand that."

"Well, he doesn't," I said, realizing immediately that Rainie was right. It's not like Jay believed in the sanctity of the institution or anything. He had ended three marriages, blown them off, not really contesting any of the terms and maintaining civil, almost friendly relations with all of his exes.

I assayed the drunkard's adamancy, pressing a finger down onto the tabletop. "I'm not sure *why* he's not talking to me, van der Gliupp,"—a hiccup had interfered—"all I can tell you is, he's not talking to me."

Jay vaulted from the piano over to our table, picking up a chair along the way, spinning it around and then straddling it as he sat down, crossing his arms across the back in a folksy manner. "Hello," he said. "How goes it, Rainie?"

"Couldn't be better," was her answer. It gave me vague misgivings. *Vague* because I was more than a little drunk, also because all of my emotions are vague. But I guess I thought that her response should have been along these lines: *Things are going so badly, Jay, that I've taken up with your miserable brother.*

Rainie turned toward me. "I thought he wasn't talking to you."

"Ah, well, if you'll notice," I pointed out in a professorial manner, "he's *not* talking to me. He's talking to you."

"So, Phil," Jay said, rotating the planet that was his head, "what's this about a novel?"

"Huh?"

"I was talking to Veronica," Jay replied, "and she said you were working on a novel."

"That's right," said van der Glick, after it became apparent that I wasn't going to respond. I was trying to remember when I'd mentioned it to Ronnie. The answer (which bubbled up from my gut rather than descended from my brain) was that I mentioned it to her all the time. At the end of many a drunken telephone conversation I'd blurt, "Just wait till I finish my book, read my novel, Ronnie, and you'll understand *everything*."

"It's an autobiographical novel."

"Really?" said Jay.

"Oh, yes. It has the 'incident' in there, and a lot about you . . ."

What, you didn't think that was me talking, did you? Oh, gosh, no. I was beyond stupefaction, plus I was busy receiving drinks from Amy, who had chosen an approach to the table that brought into her view van der Glick's hand rooting around my crotch, searching for the shrivelled penis.

"Now how, exactly," wondered Jay, "can Phil write an autobiographical novel when he has no sense of himself, and a faulty memory to boot?"

"I don't know," admitted Rainie. "But that's what he's trying to do. Like Proust. But what was it Dorothy Parker said about Proust? That reading *In Search of Lost Time* was like soaking in someone else's bathwater?"

"Who says I have a faulty memory? Thank you." That last comment was made to Amy, who shrugged to indicate that bringing me drinks was her job and in no way elective.

"I do," said Jay. Talking to me, directly to me. "I say your memory is totally fucked. Like, for example, you didn't even remember about Tom and Tony until I reminded you a few years ago."

"Wait," I said, "weren't their names Ted and Terry?"

"I knew it. I knew you were getting everything wrong."

"You're the one who told me their names were Ted and Terry!"

"Let me read it," said Jay.

"I'm not going to let you read it."

"He's worried," announced Rainie, "about using real people as fodder for his so-called fiction."

"He should be. He treats people badly enough already."

"Guys, I'm sitting right here. You shouldn't be discussing me as if I were, you know, elsewhere."

"But you *are*, Philly Four-Eyes," said Jay.

Rainie van der Glick nodded in accord. "You are elsewhere."

Then break time was over and Jay returned to the grand piano. He balanced some drinks upon it, hung his head low and began to play. It was the last set, so he abandoned his idiosyncratic renditions of classics and show tunes, dipped into his classical repertoire and came up with some real weepers. He played the first Brahms intermezzo, for example, which choked me with the strength of an anaconda. And he played Glenn Gould's transcription of the *Siegfried Idyll*, by Wagner, that great anti-Semite. I felt this was something of a low blow. Do you know the story? Cosima Wagner woke up on her birthday and there were thirteen musicians sitting on the staircase, playing this beautiful avowal of transcendent passion. *Wagner did this wonderfully romantic thing*, was Jay's implicit statement, *and he was a fuck-pig. What, exactly, does that make you?*

I awoke the next morning, although, again, I've used an overly delicate term. Rather, I was spat forth from a comatose void that was more deathlike than death. Spat forth screaming, I might add, crash-landing in a strange land. There was a naked woman beside me, one who'd obviously thrashed the whole night long. The sheets were kicked clear across the room. The woman lay on her back, her arms and legs spread, her head slapped sideways. Rainie van der Glick, my childhood friend. And here I was in her bedroom, which seemed remarkably girl-like for van der Glick, to the extent that there were stuffed animals goggling at me from their perches on book-laden shelves. The walls were lined with works of art and framed photographs. The paintings were all very realistic, all landscapes, and the photographs—which hove into view as I plucked up my spectacles from the bedside table and balanced them on my nose—were of Rainie and strangers to me. They were by and large men; was Rainie seriously involved with any of them? I wondered.

As I ruminated on this, my penis (and whereas it is hypothetical that part of my psyche is still thirteen years old, it is incontrovertible that my dick is) demanded that I study the naked woman in repose. Rainie had a fine body, but I found it somehow dissatisfying. I studied the way her breasts lolled to either side of her ribcage and I frowned, not because they were no longer young and were therefore imperfect but because Ronnie's breasts lolled differently. My penis began to roar then, a ferocious roar, although the effect, looking down upon it, was probably less than the little fellow had intended. Still, he was game, and assuming that Rainie and I had been too polluted to accomplish anything the night before, I ran my fingertips up the inside of her thigh. She stirred, swung her head to the other side. "McQuidgey," she whispered. She lifted her hands, groped the empty air, took hold of my head. "What time is it?"

I checked the clock on the stand, which was huge, the numbers of the digital readout an inch high so that, I assumed, Rainie could see them even without her spectacles. "It's 7:13."

"We've only been asleep for like twenty-two minutes." Still, she drew my head downward. I crawled on top and gentled myself into her. "Mmm," went Rainie.

It was not the most impassioned act of lovemaking, but we were both grotesquely tired and swill-stunned. When we were done ("I'm done," said Rainie van der Glick, and then I was done, too) she drifted back to sleep. I climbed out of bed and located my clothes, not all of which were in the bedchamber. My socks, for example, were in Rainie's shower stall, bone dry.

As I sat on the lip of the bathtub and pulled on my socks—an act that possessed a perverted domesticity—I wondered if Rainie would like to have me for a boyfriend. Maybe that was what her life needed, someone with whom she could take Sunday drives, stopping at antique stores and roadside fruit stands. Or it could be that I was in such rotten shape that Our Lady of Perpetual Mercy Fucks needed to devote her attention to me twenty-four/seven.

I went down in the elevator. My stomach was so tender that the short ride sickened me as vigorously as a squealing plummet on a roller coaster. Then I was on the street and blinded by the sun. It was late October and very chilly, but that didn't prevent this huge cockadoodle of light. There were churchgoers out there, sedate and well-dressed, heading toward their various houses of worship, which nauseated me far more than my descent in the elevator. I considered throwing up in the gutter, but steeled myself, only because I didn't want to hear a small voice coming from behind, "Mommy? What's wrong with that man?"

I threw my arms up into the air and prayed for a miracle, and a miracle occurred. An orange taxi pulled over to the side of the road. I loaded myself into the back seat, spoke my address and went to sleep. The cabbie woke me up gently (for a cabbie) and, surprisingly refreshed, I paid him, got out, circled around the back of Michelangelo Barker's house. There was a brief moment of panic because my house keys weren't in my pocket, but they were in the door, which was all very well and fortunate, although I couldn't really understand why they were there. Then I entered my basement apartment and saw my pages strewn about and I understood.

Remembered, I suppose, is the technical term, although I doubt it is any kind of remembrance that you people might understand. You might not understand memories that appear in a diarrheal blast, lacking form and order, splattering against the walls of your mind. Not unless you are, like me, an enthusiastic amateur alcoholic. These memories included: Jay, Rainie and me stumbling along the streets at dead of night; Jay and me sitting curbside and intoning, "Akela! We'll do our best! Dib dib dib, dob dob dob!" whilst Rainie performed some sort of interpretive dance; the three of us in my gloomy apartment sifting through the loose pages of my manuscript. Ergh, that last memory certainly disturbed me. I hope Rainie didn't find the pages that were pertinent to her, *ow!*, too late, another painful squirt of memory, this one of Rainie clutching a piece of paper and demanding, "Hey, bud, just *what* is so heartbreaking about my stabs at femininity?"

At this point my book's pages numbered perhaps one hundred and seventy, but as I scanned the room, I sensed somehow that there were not so many as that. It seemed to me that there were, oh, twenty-odd pages missing . . .

I dove for the sheets of paper, scanning them frantically for proper names: Ted, Tony (whatever the fuck) and Norman. I saw nothing. There was no accompanying trumpet of memory, but I soon knew that my brother, Jay, had carted away all the pages dealing with what I'm still bent on calling, simply, the "incident."

———

"Hello?"

"Philip. It's Milligan."

"Who?"

"Ed. Edward. Eddie."

"But you're dead."

"Right, right, right. But I try not to let it slow me down."

"Oh. I get it. This is a troubled dream."

"Well, I did use to call you all the time. Wouldn't you say it's more like half memory, half troubled dream?"

"Mostly troubled dream."

"I've been reading the Bible."

"Okay, okay. There's some memory involved."

"What I want to know is, why is there *any* troubled dream when it's, what, four-thirty in the afternoon?"

"You should talk. Mr. Nocturnal. You were always sleeping in the afternoon, fearful that the sun's rays might spoil your perfect skin."

"And it would have. The great giver of life also destroys. That's one of the Great Chuckles."

"Hmm?"

"Oh, that's kind of an inside joke. Around here, we don't say *great irony*. We say *great chuckle*. Because the Big Guy is a comedian."

"I see."

"'Isn't that Henny Youngman? No, that's God—he just thinks he's Henny Youngman!'"

"So you're in heaven, are you? Not the other place?"

"Well, it doesn't exactly work like that. You'll see."

"Please, tell me more. I'm interested."

"There is no hell. There's just this place. And it's boring. The earthly vale, that's where all the action is. That's why I don't like to see you sleeping at four-thirty in the pee-em."

"I was out last night with a friend of mine, and we had a little bit too much to drink, and then we——"

"Fornicated like silver martens?"

"How do silver martens fornicate?"

"Quickly. It's painless, but also pleasureless."

"Well, all right. We fornicated like silver martens. The point is, I didn't get much sleep, so I'm having a little nap. There's nothing wrong with that. Dagwood Bumstead has naps, right, curled up on the couch with all those little z's hovering over his head. No one thinks of Dagwood Bumstead as a slobbering degenerate."

"Dagwood fucks Blondie up the ass."

"Ha! It's good to see you haven't changed, you're still the same old Milligan."

"No, Phil. I've changed. No getting around it."

"Anyway, anyway, it's a little hard napping around here. The phone is ringing off the wall, except it's not on the wall, you know, it's one of those portable phones, so it keeps ringing off the, you know, wherever the hell I left the damn thing. My brother called about an hour ago."

"Jay."

"Yeah, Jay."

"I like Jay. He's a great musician. An artist."

"What does that mean? That I'm *not* an artist, right?"

"Phil, what you are has absolutely nothing to do with what your brother is."

"Oh, fuck, what was that, some kind of enlightened wisdom or something?"

"One has one's moments."

"Anyway, it's just not true. We had the same damn upbringing, didn't we?"

"No."

"What do you mean, *no*, dead man?"

"You had the same mom and lived in the same house, but you two had vastly different experiences . . ."

"That's what *I* said. Because he called me up, you know, and he's all *Phil, you got this wrong, you got that wrong,* and I told him, *My experience was different than yours.*"

"Oh no, in that particular case, you got everything wrong. Listen to Jay."

"We're going out tomorrow night. He wants to meet on the street, when the sun goes down. Ooo-wooo, very dramatic."

"Tomorrow night. Yes. A nice touch."

"Look, I don't mean to be rude, but to what do I owe the pleasure of this phone call from the Great Beyond? What exactly do you want?"

"I just wanted to chat. So were you out with what's her name, cute little makeup girl with the perfect butt?"

"Her name is *Bellamy*."

"Hey, don't get all, don't get all . . . *shirty*."

"And no, that didn't work out with Bellamy."

"Sure it did. It broke up your marriage, right? Isn't that what you wanted?"

"What, do you take psychology classes up in heaven?"

"I think about things, Phil. I've got a lot of time to just think."

"You think about me?"

"Sure. Because you're in crisis."

"Oh, gawd."

"So if you weren't out with Bellamy, who were you out with?"

"Rainie van der Glick."

"Ah! Our Lady of Perpetual Mercy Fucks."

"See, now, that just proves that you are nothing but grog-addled fabrication. Because there's no way you could know about that."

"That's not true. I was on her radio show, remember?"

"Oh, sweet jesus, don't remind me."

"And then we went out for a coffee and, in point of fact, had sex. But we didn't fornicate like silver martens, Phil. Not at all. It was very sweet. Tender."

"You had sex in the midst of your spiritual conversion?"

"Sure. Sex is a beautiful thing, Phil. It's one of the great joys."

"This from a man who had a, I don't even know how to describe it, a leather suspension harness in his rumpus room. There were instruments of torture, implements of perversion. You had a trunk full of wigs and an endless collection of red shoes with stiletto heels."

"But listen to what I'm saying to you, Phil. None of that was as rewarding as simply *engaging*. I had all those devices because I was afraid of contact. I had those clothes because I was afraid to be naked."

"Hold on. *You* used to wear the wigs and high heels?"

"Of course. What did you think?"

"And you had joyous sex with van der Glick?"

"We made contact."

"I'm not certain I'm believing this."

"You don't believe I had sex with Our Lady of Perpetual Mercy Fucks? Come on, Philly. She had sex with Bob Hamel, for goodness sake."

"There! You've just positively identified yourself as mere figment."

"I know Bob Hamel. *The Dullest Man in Heaven*, we call him."

"He's dead?"

"Testicular cancer. He tried to call, but you weren't around."

"Okay, look, I know why you're calling."

"See that? See that little dodge, that little sidestep, that little sashay? When guilt comes, you just step out of the way."

"You want me to feel in some way responsible for what happened to you."

"*I* want you to feel responsible? Why is this bird coming to land on *my* shoulders? Whether or not you feel responsible is your lookout."

"Well, I don't. You were fucked up. You were always fucked up. You're a fuck-up."

"Fair enough. I own what happened to me. I started reading the Bible—the one you told me to read—and I started thinking about the Good Samaritan. And Jesus Christ, of course. I started reading all these stories about self-sacrifice, and they started to change me, because you always told me I was a self-centred egotistical bastard. Which was true, quite true. And then you wrote that scene, you know, like in that movie, the one that we watched that night when we were all fucked up on *árbol de los brujos,* so I—"

"Okay, okay, I can see how I was kind of involved."

"Uh-huh. Kind of sort of."

"But, Ed, I'll be candid. I can't feel any guilt about what happened to you. I've got too much guilt already, I can't take any more. It would destroy me."

"What do you feel so guilty about? Screwing the makeup girl?"

"I guess so."

"Oh, bullshit. The only reason you had an affair with Bellamy was so you'd have an excuse to feel guilty."

"Look, I don't need this nickel-ante psychology from the Other Side. What's more, the other phone, I mean the *real* phone, is ringing somewhere. So I'm going to have to say goodbye."

"Look, you've got to forgive yourself. For whatever it is you did. I have no idea what it is, and I don't care. But you can't forgive yourself until you look at the thing, and acknowledge you were wrong. Once you've forgiven yourself for the big thing, maybe you can forgive yourself for what you did to me."

"And what then? You'll find eternal peace?"

"No. But I might win the pool."

"Okay, enough. I'm going to answer the other phone. The earthly phone."

"I'm just trying to help. You're fucking up. Pull up your socks."

"That's your great wisdom? *Pull up your socks?*"

"Basically, yeah. Turn things around. You can do it, baby. *Turn things around.*"

15 | ALL SOULS' NIGHT

"VAN DER GLICK?"

"Huh, wha?"

"You're fucking van der Glick?"

"Ronnie?"

"Oh, I'm sorry, my boner, I should have identified myself. Hello, Philip? It's Veronica, your estranged wife."

"Hi."

"You're fucking van der Glick?"

"Okay, now, let me just gather my thoughts here for a second. I was taking a nap."

"Because you were shit-faced last night?"

"I wouldn't say I was *shit-faced*."

"Jay said you guys were shit-faced. That is the exact term he used."

"You've been talking to Jay?"

"*Yes*."

"Why were you talking to Jay?"

"I don't need a reason to talk to Jay. He is my brother-in-law."

"He's your estranged brother-in-law."

"No. You are my estranged husband. Jay is my brother-in-law. He may be a little *strange*, I'll grant you that."

"Okay. And he apparently informed you that I've seen Rainie a couple of times."

"*Seen* her? Jay said she had hold of your dick the whole night."

"Jay seems to have been very chatty."

"Well, at least he let me know what was going on. When were you going to fill me in?"

"Last time I checked, Veronica, we had split up. I was thrown out of the house. You've taken up with Derwood, or whatever the youngster's name is. So I don't understand why this seems to bother you as much as it does."

"Because Rainie is a friend of mine, in case you didn't know."

"Oh, I know. I know. I wrote about it, just a second, let me see if I can find the page. Hold on."

"Phil."

"The place is a bit of a mess. You know. Just hold on. Ah! Listen. 'Rainie and Ronnie were friends, of a kind; they dined together two or three times a year and went on annual shopping campaigns.'"

"Okay, first of all, *wrong*, we see each other more than that, second of all, *bad*, I mean the writing, it seems *really* pedestrian, third of all, what the hell kind of book are you writing?"

"It's an autobiographical novel."

"It's like you're taking real people, real relationships, and making little, I don't know, little tiny versions of them so that they'll fit in your damn book."

"You may have a point there, Ronnie. You may have a bit of a point. But I don't mean to. When I write, sometimes I think I'm getting it all there, getting it all in, but when I read the pages the next day, it's . . . I don't know. Gone."

"Go back to television. Perhaps the novel is beyond you."

"Have you been sleeping with Hooper?"

"Never mind who I've been sleeping with."

"You *have*, you have, dammit, you've been sleeping with Hooper!"

"I have not been sleeping with Hooper, although I am going out to dinner with him . . ."

"*What?*"

"Not that this is any of your business, but he sent me a copy of *Baxter*, which I read and adored, so then he called and asked me out, and I said yes because I wanted to tell him how much I liked the book."

"I see. Won't that be nice. But it might have been simpler, don't you think, to rip my heart out of my chest and put it in the Cuisinart? Just keep pressing that *pulse* button?"

"John is an old friend of mine. I knew him before I knew you. I don't see the problem with my having dinner with him."

"John doesn't have dinner. John has nourishment before the strenuous rutting commences. He carbo-loads for energy and stamina. Don't be so naive."

"Hey. I am perfectly capable of resisting Hooper's advances. I have a very nice boyfriend who I wouldn't want to be *unfaithful* to—anyway, screw you, Charlie, you're the one that's fucking van der Glick."

"And what the hell do you mean, you *adored* it?"

"What?"

"*Baxter. Which I read and adored.*"

"Well, of course I loved the book. Even you could understand that."

"*Even* me, what do you mean, *even* me—despite the fact I have the emotional intelligence of thirteen-year-old?"

"Thirteen seems a little high."

"Why could *even I* understand that you loved the book?"

"Haven't you read it?"

"Of course I haven't read it."

"What do you think it's about?"

"I gather from the endless gushing in the dailies that it has something to do with the stage. A life in the theatah."

"It's about *me*, Phil."

"No, no, that one was called *Lissome Is the Naiad* or, variously, *Hellhag!*"

"What the hell are you talking about?"

"Am I in the damned novel?"

"The character Paul is not unlike you."

"But but . . . I am not fodder for Hooper's fiction."

"Look, enough about Hooper. I called to talk about van der Glick."

"Rainie van der Glick and I have been friends since we were, I'm not sure, five years old or something."

"Are you in love with her?"

"Um . . ."

"I withdraw the question. It was an asinine thing to ask. Of course you aren't in love with her."

"That's what I was going to say."

"You're not *capable* of love."

"Sure I am. I love you, don't I?"

"Yeah, well, people who love other people don't go fucking *other* people and making the people they love feel like stupid ugly idiots."

"Okay, now, listen to what I'm saying, don't attack me blindly here, but the thing is, I think what you just said is wrong. Behaviour and emotion are two different things."

"Phil, Phil. That is so pathetic."

"Anyway, like I say, you have your little boy toy, plus you're going out with Hooper, so really, I don't see what the big—Ronnie? Veronica? Oh, sure, hang up on me. That is really mature. You keep saying how I have this low-grade emotional maturity and what do you do? Hang up on me. You know what that is, Ronnie? That is *petulant*. Okay, I realize I'm being somewhat petulant right now, but at least you're not at the other end of the phone to hear me. Oh, god. Oh, god, Ronnie. Oh, god."

When I emerged from my basement apartment, I was assailed by a miniature version of Black Chester Nipes. The creature had a six-gun drawn, clutched in two tiny hands; the weapon trembled with the effort of holding it aloft. This being's face was informed by the telltale black smear, but the cloud's centre was the mouth, and after a moment I guessed it was not gunpowder residue but chocolate, chocolate that had been consumed gluttonously. I saw the rightness of Jay's choice of meeting-nights. (I understood Milligan's comment—*A nice touch*—although I tried not to think about Edward Milligan too much.) It was Halloween.

"Give me candy," said Little Black Chester.

"I don't have any."

"Then you must die, earthling." The kid had his mythologies confused, but who can blame him? Who among us have their mythologies all sorted out? He popped off a few caps, filling the air with little beads of acridity.

I stumbled off, "stumbled" because sometimes I am literally hobbled by remorse. How could I have become so self-absorbed that I failed to note the advent of Halloween? (Answer: easy.) And wouldn't the girls be heartbroken that I wasn't there to share the event with them? (Answer: not really.) I resolved to head over there as soon as the "meeting" with Jay was done.

The street was crowded with dwarf goblins and pygmy ghosts, but all was not absolutely macabre; there were also wee princesses, angels with minikin wings. There were many entities where I could recognize neither genus nor species. This may have been because I had never seen the spawning movie or television program, or it may have been because the disguisee was a ranker. This was a shared characteristic of my friends and me when we were kids—no one could ever tell what we were supposed to be on Halloween.

As a kid, Rainie always tried to be some historical personage, a woman she admired, say, Carson McCullers. Toward this end, she would climb into a dress, pull on nylons and bedaub her face with lipstick. She would appear at people's doorways and even though she was immediately recognizable as a little whore, people would send up the call out of embarrassment: "What are *you* supposed to be?" My own costuming was, admittedly, obscure; I would portray characters from *The Twilight Zone*. I would, for instance, pretend to be the little boy from the episode entitled "Third Stone from the Sun," the lad the townspeople came to believe was an alien. They believed this because he would say strange things—"I come from the third stone from the sun"—and when he was struck down by a car, he simply climbed back to his feet and walked away. Rod Serling's little plot twist here is that the kid was born without a functioning nervous system and couldn't feel pain. The odd things he said were explained to the unthinking townsfolk—*The third stone from the sun is Earth, you idiots!* He was nothing other than an ordinary little boy, which was dramatically very moving but didn't really suggest any dynamic costuming ideas, so of course I too would receive the blank stare and the dumbfounded "What are *you* supposed to be?"

When my brother stepped out of the shadows, however, about half a mile from our assigned meeting place, he looked at me, snapped his fingers and said, "Got it!"

"Huh?"

"The Trilight Zone!"

"What are you talking about?"

"I know who you're supposed to be. You're that guy, right, that librarian, who rejoiced when the world was destroyed. He believed he could therefore live forever in books."

"Time enough at last to read, read, read." This was by way of being a correction to what Jay had said.

"He organized all of the books from the library into piles on the steps. He had piles for this year, piles for the next year and the year after that . . ."

"I know all this. I'm the one who told you."

"But what happened was, he bent over to pick up a book and his glasses flew from his face. They shattered. And he could see nothing. It seems to me he says, *It's not fair, it's just not fair,* but we the viewers understood. It *is* fair. It is what he deserved."

We began to amble down the street, knee-deep in poltergeists. Jay seemed to have a destination in mind.

"By the way," I said, "thanks for ratting me out to Veronica."

"Oh," Jay said, quite seriously, "you're welcome. It was my pleasure."

"That was certainly a pleasant call to receive. *You're fucking van der Glick!* That's what she said. That's what she screamed."

"You *are* fucking van der Glick."

"So what? *She's* going out to dinner with Hooper."

"Yes? And your point?"

"It hurts."

"Ah. Good. Signs of life."

I took a moment to study Jay—because I had no idea what the hell he was talking about—when something struck me. "What are *you* supposed to be?"

He wore a suit that was dark as pitch—at least, for the most part, because at various places—elbows and knees particularly—the material was so worn that the paleness of his skin shone through. Jay owned no suits, I knew that, so he had obviously purchased this at a second-hand store, or perhaps he'd bartered with a cadaver. He complemented this suit with jesus boots that appeared to be made of, I don't know, jute or something. They looked ancient, these sandals— they seemed to have made innumerable journeys through wastelands. As odd as all this was, there was something about the plain white tee-shirt my brother wore underneath that looked odder still, something that was difficult to put one's finger on. It struck me that the collar rode too high on the front, that it covered Jay's prominent Adam's apple, and where it did, there was the bulging expression of a manufacturer's label. "Ah!" I said, because the answer to my own question occurred to me. Jay had the tee-shirt on backwards, which gave him this queerly canonical look. "You're supposed to be a priest!"

He smiled in a beatific manner.

Jay's Halloween costumes, when he was a boy, also tended to have a religious flavour. I don't know why, because he otherwise evinced no interest in the Judeo-Christian tradition. (I didn't know then that he was slipping over to the Valleyway United Church to pound away on the keyboards there.) But every October 31, Jay would appear as, oh, a shepherd or one of the Magi. One explanation might be the simplicity of these outfits—you put on a sheet, sash it with a piece of rope and carry around a big stick. There was one Halloween when he wanted to go out wearing only a diaper rendered somehow out of two knotted pillowcases and a crown made out of intertwined rose branches. And he wanted to lug over his shoulder a cross (two fence-boards nailed together). But my mother stopped him at the front door, and disallowed this costume on the grounds that he would be too cold.

"That's right," said Jay now. "I'm supposed to be a priest. So I can hear your confession."

"Ergh." That was a sound of both annoyance and fear. "Where are we going, anyway?"

"Last known address."

"What?"

"So you talked to Ronnie, huh?" said Jay, avoiding the question. "How did she seem?"

"She seemed, um, the word for how she seemed would be *livid*."

"Because of van der Glick?"

"Well, yes, I mean, that certainly brought the, um, lividity to the surface. But, hey, it's always there."

"I see, my son."

"It made me think, though."

"Good. Share your thoughts."

"Well . . . it's just that she was *so* mad, you know, *so* jealous. It made me think that she must still have feelings for me."

"It's possible. People are plenty weird. Even Ronnie."

"You don't think Ronnie's weird?"

"I just said she was."

"Yeah, but . . ."

"Let me ask you something, my son."

"Quit calling me that."

"Do you love Rainie?"

"Uh . . ."

"The reason I ask is, she loves you."

"Really?"

"Yes, my son. We in the Church are currently giving much serious thought to adding a commandment. Which would make it number, um—"

"Eleven."

"Quite so. And the eleventh commandment would be, *Thou shalt pay fucking attention.*"

We moved into a peculiar section of the downtown area. Toronto doesn't really have any slums—none that you can get to on foot, anyway, although horrific high-rise tenements circle the city like moons—but it certainly has its seedy sections. We came upon row houses, identical and hunched, dwarf dwellings that long ago were the quarters of the men who laboured for the nearby soap factory. It was very apparent that this wasn't the best part of town, because the hordes of fairies had disappeared. There were one or two lumbering trick-or-treaters, well over six feet in height, their feet enormous, balaclavas and nylons obscuring their features. These boys would leap onto the stoop, pound on the door, wrench open their pillow-cases and emit a small but emphatic grunt.

Jay stopped to light a cigarette. He struck a match and held it in cupped hands. He dipped the smoke into the flame, and then began to puff with industry. When he did remove the cigarette, he held it hoodlum-style. I saw that we were taking a smoke-break, so I lit up a little cigar and wondered why. I got the sense that the evening was orchestrated, so this little respite was obviously planned.

The answer, I suspected, lay in the building behind Jay, which was squat and strangled by ivy. It was a church, recognizable because of its two stained-glass windows, although all of the coloured panes had been replaced by dark, smoky ones. There was no light coming from them.

"First of all," said Jay, "I think you should have mentioned that I had *all* the badges."

"What?"

"I had every badge that a Wolf Cub could get. And that includes knot-tying."

"So?"

"So, you weren't the *only* accomplished knot-tier in the troop."

"Is that so?"

"Yes, my son."

"And what's your point?"

"Ah, that's the point, isn't it? *What's the point* is what's my point."

"All right, maybe you were good with knots too; the thing is, I've fictionalized to a certain degree."

"What you've fictionalized is your *life*."

I thought about that and came to the same conclusion I'd come to many times before, i.e., my brother is just a little bit nuts. "What are we doing here, Jay?"

He nodded his enormous head so emphatically that I spun around to look in the direction indicated. "Last known address," said Jay. He tossed his butt away and crossed the street.

One of the houses had a porch light burning. (The others all were dark, I guessed because the inhabitants were pretending not to be home, not wishing their rye-consumption to be disturbed by the menacing Halloweeners.) Once we achieved proximity to the little home, all hell broke loose, in the form of feline commotion and ado. Some of the pussies squawked and scattered, others yowled and raised themselves to piddy-paws, pleading for affectionate scritching. Jay nodded at the cats, offered a friendly "Meow." Then he pressed a broken plastic button that rested in a setting of rust, and from within the house we heard an ominous *bong*. Jay folded his hands together and held them chest-level.

There was no immediate reaction to the doorbell, and then no eventual one. Jay rang again, looked at me and said quietly, "Don't worry, she's home."

"*Who's* home?"

"You'll see."

I did see, after the third ringing, when a woman shouldered open the wooden door and shouted, "I don't have any candy!" The sentence

I just composed makes it sound as though I recognized this human being as female when she first appeared, but that's not really the case. The first impression was indeed of masculinity, because she was bald, for the most part, although long strands of faded golden hair clung to her skull. The voice was also no clear indicator, as it was smoke-choked and gravelly. But there was jewellery, a dress and a bizarre attempt at makeup, and although I am sophisticated enough not to be taken in by cross-dressing, there was such a cold absence of sexuality that I concluded that these trappings were adopted as a default position. It was a woman, then, a theory proven by Jay when he said, "Good evening, Mrs. Kitchen."

Suspicion clouded her features. "Yesssss?"

"I'm Jay McQuigge. I called you."

It took a moment or two for Mrs. Kitchen to summon forth the memory. "Yessss," she nodded, then she jerked a thumb at me. "Isss thisss Phil?"

"That's him," Jay agreed.

"Nice." (She elongated that "s" sound as well, but I couldn't figure out how to transcribe that stylographically.)

A cat was trying to sneak into the house, pressing against the wall and folding its body around the jamb. Mrs. Kitchen hooked a foot under its belly and propelled it off the porch and onto the small square of earth that served as a front lawn. "Damn catsss," she said. The speech impediment was caused by the fact that she lacked a number of teeth. Her mouth was peppered with gaps, and after making certain sounds her thick tongue would briefly get trapped in one of them. "Okay, boysss," she said, "come on in."

"She lived in this really weird little house," I said, "full of newspapers. It was like she'd never thrown a newspaper away in her life, and they were stacked up everywhere. The pages had turned yellow, you know, and some were so old that the paper was brown and brittle, and if you grabbed a corner of it, it just kind of snapped off and turned to dust."

My audience had various reactions. Well, let me be clear— everyone was ignoring me, but in different manners and, I suppose, for different reasons. Currer and Ellis were ignoring me because they were busy bartering, trading Halloween foodstuffs.

"Do you like these fizzy pop rocks?" asked Currer.

"Yeah," Ellis responded.

"Okay, then, I'll give you three packs of pop rocks and seven Halloween kisses if you give me those two chocolate bars."

If I hadn't been concentrating on relating the tale of my visit to Mrs. Kitchen, I might have advised Ellis to run screaming from any deal that involved Halloween kisses. This is a mysterious confection that appears once a year, a tiny block of tasteless gluten wrapped in wax paper adorned with images of batwings and broomsticks. I can't believe they're still around. When I was a lad (and maybe still today) Halloween kisses seemed somehow to be tokens of social standing. Popular children might find one or two settled at the bottom of their loot bags. Rankers seemed to find nothing *but* Halloween kisses.

Anyway, Ellis wouldn't do it, being considerably craftier than her older sister. "No Halloween kisses," she stated. "Three packs of pop rocks for one chocolate bar. *This* one."

"The other one."

"This one."

The bickering carried on until Ellis finally caved, although I believe in the end she gave up precisely the chocolate bar she wanted to give up.

So this was why my children were ignoring me. Veronica Lear, on the other hand, was busy straightening up the house. Her attitude, which I intuited from body language and a kind of icy aura that engulfed her, was this: *The house is a bit messy, besides, you are an*

*aberration, a resident of the Twilight Zone, a base and worthless creature
that somehow has acquired the ability to speak, although it would be
impossible for you to have anything of import to say, so I'll spend this time
tidying.*

"She was of the impression," I went on, "that Norman and I
were best friends. Not good friends, but *best* friends. You know what
I mean? That we'd exchanged blood and made the declaration."

No reaction from any quarter. Oh, well. It really wasn't much of
a story, anyway. I thought perhaps I could hook the kids on the
spookiness of the house, I thought maybe Ronnie might—actually, I
don't know what I thought vis-à-vis Ronnie. The truth of the matter
is, I just wanted to be with them. I had never missed a Halloween
before, not one out of the previous eleven. If you're calculating, yes,
that means I took Currer trick-or-treating when she was one year
old. I wrapped her in some fuzzy material and, on the neighbours'
stoops, held her forward like an offering to the gods. I accepted candy
on her behalf, even though she had only one tooth.

I pressed on with my story, about how Mrs. Kitchen thought I'd
been Norman's best friend, how she'd wondered why we'd never
met (should have been a tipoff), the problems she'd had raising little
Norman, he of the beautiful hair. (The hair thing came up quite a bit.
From time to time Mrs. Kitchen's face would acquire a soft, out-of-
focus aspect. "Norman had," she'd whisper, "such beautiful hair.")

"What sort of problems?" asked Jay. He was still in priest mode,
to the extent that he'd declined the offer of a drink. I'd accepted, of
course, and was given something in a coffee mug. I'm fairly certain it
was cooking sherry.

"Well, he got into trouble a few times. With other boys." That
was all Mrs. Kitchen had to say on the subject. *Trouble with other boys.*
Jay pressed and subtly cajoled ("We all get into trouble at some point
in our lives,") but Mrs. Kitchen was not forthcoming.

"Where," asked Jay finally, "does Norman live?"

"He's travelled around quite a bit," admitted his mother. "Never seemed to stay in one place too long. Mind you, they'd send him various places . . ."

"*They* would?"

"The superiors."

"Where does he live now?" Jay asked.

"Norman lives in Thunder Bay," she answered.

"Would you happen to have an address for him?"

Mrs. Kitchen went to locate the items she needed: her address book, a pencil and a piece of paper. Despite the quantity of newsprint in the household, this last item proved the hardest to find. She was gone from the kitchen for quite a few moments, a few moments during which Jay and I exchanged no words except for the following.

He glanced at me and flipped his eyebrows high on his massive forehead. "Road trip," said he.

16 | THE CREATIVE PROCESS

WE—MISS LEAR AND I—HAD BEEN A COUPLE (A BREEZY, CAREFREE couple) for about a year and a half when Veronica discovered she was pregnant. I was all right with this—I saw my life unrolling as a life will. In retrospect, I would have to concede that I was not wildly enthusiastic, and enthusiasm is probably what Ronnie wanted of me. I don't know how many times previously I had failed to be what Ronnie wanted me to be, but it didn't really matter, did it? We were simply two people who ate at restaurants, watched movies, made love, smoked cigarettes as we leafed leisurely through the Sunday papers. All that changed when the paper turned blue. After that, all of my little failures were thrown into a pile and became a cairn of bones, bleached by the sun and cleaned by maggots. Man, there's a metaphor.

I could fail on a lot of counts, too. I could fail to be attentive, romantic, empathetic, forthcoming—that was a big one, that failure to be forthcoming. You've probably sensed something of it yourself, you've probably fallen into some deep holes in this narrative and wondered where the hell you were. *Phil is not being forthcoming*.

And there were financial repercussions to the pregnancy. Ronnie and I had kept our separate residences during the year and a half, although I spent most of my time at her place. My own place was largely dedicated to my mess; I kept my mess over there, paid visits occasionally to make sure my mess was thriving. Veronica was quite clear on the fact that she wanted nothing to do with my mess. I believe she would have been happier living as some particularly ascetic Buddhist monk, reducing her surroundings to the barest of necessities. A bed, certainly, a table, a chair. When Ronnie became pregnant, we decided to move in together. We rented a place in Toronto's Riverdale, the upper two floors of an old house that sat across the street from Doggy Park. I reduced my mess as best I could, but Ronnie's eyes hardened as the van pulled up and began spewing fishing rods, press benches, bicycles, banjo cases (yes, I had duplicates of everything), record albums, books, books, books. And more books. Ronnie picked one out of a box and noted the title.

"Didn't you already read this one?"

"Yeah. It was good."

"Oh." Then silence, for Veronica could speak silence.

"Why? You don't think I should throw it out, do you?"

"Well, you've already read it."

Oh, but wait, here come the boxes of papers—yellow second sheets, coffee-stained and ash-flecked.

"What's all that, Phil?"

"That? That's my, my, *work*. My plays."

"Oh." Silence.

"You know, all the various drafts. And all the plays I've started and bogged down in."

"Why do you keep them?"

"Because I might finish them one day."

"Oh."

I haven't yet, as you know. At the time Ronnie became pregnant I was finishing a play entitled *Low Man*, which was kind of my take on *Death of a Salesman*. Loman, you see, although my title referred to the low man on a totem pole. It was quite a bit like David Mamet's *Glengarry Glen Ross*, which it predates (I point out hastily) by a couple of years. Except that I did not understand that world as well as Mamet, and my dramatic sense is not as strong as his, and my dialogue isn't as good. The only aspect in which my play may have the edge is that I have a woman in *Low Man*, the young dogsbody who files papers and fetches coffee. It was a good part, written with Veronica Lear in mind, although by the time the play was actually in production, her stomach was ballooning (as were her breasts, in a manner that still makes my heart ache) and the part went instead to a newcomer, fresh out of the academy, named Paula Beecher. Paula, as you may know, went on to play Harriet in *Padre*, a sad piece of synchronicity that has plagued me for years. Not that there was ever anything inappropriate with our relationship—she's happily married, Paula is, although never to the same person for more than two years in a row—but as far as Ronnie is concerned, Paula was the career-ender. In Ronnie's mind, it's almost as though Paula were waiting in the wings, and the instant Ronnie's pregnancy became visible, she rushed onstage and shoved my wife into the shadows. I should therefore harbour resentment against Ms. Beecher, which I clearly don't, or else why would I cast her in *Padre?*—another bone for the pile.

Low Man didn't fare very well. The Toronto reviewers could sense *Glengarry Glen Ross* in the futuristic ether; they knew there was a good play somewhere in the material, but they were unified in their opinion that I hadn't written it. I'd had failures before, and I was fairly thick-skinned. (For one thing, the criticism gave me an excuse for flamboyant drunkenness; for another, I think deep down I agreed with it.) But the meagreness of the royalty cheques suddenly became significant. How was I going to support a wife and a child on the backs of a handful of theatregoers? In my memory, I was pondering that question when the telephone rang.

"Mr. McQuigge? William Beckett."

"Yes?"

"I was wondering if you'd care to go along to lunch."

I went along to lunch, but Beckett didn't actually eat anything; instead, he watched me eat my club sandwich with a certain revolted fascination. And I'll mention that in all the years I've known him, I've never ever witnessed him eat. So, although Beckett demurs and protests, there is evidence that he truly is Beelzebub, Overlord of Darkness.

"Television," he told me, "is a river of money into which we must jump."

"That sounds good," I agreed.

"I've been green-lit on *Sneaks*," he told me, not concerned with the look of bafflement that washed across my face. "A series of some little charm and vast amounts of twaddle. The premise? Simplicity itself. Two cat burglars, a man and a woman, lark about cat burgling. They once were married, have now separated, but need the other's skill in order to successfully ply their larcenous trade. He is possessed of wondrous fingertips, you see, and can open any safe. She is superbly athletic and can gain entry to any loft or aerie. So they continue to work together, although they bicker and argue constantly. Does this appeal to you?"

"Um . . . does *what* appeal to me?"

"The notion."

"Well, um, do they argue and bicker while they're cat burgling?"

"Yes, indeed."

"But isn't the point of cat burglary to be as quiet as possible?"

"Mmm. Quite. But we don't worry about such things inside the box. For one thing, Philip, there is no such creature as a cat burglar. There are great heaving louts who smash out windows, take what they believe they can pawn, make themselves a sandwich and defecate on the carpeting for good measure. So don't worry about the bickering. For another thing, that's precisely the point, that's the premise, that's the brand, because every week our heroes, through their bickering, awaken the inhabitants. They thus become involved in other lives."

"I get it. I guess."

"I am in the process of assembling the writing team. And I am offering you the position of story editor."

"Sorry, I'm a playwright."

I didn't really say that. I wonder how my life might have unfolded had I said that. I might be sitting in a little cabin right now, my writing place; through the window I can see the big house; Ronnie is tending to her flowers; the children are playing in the garden. But what I said was, "How much would that pay?" and the answer was totally mind-boggling—at least, I allowed my mind to be boggled because 1) I had a pregnant partner and 2) perhaps it was my destiny. "You are entering another dimension of time and space . . ."

Ronnie's reaction to news of my employment was complex and rather more muted than I might have foreseen. She twisted her mouth way off to the side of her face, something she does when perplexed or involved in cogitation. "Sounds kind of like a dumb show," she adjudged. "Maybe there's a part for me." She was not feeling very good about herself right then. Her body was exploding with fat and hormones, after all. I remember that around this time we went shopping for maternity dresses (her regular wardrobe now confined to storage containers) and she tossed the store's offerings into the air, disdainful of all the pastels. "Don't you have anything that's like, you know, *black?*" she demanded of the salesgirl.

I shall be brief about my career in the television bidna. (*Why start now*, I can hear you demanding, as if you had all been sleeping with John Hooper, as I suspect Ronnie has. The only reason I have for thinking my wife may *not* have been sleeping with Hooper is every bit as sickening as the notion that she has; she has a boyfriend. Ronnie still has plans to take this Mexican vacation with her young Kerwin, the priapic philosophy student. I'll let you in on a little secret, though; I have a few travel plans of my own. Or rather, in conjunction with my brother.) (Oh, oh, getting back to that, there is a grand literary sense in which you *have* all been sleeping with Snooty Hooper, commingling with him on some infinite intellectual mattress, because his book *Baxter* is setting sales records all across this grand nation. The Giller Prize announcement will be made in a few days. If I were smart, I'd find some bespectacled bookie and put a lot of money down on Hooper, but I, even I, yes it's true, despite all odds and against all rational thinking, even I have my pride.) All right, my television career, my curriculum vitae: the show *Sneaks* was something of a hit, due mostly to the chemistry between the two leads, Gart Sweeney and Thea King. (Off-camera, of course, the two could not abide each other.) I was Story Editor for one season, Executive Story Editor for the next, Co-Producer for the third, and then William Beckett launched another series, the ambitious but ultimately abysmal *Poe*. (The premise of *Poe* is odd for television, and pure William Beckett. The series supposes that, when not scribbling poetry and short stories, Edgar Allan Poe becomes involved, on a weekly basis, in mysteries and intrigues, which he solves using his massive intellect and vast amounts of laudanum. That show was scuppered by a failure to cast the leading role properly; Larry Boyle was pudgy and a little silly-looking, and no amount of dark makeup could lend a sinister aspect to his mien.) Anyway, when Beckett left *Sneaks* to start *Poe*, he appointed me his successor as show-runner. This was a stroke of some luck (I guess) because a) there was oodles more money, b) the show was already running pretty smoothly and c) because of the Byzantine intricacies of the Canadian television funding system, the fourth season of *Sneaks* was always understood to be its last, so I was placed in a fail-safe position. In point of fact, I didn't run *Sneaks* at all well, but I made it through the season and earned my stripes, as it were.

Meanwhile, another star was in ascendancy. Edward Milligan, as hard as this may be to credit, began his career on the stage in his native Calgary. He was in exactly one play, David Mamet's *American Buffalo*, filling the smallish role of Bobby. In the audience one night was the American film director Joel Schumacher, and I have no idea what he was doing in Calgary, let alone in that theatre, but he rushed backstage as soon as the curtain came down and offered Milligan the lead in his next movie. That movie never got financed, but by the time it didn't get financed Milligan was already in Hollywood. He spent a few years there, getting small parts in some good pictures, larger ones in some stinkers, and although by American standards his career came a cropper, up north here the industry developed a certain pride in him. So a call was put out to his agent—*Come back home, Edward Milligan, and you can star in your own television show.*

And another call was placed to yours truly: *Develop a show for Edward Milligan.*

The two of us were brought together over lunch. Carla Dowbiggin was there, as well as Bill Veerstuck (the network's head of development) and some guy named Jimmy. I didn't know who the hell Jimmy was, and I'm not certain that Carla or Bill did either, and it is possible that he was simply some enterprising scalawag who managed to cadge a free meal.

Milligan was late, what else, so I spent an hour spinning my wheels and trotting out various half-baked pitches, because, really, when I sat down at the table, I had no ideas for a television series.

I did have, back home, a four-year-old and a newly pregnant wife, so I was plenty desperate. "How about a medical show?" I wondered aloud. "Milligan plays a doctor. Um, a young intern. Kind of like Dr. Kildare, but, um . . . hey, why don't we redo *Dr. Kildare*? You know, that could work. It was a very popular show. Or Ben Casey. Or, I know, Milligan could play a young intern in a *psychiatric hospital*. Yeah, yeah. And every week, he becomes involved with another patient, not *involved* involved, you know, but, um . . ."

Milligan entered the restaurant, looked around, saw us and smiled. He approached the table eagerly. Introductions were made, and as I shook his hand, I noted that he had a certain raffish quality. "You know what?" I said as we all sat back down. "I do have one idea that might work."

———

"Hello?"

"Am I speaking to Mister Peter Paul Mendicott?"

"No."

"Oh. Well, I'm sorry, but I was told I might reach him at this number."

"You might. But that isn't what you asked. You asked if you were speaking to the man."

"Right. Is Mr. Mendicott there?"

"Of course he's here."

"Mm-hmm. And, um, may I please speak to him?"

"No."

"Our conversation isn't going well, is it?"

"Pee-Pee doesn't exactly speak. You can't smoke roll-your-owns all your life and expect to *speak* at his age. I mean, he is hooked up to so much breathing apparatus that I spend half my day just trying to locate him. He's about twelve pounds of wrinkles and he communicates mostly through faint wheezes and huge blasting farts."

"Listen, I don't mean to, I don't know, *pry,* but are you a man or a woman?"

"I get that a lot."

"It's hard to tell just from your voice."

"I am aware."

"So, ah . . . ?"

"Here's the thing. Until we proceed further in this conversation, I can't see how it makes any difference."

"Fair enough. Right. Well, here's the thing. My name is Phil McQuigge."

"Phil fucking McQuigge?"

"Er, yes."

"Executive Producer and, nyah-nyah, creator of *Padre?*"

"Um . . . formerly those things. At present I am a novelist."

"Hold on. I'll get Pee-Pee."

"I thought he couldn't speak."

"He can *listen*. I can put on the speakerphone and he can listen to whatever it is you have to say."

"Is Pee-Pee, Mr. Mendicott, aware of the television show *Padre?*"

"What the fuck do you think has kept him alive for the past couple of years?"

"I don't get you. And before you explain, I really need to know now if I'm speaking to a man or a woman."

"Are those my only two choices?"

"Hmm?"

"I'm transitional, baby. I'm surfing the continuum."

"Oh. Is Carson City, Nevada, the best place to be for a person like you?"

"The clinic is here."

"Ah."

"And it's not like there's any nightlife. It's not like I ever go out, anyway, except to pick up meds. Pee-Pee and I stay inside, in this fucking adobe hut. We watch television. All day and all night long. We have a satellite dish so huge that at least once a month extraterrestrials land in the backyard seeking to make contact. We have video, DVD, hey, we have a goddam Beta player. So that's what we do, all day, all night long. We watch television."

"Do you ever see that show, um, *The Twilight Zone?*"

"Sure. Around here that's like reality teevee."

"Ever see the one where this librarian . . ."

"McQuigge, you're attempting to change the subject."

"No, no, I was just conversing . . ."

"So we see this listing one night. You know. '*Padre*. A clergyman tries to tame the Wild West.'"

"Only two people in the whole United States watched the show, just my luck it's you guys."

"And Pee-Pee watches for a few moments, you know, and then he says, *That fucking cunt.*"

"Let me remind you, young, um, person, that Father White was only a secondary character."

"In the *movie*, yeah."

"How so?"

"Did you never read the novel?"

"No, and kindly remove that sanctimonious tone from your voice. Do you think I haven't tried to find it? I have searched every used-book bin in this city. I have hired a book search service, it cost me hundreds of dollars, I believe the young man was ultimately, I don't know, devoured by crocs somewhere in Africa. So don't get shirty with me."

"*Mea culpa*. The point is, Father White is the hero of the novel. Johnny Mungo isn't even *in* the book. He was just added for the movie."

"Who added him?"

"Well, Pee-Pee did. But it was not an aesthetic choice. It was, um, look, the fact of the matter is, Mark Goode was his little bumboy. And you know what love can do. Turn our heads a-fucking-round."

"What's that?"

"Hmm?"

"What's that sound? It sounds like a toilet flushing in some inter-dimensional black hole."

"I have entered the teevee room. I have put on the speakerphone. That sound you so eloquently describe emanates from Mr. Peter Paul Mendicott."

"Hello, sir!"

"¨ . . . ¨ ¿"

"I'll tell you who it is, Pee-Pee. That is Philip McQuigge!"

"¡"

"Uh-huh. I managed to track him down for you . . ."

"Hey."

"Play along, Phil. The old fart rewrites his will about eight times a day."

"Mr. Mendicott. Here's the thing. When I was a small child, I went with the other rankers to the Galaxy Odeon. *The Bullet and the Cross* was the matinee. We watched that movie, sir, and we, um, cried. We wept. And I guess I decided then, on that day, that *that* was what I wanted to do with my life, make, you know, art that made people weep. I haven't done that. I have not accomplished that.

"Anyway, when I had the opportunity to create my own show, this idea popped into my mind, *Padre*, and I was too, I was too, I don't know, self-absorbed or egotistical or some damn thing to ever consider that it wasn't my idea. And I'm sorry. And not only that, not only that, but my one success for the stage, *The Hawaiian,* well, what happens is that this girl, who was played stunningly by my estranged wife, is taken hostage, gun to head type of thing, and she, well, she does what Father White does. I stole it. And I kind of stole it for what turned out to be the last episode of *Padre,* but I changed it, but the actor, his name was Edward Milligan, he . . . well, it was very, very sad. At any rate, I apologize to you. Sir. I am very sorry. I just . . ."

"It's all right, Phil. He's gone."

"What do you mean, he walked out of the room?"

"No. No. I mean, um . . . *release.*"

"But that's . . . that's terrible."

"Are you kidding? Are you kidding, Phil? Release is what we've been waiting for."

"You're telling me that he just died? Just now? As I was talking to him?"

"I'd better go. I've got things to do. Procedures to follow."

"I feel just awful."

"Don't. Don't at all. You just did a good thing. Try to make it the first of many."

17 | THE PLATE

ALL RIGHT, I SEE NOW THERE IS A PLATE I HAVE TO SPIN. THOSE OF you
who don't quite grok the metaphor never spent Sunday evenings
watching *The Ed Sullivan Show*. That is how my family spent its
Sunday evenings, or so I assert, with a large measure of wilful self-
deception. For although I sat cross-legged in front of the television
set, my hands cupping my chubby knees, the rest of the family was
otherwise occupied. My mother would be on the sofa behind me,
reading a novel, drinking a drink. My brother, if he was in the house
at all, would be, I don't know, conducting little experiments; for
example, he spent many hours trying to ascertain exactly how mal-
leable his face was. Jay would invert his eyelids, fold his ears, pinch
his nostrils, tug at the edges of his mouth. Sometimes he would wrap
Scotch tape around his massive head, flattening and deforming all of
his features. Although this may sound like the result of bottomless
boredom, that wouldn't account for the absorption my brother
found in such activities. Anyway, if he was just bored, why didn't he
watch television like a normal kid? "Hey, Jay!" I would holler, as
soon as Mr. Sullivan had completed his introduction. "It's Topo
Gigio, the cute little Italian mouse!"

"Hey, a lion tamer!"

"Hey, a plate spinner!"

Plate spinners were my favourite. The stage sprouted long wooden poles; the performer would enter with a stackful of plates (or else have the plates tossed to him by his assistant, who wore a little leotard that cleaved the backside and revealed many square inches of bare buttock, which went unmentioned, seemingly unnoticed except by me) which the plate-artiste would set, one by one, atop the poles. He'd place a plate, flick the rim a few times, set the thing into motion and centrifugal suspension, and then move on. A good plate twirler might have as many as twenty-five plates and poles, and as he worked on, say, the fifteenth, the first would be slowing and wobbling and threatening to drop and shatter, and the performer would dash back and give it a few quick flicks. Then on to the sixteenth, back to the second (give that first one a little extra torque, just for good meas-ure), back to the seventeenth (for some reason the eighth would need some quick attention!), and soon the man was dashing all around the stage, and plates were spinning and wobbling and, oh!, every so often one would drop and the man would dive and catch it before it hit, an act the audience awarded with great huzzahs. It has only just dawned on me now that I was receiving, not just entertainment, but some skewed notion of how to live my adult life-to-be. Maybe it was the presence of the bare-buttocked assistant. (And of course, I never considered what happened after Ed Sullivan threw up his hands and invoked applause, I never considered that behind the fallen curtain every single fucking plate was shattering to little bitsies.)

At any rate, plate-twirling certainly has an analogue in novel-writing, and I see now that a plate is wobbling, so let me rush back, let me remind you of the scene in the makeup trailer, on the set of *Padre*, wherein I more or less dared Edward Milligan to read the Bible. Okay, you got that? (Flick, flick.)

Now we can proceed to an evening perhaps three days later. I have crawled into bed beside Ronnie, and, despite the fact that I have just recently spent my seed (you'll soon appreciate the Biblical tone) with Bellamy, I reach up under my wife's nightshirt and cup her right breast in my hand. Ronnie stirs, purrs, presses herself back up against me (although she remains an awfully long way from wakefulness) and I am content. I have these small moments of contentment, they are really all I can hope for, because if I were to look around I would see naught but wobbling plates.

The telephone rings, and I leap out of bed, wondering who the hell it could be. My brother, Jay, is my best bet, as he sometimes misplaces time at the bottom of a whiskey glass. So I snap up the phone in the master bedroom, press it tightly against my face and whisper, "Hello?"

"Phil? It's Ed."

"Milligan?"

"Yeah, sure. Milligan."

"You have to be on the set in four hours."

"Yeah, I know, but I can't sleep. Listen, listen to this. *A certain man was going down from Jerusalem to Jericho, and he fell among robbers, who both stripped him and beat him, and departed, leaving him half dead. By chance a certain priest was going down that way. When he saw him, he passed by on the other side.*"

"Ed? Why are reading me this?"

"The priest passed by on the *other* side."

"Yeah. Okay, listen. Take that dope you have, flush it down the toilet. Actually, save a little bit for me to try, it seems to be really top-notch . . ."

"I'm not doing any dope, Phil. I was just lying in bed here, and I thought I'd look at this Bible. Okay, so then a Levite passes by on the other side. But the Samma-ritten, I mean the Samaritan, um, *he was moved with compassion, came to him, and bound up his wounds, pouring on oil and wine.* I didn't know wine was good for that sort of thing, you can really learn a lot from the Bible."

"I don't think it really functions very well as a first-aid manual."

"Look, Phil. Don't, you know, *mock* me. Please don't mock me. Because this story, it's like . . . you know, you try to divide the world up into good and bad people. You know? It's like this choice you're given, *You gonna be good, you gonna be bad?* And it's easier to be bad, right? It's more fun. But in this story, the good person, the priest, he just passes by on the other side. So like, where does that leave us? There are no good or bad people, there are just people and some can be moved by this, this, *compassion*. Doesn't that make you feel better?"

"Why would it make me feel better?"

"Because you think you're such a bad person."

"I don't think I'm a bad person."

"Bull-fucking-whipdip. You think you're the lowest of the low, and the only reason you can stand having me around is that I'm a lot worse than you are."

"Look, Milligan, I was in bed."

"With your wife, your beautiful wife?"

"Yes, with my wife, my beau—my wife."

"Do you love her?"

"Of course I do."

"Then why are you laying the pud to Makeup?"

"Milligan!"

"I'll tell you why. Because it's a monstrous thing to do, *ergo*, you're a monster."

My wife, my beautiful wife, is struggling to resurface into the land of wakey-wakey. "Phil? What's going on?" I think I woke her up when I whispered/bellowed, "Milligan!"

The next day, on-set, Milligan seemed to be his old obnoxious self, and I was convinced that his nocturnal phone call was the result of space-age pharmaceuticals. I found him fighting bitterly, savagely, with Jimmy Yu, *Padre*'s most frequent director. "You're whacked!" Milligan was hollering. "Just totally fucking whack-o."

I couldn't read all too much into that particular statement, given that it was incontrovertible. Jimmy possesses no grip on sanity, doesn't even attempt it. One only has to look at him; they say appearances can be deceiving, but in my experience this is not the case, certainly not the case with Yu. Jimmy sports a kind of inverse monk's tonsure, shaving his head except for the crown, from which blooms a thick plume dyed on a daily basis, although amateurishly, so that it is mottled and variegated. He is the only person I've ever encountered whose spectacles are thicker than my own. My lenses make my eyes look distorted and large. Jimmy's cause his to disappear, and when you look at him head-on, you see nothing but flesh-coloured clouds where the orbs should be. He's fortunate in that nature saddled him with a huge pair of ears and a prodigious nose, as anything smaller would be unable to deal with the specs.

Jimmy is from Hong Kong originally—specifically, a film studio in Hong Kong, one that specialized in martial arts movies. His father was a director and his mother an actress (indeed, his mother was Nan Yu, famous for her role as White Breast, a fierce warrior who often battled with a breast exposed, I suppose for tactical reasons), and although there was a family apartment nearby none of the Yus ever left the sets. Not young Jimmy, at any rate, who still doesn't truly believe that there is existence beyond the sound stage. We (by "we" I mean the producers of *Padre*) supplied him with a hotel room, quite a nice hotel room, but he went there only reluctantly, after being tossed out of the production facilities by Security. (Despite which, he managed to run up an astronomical pay-per-view movie bill.) When he is editing (Jimmy is truly a filmmaker, he does it all himself and trusts no one) he sleeps and eats in the editing suite, although only to the tune of twenty-odd minutes a night and a few handfuls of peanuts.

This may sound like artistic dedication rather than insanity, but trust me, it's insanity. Jimmy is in the grip of the illusion that he is reinventing cinema, marking his page in movie history, every second of every day. Therefore, the simplest shot (Milligan standing in front of his little parish church, for example) is undertaken with Eisensteinian enthusiasm. Yu will mount huge attacks; he will holler into being a phalanx of klieg lights and booms; he will lead the charge himself with the 35-millimetre camera raised above his head. Again, this may sound admirable but it is fundamentally irritating, and finally maddening, because Jimmy lacks both age-appropriate social skills and much of the English language. Although he's lived in North America for ten years, he abandoned his acquisition of the tongue after mastering, oh, thirty-five words, not all of which are applicable to the film and television business. ("Buttocks," for example, which he employs in a variety of ways. When angry at the grips, Jimmy will shriek, "Buttocks!" We don't know if this is the part of their anatomy he is threatening or if it is just an all-purpose cry of frustration.) The word he shouts most is "Right!" which serves duty both as "correct" and, although it is racially insensitive to mention this, "light."

So when I heard Jimmy scream, "More right!" and Milligan assert, "You're whacked," I just continued walking, because all was as it should be (or just *was*). But then I heard Ed Milligan say, "You know, these people have *feelings*." I stumbled a bit, raced out to the makeup trailer, indulged myself in the very teenage activity of feeling up Bellamy.

At some point in the afternoon I ventured back to the set, where I spied Milligan and Jimmy Yu sitting in a corner, talking quietly, their foreheads almost touching. I grabbed some food from the crafts table and wandered close enough to overhear Milligan say, "Vanity of vanities, Jimbo. All is vanity."

"Van-nitty," repeated Yu, as though he was willing to add this new word to his vocabulary.

"Yeah, yeah, because, check this out, what profit hath a man of all his labour under the sun? Because, like, one generation passeth away, and another generation cometh. Get it? This is all so, so . . . *ephemeral.*"

Jimmy Yu nodded and attempted to repeat the word "ephemeral," although I am unable to transcribe this utterance.

Well, it could be that after all these pages (there's at least a couple hundred scattered about my gloomy basement bachelor) I've finally learned something about novel-writing, because I am not going to follow this particular narrative thread to its end just yet. (At any rate, I have wobbling plates to attend to.) For now I will only tell you that Milligan continued to read the Bible. He became a born-again Christian. He appeared on Rainie van der Glick's radio show and proclaimed himself so, which caused the ratings of *Padre* to plummet. My, my, people are strange. Mind you, he continued to ingest huge quantities of drugs, which, in combination with his own self-hatred and twisted emotional palette, led him to a very strange place.

And he gleefully took me along.

I'm going to spin another plate here, with your kind indulgence, a plate off toward stage left, and tell you that earlier this evening I entered Birds of a Feather and sat down at a little table near the back. Amy presented herself quite a while thereafter, having left me to stew in my own juices (an apt metaphor) for fifteen or twenty minutes. She pointed a finger, as though trying to place me. "The regular?"

"No, uh, half the regular. Just the beer portion, please. Amy."

"Your bro' isn't here tonight, you know."

"Oh, yeah, I know. He has plans and preparations to make. We're going on a road trip."

"Huh." She didn't ask where we were going; in fact, she enunciated that single syllable with such manifest lack of interest that I inferred I was never to bring up the subject of my trip, or travel in general, again. So it was quickly on to Plan B. "So . . . I read *Barchester Towers*."

"Really."

"Really." Not really. I'd read maybe two hundred pages and scanned the Coles Notes.

"I'll get your beer." And then Amy was gone.

This wasn't going well; indeed, the whole notion was misbegotten, and I'm sure many of you find it off-putting. There's no getting around the fact that I was a few years older than her—more than a few—hey, let's face it, I was an old goat, a bleating ungulate. But, um, maybe we as a society should be a little less sanctimonious as regards the workings of the human heart, and those who are condemnatory should book tickets for the *Jerry Springer Show*, where anyone can hurl stones at the slack-jawed sinners.

Okay, all right, perhaps a little too sensitive there.

Amy returned with my beer. "So . . . ?"

"So?"

"So, what did you think of *Barchester Towers*?"

"Well, um . . . the names were weird."

"Eh?"

"Mr. Quiverful. Omicron Pie. These are like teevee names."

Amy placed her salver on the tabletop, slipped into the seat across from me. "Teevee names? What's that all about?"

"Oh, well, in these litigious times, you can't use real, *realistic* names on television. I couldn't call someone, I don't know, Jack Winston, because Clearances would come back and say that there's a guy in Akron, Ohio, named Jack Winston, and he's in the same business or whatever, and he could enjoin production of the show, so you have to change the name. You have to come up with a name that nobody has. Omicron Pie is good."

"Huh. Interesting."

Really? Was it? Or was Amy just being polite, in which case, why? Maybe I hadn't lost too much ground that evening with Rainie.

"Yeah, I remember you saying you worked in television. *Padre*, right? With the star that—"

"That's the one."

"So . . . what's your favourite teevee show?"

"My—? Oh, gosh. Don't you have to—?" I gestured at the bar's patrons; they didn't seem to total more than about seven people.

"No, I'm good for a few minutes."

"Well, then, I'll answer unequivocally. *The Twilight Zone*."

"Yeah! Great show. I'll tell you what my favourite episode is, 'A World of His Own.'"

"You're not old enough to have a favourite *Twilight Zone* episode."

"I'm probably not as young as you think I am. And anyway, you can rent all the seasons, you know, at the video store. I like old things. Old movies, old television shows, old novels."

"So 'A World of His Own.'"

"About the writer who talks into the tape recorder, right, the Dictaphone, and everything he describes becomes real. And then to destroy whatever it is, he just has to throw the tape into the fire."

"It's a good one, all right. His wife catches him with some blonde, and he tells her about the magic Dictaphone. She doesn't believe him, so he throws the tape about the blonde into the fire and she disappears."

"Then he takes out this tape that describes his wife, and it ends up in the fire—"

"Uh-huh, but remorse gets the better of him, so he gets on the

Dictaphone and starts describing his wife, and then he has second thoughts—"

"And starts describing the blonde again. I like little twists like that."

"I should point out, though, that the teleplay was by Richard Matheson. It's not a Rod Serling script."

"Uh-huh. And that's important?"

"Well, kind of. I don't know. What's your doctoral thesis about?"

"I'm calling it *The Power and the Glory; Heterodoxy in the Novels of Anthony Trollope*. It's about the conflict between spiritualism and social status in the clergy."

"Oh, yeah. That's what *Padre* was about, too. Except *Padre* was a pile of shit."

"That guy was cute, though."

"Yeah, he was cute."

"So, Phil, I should get back to work. It was nice talking to you."

"Yeah. Listen, I'm going away for a few days, but maybe when I get back, if you have a night off, we could have dinner or something."

Amy wrote down her number on a napkin, shoved it across the table. "Sounds good. What's the matter?"

"Huh?"

"You look funny."

"Well, I'm . . . I'm just a little bit flabbergasted here."

"Oh. Good. I'm all for flabbergastation."

———

"And I've made quite a few dinners, and frozen them, and they're all labelled, you know, chicken cacciatore or veal scaloppini or whatever."

"I see. So the children only eat foreign food?"

"Why are you being so snarky?"

"Snarky? *Moi?*"

"*Toi.*"

"Well, it's just that, you know, I feel this whole situation is bad enough without you treating me as though I were totally incompetent."

"For one thing, I am only trying to be helpful. For another, you brought this situation upon yourself."

"I brought upon myself the situation of you larking off to Mexico with your young lover?"

"Yes, you did. And lastly, do you realize that's probably the only time you ever actually told me what was bothering you?"

"It's the first time you've ever gone on a romantic holiday with your young lover. And do you realize that we never went on a romantic holiday?"

"Whose fault is that?"

"You're saying it's my fault?"

"You were always working."

"I was always working because we always needed money."

"And you resent me for that."

"I resent your resentment about the fact that I was always working, yeah."

"You know what? Maybe we should go talk to a   ellor."

"What was that?"

"We could try to work ou   f these issues."

"Something funny's going on with my phone."

"Even if we rema   arated."

"There are strange little blasts of silence."

"Oh. M   ou have another call."

"Really? What do I do?"

"Put me on hold and answ   one."

"I don't know how."

"Hit the talk button again."

"Okay. Hello? Who is this?"

"It's still me, doofus supremo. Hit the *talk* button."

"Hello?"

"Okay. I got a car."

"Jay?"

"She's a real beauty. A 1970 Dodge Super Bee. Three-eighty-three magnum, a 727 transmission . . ."

"What does all that mean?"

"Fucked if I know."

"Hold on, hold on. Don't go away. Hello?"

"Yeah, I know. Whoever it is is more important than me. Who is it, anyway? Your girlfriend Rainie?"

"No, um . . . listen, did you say *even if we remain separated?*"

"Uh . . . I may have."

"But that would imply our separation is not a done deal."

"I only meant that seeing a counsellor could only be helpful, even in separation. I certainly didn't imply there was any chance of reconciliation."

"Yes, you did, Ronnie."

"That may have been what you *inferred*."

"You're seeking refuge in syntax. That's a good sign."

"Phil . . . I'm in love with Kerwin."

"Is that so?"

"Okay, okay, okay, maybe I'm not in love with Kerwin, but that doesn't mean that you and I have any sort of a future, except as co-parents."

"Right."

"It doesn't."

"Okay, babe, I've got my little brother on the other line. Or on the same line, whatever, I didn't even know my phone could do this. I'll talk to you soon. Bye-bye."

"Bye."

"Hello?"

"The big thing is this. At some point during the journey—I'm thinking on the return, near Sudbury—the odometer's going to click over. Nothing but zeroes. Flat line. A brand new beginning."

"It's got a hundred thousand miles on it?"

"Almost *three* hundred thou. She's a trooper."

"Where did you get this thing?"

"Bought it from a musician friend of mine."

"How much?"

"Two hundred bucks. A steal."

"We're doomed."

"Hey, don't sweat it."

"I'm just worried about, you know, I think this may be a *crime.*"

"Trying to reclaim the spiritual integrity of your existence is all of a sudden a crime?"

"I'm afraid it might technically be kidnapping. I mean, I am the girls' father, but if their mother hasn't given her explicit approval, especially now that we're separated—"

"If you want to bail out, bail. You don't need a reason. Especially not a stupid one."

"I'm just saying, maybe it's not a good idea."

"Oh, it's a good idea, Phil. It's *necessary*. All of these things—these things that happened to you, these memories—you've just been throwing them into a big pit. Covering them over with dirt. That's how you been dealing with this shit. But the thing is, it's all been toxic waste, man. You've destroyed the table water."

"Huh?"

"You know what I mean."

"The water table?"

"Right. So all the land is now, you know, poison. No healthy crops can grow."

"Uh-huh. I think you might want to turn that metaphor loose now, Jay."

"If nothing else, you should want to actually get a couple of details right for your goddam book. I mean, it's an autobiographical novel, you'd think you'd want to get some authentic memories into it."

"I've got plenty of authentic memories in there."

"You thought their names were Tom and Tony."

"That's what you said they were!"

"Ted and Terry."

"I guess it doesn't matter what their names were."

"Yeah, it does. It matters. Because, Phil, this thing has fucked us up."

"I wouldn't say that."

"Yeah, I know you wouldn't say that. Because you're an emotional imbecile, that's why you wouldn't say that. But you have fucked up."

"Look, I may have made a few poor life decisions . . ."

"Shut up, Phil. I'm not trying to be hard on you. I fucked up every bit as badly. I'm a two-bit fern-bar pianist who can't play a major seventh without weeping like an infant. Let's face it, Phil, we both have a warped world view, and what warped it was two greaseballs named Tom and Tony."

"All right."

"All right."

"But I still think their names were Ted and Terry."

"I'll see you Monday morning."

18 | THE WINDOW

IN THE ARGOT OF FILMMAKING, THE LAST SHOT TAKEN EACH DAY IS called "the window." Like much else in that curious world, the reason behind this is unclear. I myself endorse the theory (not that I don't think it's fanciful) that the term stems from the fact that at the end of many old romantic movies, when the couple kiss to seal their happy fate, the camera coyly moves away and ends up looking through a window.

Industry grinds on non-stop for several months in the television series business, so the daily window doesn't generate much excitement. But when the schedule reaches the end, and freedom looms, the crew do get quite excited about the window, the shot that will send them off to various locations around the world where they can drink heavily. So the crew began to get jazzed and giddy when they were handed the script that was numbered "626," representing the last of the hours, the twenty-sixth of the sixth season, that were owed to the network. It was a six-day shoot, as opposed to a seven, because overages (mostly caused by Jimmy Yu) had forced us to cut corners. Moreover, it was a bottle show, a drama contained within the flimsy walls of our standing sets, largely within the small ersatz church. I wrote this one myself, and I was not challenged by the limitations,

I was rather liberated by them. I had a feeling that I could write a little contained drama that would seem not unlike Playhouse 90 or any
of those live television shows written by guys like Paddy Chayefsky
and Gore Vidal. Or even by my hero, the great Rod Serling.
Typically, I recycled material. So, as in *The Hawaiian*, I introduced
into a quiet setting (the little church, in this case, as opposed to the
hopeless barroom) a deranged lunatic who had just killed people.

I borrowed more than that. The lunatic's name is Oscar, as it was
in *The Hawaiian*, and the people he's killed are likewise his own parents. I even cast the original actor's son to play this newer version.
The first Oscar, Michael Poole, had gone on to no great distinction
(other than the fact he kept working, which is something) but his son,
Nicholas, was emerging as one of the country's great talents. He'd
already been in two features. For the most part he disdained television
work, but it was a pretty juicy role, his character being in virtually
every shot, so young Nick signed on. The script was talky, as opposed
to action-packed, and although this was not Jimmy Yu's specialty,
something sparked in him and he was brilliant. Yu moved the camera
with sinister grace, pushing in on young Nicky's face relentlessly,
refusing to back away from the soul-tarring anguish. Watching the
dailies, everyone got very excited; we would view all of the takes from
every scene, eager to peel back layers and discover nuances.

And so the sixth day, the day of the window, found us filled with
good spirits, and as there was no longer any writing to be done, and
very few production wrinkles to be ironed out (in television land
there are always some), most of the production staff crowded onto
the set. Dirk Mayhew was there, and I know you don't remember
who he is, but he's the Production Manager who had, for the past six
years, done little other than complain bitterly about Jimmy Yu's
penchants and proclivities. On this day he was serene. "I have to
admit," Dirk marvelled as he watched Jimmy work, "the man is a

genius." The Supervising Producer, Stevie Medjuck, was likewise overbrimming with compliments. "That kid is just wonderful," he said, nodding toward Nicky Poole. "And Milligan is doing the best work of his life."

He was?

I hadn't really noticed Milligan, or remarked upon his behaviour, which should have been a huge heads-up right there. Why wasn't he industriously trying to steal young Poole's thunder? Milligan was not a generous actor, by any stretch of the imagination. For example, he didn't hang around to feed lines on the turnarounds. I'll explain: let's suppose that the scene being filmed involves Milligan and another actor, say, Paula Beecher, who was in my play *Low Man* and for that reason represented a bleached bone, albeit a smallish one, on my marriage's cairn. First there would be what is called a master. The camera would be placed at a distance sufficient to film both Milligan and Paula as they had their exchange. Then there would be coverage. The camera would be moved closer so that the frame held Milligan's face, the exchange repeated. Then they would turn the camera around and film Paula. Unless this shot was composed so that some portion of Milligan was evident, perhaps the crescent of his glorious profile, Milligan would hurry off to his trailer. Paula Beecher would be fed lines by the script supervisor, and she would have to react to, usually, a clenched fist held aloft by a crew member, representing where Milligan and his haunting eyes should have been.

But on this day, the day of the window, Milligan never left the set. He stayed for all the turnarounds; moreover, he delivered his off-screen lines with emotion, encouraging the actor being filmed to dig around inside and come up with a little extra heat. Milligan even stayed on-set after blocking. (Jimmy Yu would choreograph the actors' movements during rehearsal; then the first team would be released and stand-ins brought in for the purposes of lighting and the practice of camera moves.) During these intervals, which could be longish (lighting seems to proceed at a glacial pace), Milligan would drift around, nodding, smiling at people, sharing jokes with the gaffers—in short, all manner of little human stuff. But he was also radiating a kind of childish excitement, pent-up and powerful. When there was any sort of a noise, his head would snap around—as though he were waiting for something, as though he knew that at some point that day a parade was due, and he was ever on the alert for the clowns and baton twirlers.

This all struck me as a little odd. Then again, it was nothing that couldn't be explained by a little miscalculation on the pharmaceutical front, even by too much coffee. (Indeed, the coroner's list of drugs ingested was long and comprehensive. It included exotic fare like *árbol de los brujos*, but what really fucked Milligan up, I believe, was some twisted manifestation of the Holy Spirit.) I'll admit that I wasn't as focused on Milligan as it might seem, because it was impossible to keep one's eyes off Nicky Poole. There are an awful lot of good actors, it seems to me, but only a handful of great ones. Marlon Brando, Sean Penn, Mickey Rooney . . . yes, I'm serious about the Mick. For one thing, think of the range. He can play young kids, he can play old, fat men. All right, that's a joke, but you should endeavour to watch Rod Serling's *The Comedian*, which was a Playhouse 90 starring Rooney as a comic who makes the lives of the people around him a living hell.

Well, I've progressed this far in my novel-writing, I no longer care or am apologetic when I make these tangential leaps. After all, life is like that, isn't it, tangential. Often things connect, but not at first. So I will tell you that Bellamy stood off to one side, as though at attention, a clear plastic makeup bag nestled in her hands. She stood there awaiting the call "Final touches!" at which point she would dart onto the set, digging into the bag and producing brushes and powder puffs. She would minister to the talent, dulling the sheen of their beautiful faces, until ushered off the set by the first AD. In watching her do this, I was reminded of the one time I had slept over at her house— reminded of it without remembering the circumstances; how did it happen that no one at my home missed me for an entire night?— when, in the morning, Bellamy applied her own makeup. In her tiny one-bedroom, the bathroom contained only the toilet and shower; the sink, surmounted by an improbably massive medicine cabinet, stood outside that door. Bellamy, having showered, emerged radiantly naked, and began to do her face. I was surprised, frankly, at the labour involved. She always seemed so natural, but now I saw that this effect was the result of many pains taken. She powdered and rouged (I'm at sea here with the technicalities) and I lay in her minuscule bed and stared at her bottom and marvelled at the way her breasts bobbed in accordance with her arm actions. And I guess it occurred to me that the whole affair had been undertaken to afford me this, whatever it was, perhaps a moment of luscious tranquility, perhaps a memory that might spark a toothless smile as I lay upon my deathbed. I'm not sure. I'm certain that the affair was not undertaken to accomplish the scuppering of my marriage, because even in that moment Bellamy's beauty was not as profound to me as my wife's, not as perfect or affecting.

There on the set, though, Bellamy returned from her work and took up her post outside of camera range. She caught my eyes, winked and smiled. Something inside me went clammy with realization, the wink indicating that we shared something deep, the smile hinting at real affection, maybe even what would pass for love in the mind of a twenty-eight-year-old woman.

"Hiya."

I turned and saw my wife.

Ronnie's hair was still wet, meaning she'd been to the gym, and on her face there was a broad smile, and something inside me went clammier still.

We'd done something that morning we hadn't done in what seemed like years, that is, made love. Sometime pre-dawn, we'd both been startled into half-consciousness by a sound from the outdoors, a raccoon shoving the lid off a trash can or some such thing. I was possessed of what so often eluded me in more alert states, an erection, which pressed against my wife's thigh, and she took hold of it and we were both muzzy enough not to overthink the situation and before long we were going at each other with enthusiasm. That is enough said about the physicalities. I will provide a little more detail about the workings of my heart, although you know by now that I have no real insight. Those feelings and thoughts that should have crystallized (I love my wife, I am not going to leave her for Bellamy, I should tell Bellamy this before she is too invested emotionally, etc.) remained vague and inchoate. But they existed, I swear to you they did.

All of that is a bit moot, because Ed Milligan came walking over with a strange look in his eyes as Ronnie and I were in the midst of the following exchange.

> McQUIGGE
> Hi. What are you doing here?

> VERONICA
> I came for the window.

> McQUIGGE
> Really?

> VERONICA
> Sure. Isn't that the tradition?
> Everyone, all the front office

staff and all the spouses,
everybody gathers together for
the window?

> McQUIGGE
> Uh, yeah. You've just never
> done it before.

I think I'll continue in this format, because it affords distance . . .

> MILLIGAN
> Hey there, hi there, ho there!

> VERONICA
> Hi, Ed. How are you?

> MILLIGAN
> I'm wonderful, Veronica. I'm in
> a state of flux. Veronica, I'm
> learning a lot about mercy and
> grace. I'm learning a lot about
> forgiveness.

> VERONICA
> Uh-huh?

> McQUIGGE
> Shouldn't you be running lines
> or something?

MILLIGAN ignores McQUIGGE. He turns VERONICA by the
shoulder, gently, directs her attention toward
BELLAMY.

                    MILLIGAN
        You see that woman over there?

                    VERONICA
        The cute young girl?

                    MILLIGAN
        Yes, exactly, the cute young
        girl.

                    VERONICA
        What about her?

                    MILLIGAN
        Phil's having an affair with
        her. So you have a wonderful
        opportunity to forgive him!

                    FIRST AD
          Okay, everybody! It's the
        window!

    And a huge huzzah went up from the assembled.
    Milligan smiled, kept his hand on Veronica's shoulder, placed
his other on mine. "Everything's going to be all right," he
repeated.

All right, here's scene 72A from the double-white version of episode 626.

```
INT. CHURCH—CONTINUOUS

OSCAR grabs GABE, places the gun to his head, spins
him around so that they face the congregation.

                    OSCAR
        I don't want to kill him, but I
        will!

                    GABE
        I don't think you will, son.

                    OSCAR
        I will if I have to.

                    GABE
        No, you won't. Because you
        don't have that much hatred in
        your heart. There's a little
        bit of love in there, I've seen
        it, I saw the way you looked at
        Juanita there . . .
```

Well, it hardly matters at this point what crap I scripted for Milligan to say, because he never said any of it. What he did say was "Hey, Phil? You know what would be better? If I did like in that movie!"

Okay, here's some of the stuff that came up at the coroner's inquest. First of all, why was the gun loaded, even if with blanks? Well, the way I wrote the scene, the Padre's speech is so persuasive that Oscar ultimately turns the gun against himself. (Anything is possible in teevee land.) Padre wrestles the gun away, but not before it discharges, because your typical Padre fan enjoys loud noises every now and again. Anyway, given the time constraints, Yu was attempting to shoot the whole scene as a oner—a continuous unbroken shot—instead of cutting and then loading the gun with blanks and then picking that up in coverage. This was stupid, reckless and irresponsible, and is the main reason I've been drummed out of the business. The fact that I didn't know about it (it wasn't discussed at any of the production meetings, Yu came up with the notion the morning of day six) was no excuse, because I should have. (The eleventh commandment: thou shalt pay fucking attention.) Next, Willy Props had to take the stand, and explain to the assembled what, exactly, "blanks" are. Willy told us how paper wadding is used to seal the gunpowder into the shell and that this wadding is propelled out of the barrel with considerable force. When asked if Mr. Milligan would have been aware of this, Willy shrugged and muttered, "I guess he forgot," because, of course, Milligan was an expert in small arms. Then a procession of medical doctors explained how, when the wadding impacted against his temple, Milligan's skull was shattered and a tiny piece of bone got driven into his brain. He lay in a coma for twenty-seven hours, until it was concluded there was no sign of brain activity, and then life-support was withdrawn.

Much of the inquiry was given over to ascertaining Milligan's mental state when the "accident" happened. It came out that his mind had been imperfectly wired throughout his life. We were all astounded to hear of his extended stays in facilities, the first at the age of fourteen. We were further astounded to hear of suicide attempts, earnest ones. Milligan seemed to us to be consumed by self-love, but that was mere flummery.

I spent a total of three and a half hours on the stand. I talked endlessly about the intricacies of television production, I detailed my history with Edward Milligan. I managed to not mention *The Bullet and the Cross*. I did not tell the coroner's inquest how, one moonless night, I'd screened the film for Edward Milligan. I thought he'd slept through the last half. Apparently I was mistaken.

Milligan, that day, took his position behind the flimsy pulpit. Nicky Poole wrapped one arm around Ed's chest and pressed the end of the revolver's barrel against his temple.

Veronica did not speak or move away. My wife was rigid with fury; I knew there would be moments, perhaps even minutes, before she summoned the wherewithal to act. I wasn't sure what she would do. What she did do, many hours later, was calmly ask me to gather up my stuff—all of my *goddam shit*, as she put it—and move out of the house. This was hours later, as I say, because in the interim there were countless policemen and detectives to talk to, telephone calls to be made, statements to be issued to the press.

"Hey, Phil? You know what would be better? If I did like in that movie!" Edward Milligan looked at me with unbounded delight. Then he reached up and squeezed Nicky Poole's finger, pulling the trigger, and thus shambling off in search of the Pearly Gates.

PART FOUR

THE SEARCH FOR
NORMAN KITCHEN

"HELLO?"

"Veronica?"

"No. Of course it's not Veronica. Does it sound like Veronica, dickhead?"

"This is John Hooper."

"I know who it is. Why do you think I called you *dickhead?*"

"Is this Phil?"

"Yes, it's Phil. Who else would it be? You called my house, after all."

"But you don't live there any more."

"Well . . . point, Hooper. So, what, you're used to calling here, are you, and when the phone is answered, you're used to it being Veronica?"

"She left a message to call her back."

"Did she now?"

"Is she there?"

"She is here, more or less. But I don't think she can talk to you. She's rushing around, cramming things into a little carry-on bag. Let me describe the scene. Ronnie is roaming about the house with relentless energy. The airport limo waits, the driver napping in the front seat. Kerwin, Ronnie's young boyfriend, a doctoral candidate in the exciting, challenging field of philosophy, is standing in the foyer, trying to avoid eye contact with me, although I don't allow that, I don't put up with that, I ask him silly questions, inconsequential questions—have you ever been to Mexico before, who is the current Mexican president, how much did those shoes cost?—and I pin him to the wall with my eyeballs and watch him squirm. I should be getting back to that, I don't really have time to shoot the breeze with you, Hooper."

"Fine. Just tell Ronnie, you know, thanks!"

"All right, we can shoot the breeze a little. What do you mean, *thanks?*"

"Well, she left a message congratulating me."

"Why?"

"Oh, you know. The Giller."

"She congratulated you on your Giller nomination?"

"I . . . I won, Phil."

"You won the Giller Prize?"

"Yes."

"For fiction?"

"That's what they give it for."

"Oh."

"I was as surprised as anybody."

"Gee, that's swell, Hooper."

"Umm . . . thanks."

"No, listen. Listen, John. That's . . . that's wonderful. Really."

"I was very pleased. How's your novel coming along?"

"You don't have to pretend to care."

"I do care. I liked what I read of it. All except for the television stuff. But I'm sure you've moved away from that. Written about other things."

"That I have, that I have. I have written about, oh, the incident, and the rankers, and I even managed to work in my admiration for Mickey Rooney. I've laid all the pipe, as we say in the television business. Now it's time to go, go, go. I'm in the present tense, baby. I'm writing this on my little laptop. I'm in an old dilapidated car that's headed up Highway 400. My brother's driving and the girls are bickering in the back seat."

"I don't get you, Phil."

"No, you wouldn't. So . . . the goddam Giller fucking Prize, huh? Maybe I should read your book."

"You haven't read it?"

"No, no, no. Veronica—who, incidentally, finally seems ready to vacate the premises—told me that there was a character based on me, a character with some silly name, Paul or something."

"Uh-huh. I did base him on you."

"Well, there you go. I could hardly read the book, otherwise I would be forced to sue your ass."

"Sue me?"

"It's the old 'you can't use people as fodder for your fiction' chestnut."

"I really don't see how you could sue me, Phil. Paul is the most sympathetic character in the novel."

"I don't need your . . . he is?"

"Yeah. I mean, he has issues and everything . . ."

"Did he fuck up his life?"

"Mmm, yeah, sure."

"Good."

"Good?"

"Verisimilitude and all that."

"Right."

"But I should let you know, John—and this might affect your next book—there is a reclamation project in the works."

—

After I hang up on Hooper, I join my wife and her young boyfriend in the foyer. She is going through the pre-vacation litany, some of which is murmured gently, some of which is directed at Kerwin, who supplies the obligatory responses. "Yes, Veronica," he says. "We have the tickets, Veronica." I know that he means this usage of "Veronica" to impress upon me an urbane intimacy, but upon my ears it falls as clunkily as "Mrs. McQuigge." Another doomed relationship.

"All right," Veronica says, turning to me. "I guess that's it."

"Have a great time!"

"Yeah." Ronnie nods, bites her bottom lip. "So you'll pick up the kids after school?"

"Ronnie, I've done this before. I've executed my parental duties quite successfully for years. Just because you're out of the country doesn't mean I'm all of a sudden going to become irresponsible and ignore our daughters' well-being."

Ronnie nods, unconvinced, as well she might be, because the kids are in the back seat right now. Currer is fast asleep, the side of her head pressed against the window. Her sleep seems profound. I am reminded of this little factoid, that after police arrest a suspect, they throw him into a little room and watch what he does through a one-way mirror. Innocent people pace nervously; guilty people fall asleep. I'm not saying Currer has a guilty conscience, I'm saying there seems to be a sense of relief, of release. Ellis, on the other hand, is wide awake, caught up in the spirit of adventure. It was hard to spring Ellis out of the Big House. At Currer's middle school, they handed her over without a fight. They didn't even mind the vagueness of my plans, my lame explanation as to why she wouldn't be attending for the rest of the week. "Family business," was all I said, which, for all they knew, could mean that I intended to lock Currer up in a sweatshop and force her to operate some potentially lethal steam-driven punch for seventeen hours a day. The women (there were three, but they seemed to function as a single entity) shrugged, flipped on the intercom and commanded Currer McQuigge to report to the office. At Ellis's school, on the other hand, I encountered the fearsome Miss Ogilvy, whose hackles bolted upright at the irregularity of it all.

"She'll be gone for the whole week?" Miss Ogilvy demanded, as though a week were some unit of geographical time that was but barely comprehensible to the human brain.

"Yes. But she'll be back next Monday."

"*Next* Monday?"

"Er . . . yes."

"Do you have a note from her mother?"

"Her mother is not *here*. Her mother is in *Mexico*." I freighted that word mightily, managing to suggest the sordid libidinous behaviour that I was certain was ongoing, or would be as soon as the plane landed. I barely managed to suppress the phrase "with her young lover," which would have been too slimy even for me.

Miss Ogilvy shook her head. "I'm not sure about all this."

"But but . . . it's by way of being an emergency."

"Hmm. What sort of emergency?"

Ah, good question. The word "spiritual" sprang to mind, but it wouldn't signify to Miss Ogilvy. "Medical" wouldn't really work either—I knew that the battleship had already spotted Jay parked out front of the school in the 1970 Dodge Super Bee. The automobile was nothing but ancient brown metal and pimpled chrome. Jay sat in the driver's seat, drumming his fingers with the suppressed anxiety of a wheelman at a bank job. "We have to go visit a sick relative in Thunder Bay," I said tentatively.

"How sick?"

"Very sick."

"Is this," asked Miss Ogilvy, "a matter of life and death?"

"Yes! Yes, it goddam *is*."

"I know you can handle things," Ronnie says, "but it's a mother's job to worry about her children."

(I want to finish writing about what happened this morning, this scene with Ronnie and her lover Kerwin, the priapic student of philosophy. Then we'll be caught up with the present, and there's nothing but kilometres of empty highway ahead.)

I turn toward Kerwin. "So . . . which province of Mexico are you going to be in?"

"Oh, ah, say, I'm not sure."

He's got a slight accent, one I can't place—at least, I couldn't finger the country of origin on a map. Whichever country it is, Kerwin and his people come from the poncey upper crust.

"Wait a sec." I snap my pudgy fingers. "Mexico doesn't have provinces. It has states."

"Right, right."

"How many states does it have, again?"

"Um, ah, say, I'm not certain."

"Phil . . ." This from Veronica.

"Thirty-one," say I.

"Ah!"

"Thirty-one states and one federal district, let's not forget that!"

"Philip, we are leaving now." My wife flings her carry-on bag over her shoulder, picks up a valise, nods to Kerwin that he should deal with the big suitcase. It's a huge thing. I think that when Ronnie packs for a week-long vacation, she thinks along these lines: *What if, while I'm away, there is a world war and near-total global annihilation, and I am forced to live out the rest of my life in some strange, desolate land?* That is why she has packed her entire wardrobe and most of the kitchen appliances. Kerwin bends down to get the suitcase, but I beat him to it. I suppose my limbic brain is in action here; I lift the thing and start for the door, but what I really want to do is hoist it over my head and let out a few good monkey-hoots. Besides, I really don't think he could manage it. Kerwin only weighs about eighty-three pounds.

Out the front door, down the steps—my shoulder is aching within seconds, and left to my own devices I would take a little rest, just a short twenty-minute one—and out onto the sidewalk. The limo driver wakes up with a start, pops the trunk, and between the four of us we get the luggage stowed away. Now it's time for good-byes, and I'm not at all sure how these are going to play out.

Kerwin offers his hand. He is a handsome enough lad, if that's what you're wondering, although the word "wan" springs to mind. "Wan" and "fey." There is a Keatsian quality to him; he is pinch-chested and his skin is virtually transparent. Kerwin is in his late twenties but seems to have overstayed his life expectancy already—all right, I may be overstating the case, but I'm sensitive to such things. Veronica seems to be announcing to the world, "See? I really don't like burly guys at all." At any rate, I accept the proffered hand and squeeze with an ounce or two of unnecessary force, just enough to elicit the smallest, most fleeting of grimaces. I am very pleased.

I turn toward my estranged wife. Before I can say anything—not that I have anything to say—she kisses me on the lips. "When I get back," she says, "we'll talk."

As soon as the airport limo takes the corner, the Dodge Super Bee's engine howls and it crawls up the street to collect me.

"Van der . . . Glick?"

"Now this is very interesting, friends, here on the line is none other than Philip McQuigge."

"But I was going to say, you don't have to—"

"The creator and producer of *Padre*."

"—say who I am or what I do or anything."

"I was expecting Phil to call me at some point, but I assumed that it would be a more *private* call, but no, he decided to call while I was on the air, so let's ride this donkey, see where we end up. What's the deal, Phil?"

"Well, I'm on my cellphone, I'm sitting in a car with my brother, Jay, and my two lovely daughters, and we're going on a road trip!"

"Uh-huh. And are you fleeing from *me*, Phil?"

"No, no, not at all."

"Because I'm a big girl. I don't do the heartbreak thing. I don't lose sleep, I don't skip a beat. I have a couple of extra drinks, move the file to trash and hit delete."

"Yeah, well . . . I didn't think we would discuss, you know, *that*."

"That?"

"Our, um, relationship."

"Oh, was that a *relationship*? It went by too fast for me to tell."

"Van der Glick, I don't know what it was. And whatever it was, I never said it was over."

"Which gets us back to this point, I was expecting a phone call."

"Uh-huh."

"And another thing. It's not an especially optimistic sign that you call me *van der Glick*."

"All right. Rainie. I'm calling you now, Rainie."

"While I'm on air."

"Right."

"Okay, so look, the producer is hollering in my ear right now, apparently this conversation is about as interesting as listening to farts dissipate. So. You're on a road trip, huh? Where are you off to?"

"We're going to Thunder Bay, Ontario."

"And what's in Thunder Bay?"

"Not what. Who. Norman Kitchen."

"The kid with the nice hair?"

"Do you remember him?"

"No, I read about him in your book that night you and me and Jay were out on the town. So . . . you guys are going to try to find out what happened."

"Yeah. Find out what happened to Norman Kitchen."

"And in doing so, you might find peace. And then maybe your emotional self, your *spirit*, would not be bitter and twisted. You might be capable of true friendship, affection, even love. You might be able to connect to another human being in some manner more profound and fundamental than a mere bumping of uglies. Is that the idea?"

"Er . . . something like that."

"Well, tell you what, Phil. You let me know how that works out for you."

We stop for coffee and cold drinks in Pointe au Baril. The town sits on the edge of Georgian Bay and services the needs of those with cottages on the sun-spackled islands, which is to say, the hopelessly rich. I am not all that surprised to see William Beckett in the service centre/local store. I am surprised to see him burdened down with the trappings of domesticity, a two-four of disposable diapers and count-less bags of homogenized milk. "McQuigge!" he shouts happily. "A fortuitous encounter."

"Hello, William."

"McQuigge, as delighted as I am to see you, and eager to engage in chummy colloquy, I must, unfortunately, evoke the dread spectre of commerce and ask once again—"

"Willy?" A woman emerges from the aisles, a spectacular woman who would seem to have been created by a think tank made up exclusively of fourteen-year-old boys. "Do you want to rent a movie?" She has a baby tucked under her arm, red-faced and squalling.

"Yes!" says William Beckett enthusiastically. "We must have a movie! Perhaps a farce or historical melodrama. Or a Japanese psycho-sexual thriller, subtitled of course, I'll have nothing to do with dubbing."

"Okay, what they have here is *Pretty Woman*."

"Ah. An excellent diversion."

"Hi, I'm Peg." She proffers her free, left hand. I introduce myself and my family. My children coo over the baby; Jay is agape and trembling before this woman, Peg.

"At any rate, McQuigge. *Mr. Eldritch* is scant days away from production, and I have yet to amass a satisfactory writing team. The Room seems empty, Philip, without your presence."

The Room: more television argot. It doesn't refer to an actual room, although the Room usually takes place in a room. The Room is what happens when the writing team gets together to bandy about story ideas. It's a bit like when kids get together to discuss, for example, how badly Superman would kick Batman's ass, except that it pays thousands of dollars per day.

"As I told you before, this is an anthology series, not unlike your beloved *Twilight Zone*. Do you know how hard it was to get an anthology series on the air, Philip? Does that mean nothing to you?"

"And you said before that you'd make me a co-producer?"

"Did I?"

"You did."

"Well, I . . . I suppose that could be worked out."

"Well, as it happens, William, in a few days, I think I'll be . . . I'm hoping, *praying* that I'll be . . . at liberty."

"Daddy?"

"Yes?"

"Do you love Mommy?"

"Well, sure I love Mommy."

A few kilometres pass under the tires.

"Daddy?"

"Yes?"

"Does she love you?"

"Well, that gets a little more complicated. You see, um, situations arise . . . events transpire . . ."

"Tell 'em, Phil."

"Keep out of this, Jay."

"Tell 'em, Philly Four-Eyes."

"Daddy?"

"Yes?"

"Why did Uncle Jay call you Philly Four-Eyes?"

"Well, I think he's trying to make a point."

"What kind of a point?"

"Sorry, Currer, you can't say anything. I don't think this technique works when there are four people speaking."

"What are you talking about? Why aren't I allowed to say anything?"

"Daddy?"

"Yes?"

"What was the point that Uncle Jay was trying to make?"

"Oh, well, by calling me Philly Four-Eyes he was alluding—"

"What's alluding?"

"He was referring to something else, he was reminding me of something. Uncle Jay was trying to say that when I was a kid something happened and that maybe other stuff that has happened happened because that happened."

"So, like, I'm supposed to not say anything all the way to Thunder Bay?"

"No, no. Sure you can say things, Currer. But I'm trying to get this down on paper, at least, into the little pooter here . . ."

"Daddy's acting weird."

"Daddy's acting weird."

"Daddy's acting weird."

"Come on, Jay. This was your idea."

"You're acting weird because you never just speak, the kids ask you questions and you sound like you're answering them, but nothing of emotional substance ever comes out of your mouth."

"Oh, for god's sake . . ."

"He's right, Daddy. I know I'm not supposed to say anything, but when Uncle Jay said that, I said, *That's right*. He's right."

"Didn't I just say that I loved Mommy? Er, um, Veronica?"

"You said, 'Sure, I love Mommy.' Like you might say, 'Sure, I love peanut butter sammitches.'"

"Daddy?"

"Yes?"

"Why does it get more complicated?"

"Hmmm?"

"If Mommy loves you it gets more complicated."

"No, the notion of her loving me is a complicated one . . ."

"Jesus, Philly Four-Eyes. *Notion?* The notion of love?"

"Can't you just concentrate on driving?"

"But it seems like such a weak, wishy-washy word to use in conjunction with love. Especially with you being a writer and all."

"Is that a dig?"

"Probably. Everything I say is a little dig. I'm trying to get some profound responses out of you."

"Why are you trying to do that, Uncle Jay?"

"Because Philly Four-Eyes is *fucked*."

"Hahahaha!!"

"Jay. Watch your language."

"Philly Four-Eyes is fucked!!"

"See now, I have no idea which one of you said that."

Night falls; we keep driving, through Espanola, Webbwood (population six hundred, but one of those six hundred was Canada's first woman mayor), through Ironwood. It is nearly ten o'clock when we pull into the parking lot of the Shady Rest Motel. Jay turns off the ignition, leans his huge forehead against the steering wheel and seems about to fall asleep right then and there. The children are in advanced stages of catatonia. I look about. I suspect the motel is employing the word "shady" in its colloquial rather than literal sense, because there are no trees to be seen. Indeed, the terrain looks about as hospitable as the moon. I call out, "We're here!" with stagy enthusiasm. The four of us tumble out of the car.

The man behind the check-in counter gives the impression that he has just axe-murdered the motel's owner (and family, and family pet) and is going through these procedures of hostelry so as not to arouse suspicion. He knows where nothing is. In searching for the information cards, for example, he pulls open and then slams shut every drawer he can lay his hands on, then does a second round of searches, before coming up with them. We want two rooms and request a fold-out cot in one. The axe murderer doesn't process this information, as far as we can tell, but concentrates on chewing his gum. Jay fills out one card, I do the other. (I can see out of the corner of my eye that Jay is giving his name as "Claude Balls," a joke from our childhood. Mr. Balls is the putative author of a book entitled *The Tiger's Revenge*.) "Uh," says the axe murderer, "do you have a car?" Well, you know, of course we have a car, but the four of us are too stunned by the question to offer up an immediate response.

The axe murderer grows annoyed. "*Do you?*"

"Daddy," says Ellis, "I want to go to bed."

He sat in the middle of the room. There was no one else in the little motel tavern, which, by the way, was called the Luau Lounge. I didn't know that until Jay and I were steps away from the front door (which still had its summertime screen, dead mosquitoes coating the surface). Then I saw the twisted neon tube suspended there in obscurity, the noble gas all dead or depleted. "The Luau Lounge," it seemed to read, which was unlikely, given the latitude and the bleakness of the landscape, but stepping into the bar proper, I saw decorative leis and ukuleles hanging on the walls. There was a rather crudely painted mural depicting a grass-skirted girl, her breasts covered coyly by coconut shells. This, of course, is getting mighty close to the *Twilight Zone*—some of you may recall the eponymous barroom from my play *The Hawaiian*. But before I could react (bailing seemed an apt response, hurrying back to the room that contained my two slumbering daughters), the stranger yelled, "Hey there, hi there, ho there!"

He sat, as I've said, in the middle of the room, even though no other table was claimed. This choice seemed prompted by consideration of sightlines, of conspicuousness, of access to both the centre and the reaches; he was obviously not willing to entertain thoughts of people coming into the Luau Lounge without dealing with him. Even though there was something languid in his pose, he fair bristled with energy and expectation. He wanted interaction.

Todd (I will name him now, even though proper introductions weren't made for maybe twenty minutes) was a large, doughy man. He seemed preternaturally pale, but that could have had something to do with the lighting. The effect may have been exacerbated by his hair, which was bone white. It was bone white, but Todd had plenty of it, and he attended to it with some care. The sides were swept back, while the hair on top was pushed forward and then rolled into a huge pompadour. This hairstyle, the mere existence of it, made Todd at least sixty years of age, but his face was unlined, his cheeks gleamed like a cherub's. He looked for all the world like a six-year-old, despite dark bags underneath his light and damp blue eyes.

"Hey there, hi there, ho there!" he hailed us again. Jay virtually bounded over to his table and sat down. I took my time. I felt vaguely ill, so for a moment I imagined, forced myself to imagine, my wife and young Kerwin in Mexico, which made my nausea seem more accountable.

"Know where that's from?" Todd demanded as we took our seats.

"Know where what's from?"

"That, um, 'hey there, hi there, ho there.' Hey! Answer like in *Jeopardy*. Know what I mean? Answer in the form of a question. Sometimes," Todd said, growing serious, "they don't answer in the form of a question and Alex Trebek doesn't say anything. Sometimes he does, sometimes he won't give them the points, but sometimes he doesn't say anything and I'm like, 'Hey! That wasn't in the form of a question!' Okay? But it's like anything else, you know, if he likes you, you're golden. Or if you're a *chiquita*, because I've heard that Alex Trebek is Mr. Studly Jackhammer. Lay the pud, baby. Lay the pud. So?"

"So?"

"Yeah, so, where's it from?"

"Oh, it's from . . ."

"Answer in the form of question! Because I'm not Alex Trebek and I don't like you and I don't want to lay the pud to you. Go."

"What is The Mickey Mouse Club?"

"Correct-a-mundo. Now, the bartender, whose name is Les, he has diarrhea. If you ate at this place, you'd have diarrhea too. Lucky for you the cook has gone home. But so has Les. But I can get you drinks, because they trust me. What'll it be?"

We both ordered a beer, and I was very tempted to ask for a double shot of single malt with a cube of ice, but then I was overcome by a vast sense of futility. Only then did I silently broach to myself the subject of my drinking too much. I understand that you have had to weather many binges and hangovers, and I am assuming a patience that you may well not possess. But as I watched Todd lurch toward the bar, it did occur to me that I drank too much, and that to forgo the single malt might well do me a world of good.

"Know why they trust me?" Todd was standing behind the bar now, trying to work out the mysteries of beer fridges.

"Why's that?" asked Jay.

"Because I've been here for seven weeks. In room number twelve. That's the world's record. There was one guy who stayed here for like five weeks, he was a truck driver and something fucked up in his truck and they had to ship him a new part and he had to wait for five weeks. I don't know what kind of truck part it could have been, a dilithium crystal or something." Todd managed to grab three frosty bottles that he trapped with both arms, pinning them to his chest. He headed back toward our table. "But me, I've been here for seven weeks. Over two months. And fucking counting, baby." Todd pushed a chair aside with his hips, bent over and dropped the bottles. "Brewskis, fellas. Let's get pissed."

"Why have you been here so long?" asked Jay.

"That would be because, um, mind your own fucking business."

"Sure, okay." Jay twisted the cap off his beer, raised it to his lips.

"Know what a cunt is?" demanded Todd.

Jay raised an eyebrow. "Want to field that one, Phil?"

"Um . . .," I began.

"Let's not," said Todd emphatically, "talk about cunts."

"Okay, fine, good," I agreed.

"Let's talk some more about television."

"Were we talking about television?"

"Hey. I'm going to ask you guys some questions, and you have to answer in the form of a question—so I mean, I'll be giving you some *answers,* right, just like Alex Pretty-Boy Trebek—and you give the answer and it will be fun and have nothing to do with cunts. Okay. Who wants to go first?"

"Jay."

"Phil."

"Toss-up! Gloria Winters."

I waited for Jay to answer (in the form of a question) but it dawned on me that Jay wouldn't know, Jay would have no fucking idea. He only watched television for two minutes, which was how long it took Mickey Mantle to strike out at bat. So I sighed and muttered, "Who played Sky King's niece, Penny?"

"Penny," agreed Todd, nodding wistfully. "She had great tits, didn't she?"

I shrugged. "I was just a kid."

"So what?"

I suppose I meant that I never noticed Ms. Winters's breasts, but that's not entirely accurate, because when she appeared in a white shirt with the top two buttons insouciantly unfastened, I noticed a quickening within and a tingling sensation along the length, what length there was, of my little dickie. Penny was blonde and wide-eyed with a sort of perpetually goosed wonder, and Sky King had to rescue her from some life-threatening predicament practically every week.

"Okay, so here goes," said Todd. "This was Peter Graves's—of *Mission: Imposseebla* fame—anyhoo, this was his first television series. Enhh! Guy with the glasses?"

"What was *Fury*?"

"Bingo, goodonya."

During this session, beer was consumed, not in any great quantity. Even Todd, although drunk and intent on oblivion, did not drink all that much. Mind you, I guess the story on Todd was that his blood was already forty-proof and just required periodic topping up.

After maybe an hour and a half, Jay and I toddled off to our rooms. I was tired, and a little muzzy, and when I stepped inside the motel room I was startled by popping sounds and distant-seeming scratches. I realized that my daughters were snoring, and I was rendered, um, heartbroken. I drew in a breath and began to sing, as quietly as I could . . .

> *Little Miss Muffet sat on a tuffet,*
> *Eating her curds and whey . . .*
> *Along came a spider and sat down beside her . . .*
> *He threw her out the window.*
> *The window, the window, he threw her out the window . . .*

All right, time for bed. Why this little Todd episode at all, you wonder? Surely not to drive home the fact that I have in my time watched way too much television? It's true that Todd never stumped me, although once I purposefully misanswered a question because I felt I was embarrassing him. Jay sat silently through the entire proceeding. At least, he was for the most part silent, although over the course of the hour and half he and Todd had the following conversation, which I shall accordion and abbreviate so you get the gist:

JAY

This is bullshit.

TODD

What is?

JAY

When are you going to tell us
about your broken heart?

TODD

Fuck you.

JAY

Sorry, man. I saw it. You let
your guard down, and I saw it.

TODD

You don't know what the fuck
you're talking about.

JAY

Sure I do.

TODD

Are you some kind of a faggot?

JAY

You should just tell us about
it. Maybe we can help.

```
            TODD
It's time for another Jeopardy-
style answer and question.
Philly Four-Eyes?


            PHIL
Shoot.


            TODD
Who starred in the classic
Twilight Zone episode "Time
Enough at Last"?
```

And it occurs to me the next morning, as the Dodge Super Bee continues along the Trans-Canada Highway, that I may be obeying my mother's command, issued after watching that first *Twilight Zone* all those years ago. You may not recall—it was many pages back, although I will confess that my book has not achieved the heft I had envisioned. When I first thought to write an account of my life, I imagined a book of weight, a volume of sheer volume, something that would make even Hooper gulp with envy and awe. Anyway, you may not recall this, but my mother was dissatisfied with the ending of "Time Enough at Last," even though it is one of Rod Serling's most splendid plot twists. But not everyone likes plot twists, you know, some people think many writers (including God, the Great Author Above) are too clever for their own good. So my mother rankled at the ending—when Henry Bemis had ordered and arranged the books on the library steps, but then his glasses got pitched off and smashed. She had many ideas on how to fix things—Bemis might be able to grind his own corrective lenses—but her soundest piece of advice was the one I am trying to act upon now: check all the dead bodies for appropriate spectacles.

I believe I'll share this nugget of sagacity with my offspring.

"What the hell is *that* supposed to mean?"

"Currer, watch your language."

"Watch *my* language? Daddy, the bathroom in the motel last night had the f-word written all over it."

"Hey, come to think of it, mine did, too."

"Yeah, Daddy, the bathroom walls said, *fuck, fuck, fuck, fuck* . . ."

"I saw, Ellis."

"So what the hell is it supposed to mean?"

"Well, you see, the way the story ended, the way Mr. Serling wrote it, it was about the death of hope. But you should never let hope die."

"Did you let hope die, Daddy?"

"Well . . ."

"Answer the question, Daddy."

"I'm thinking about it, Jay."

"I'll answer the question for Daddy. *Yes.*"

"There may have been some situations where I have seen the futility of—"

"Did you ever notice, Phil, that the more personal, the more *intimate* a conversation becomes, the way you talk gets poncier and poncier?"

"Um . . . I *had* noticed, actually."

"Why did Daddy let hope die?"

"Well . . . do you guys know who Albert Einstein is?"

"Yes!"

"Yes!"

"Who is he, then?"

"Okay, remind us of who he is."

"Well, he was a scientist. He was the man who figured out that $e = mc^2$, and while no one knows exactly what that means, it explains everything. Anyway, Albert Einstein said that the most important question anyone can ask themselves is, is the universe a friendly or an unfriendly place? Take it, Phil. And don't answer in the form of a question."

"I've never really thought about it."

"Yeah, you know, the thing is, you shouldn't have to think about it."

"I think it's friendly."

"Why do you think that, Currer?"

"I don't know. You said I shouldn't have to think about it, Uncle Jay."

"Okay, fair enough."

"I think the universe is friendly, and I know why."

"You go, Ellis-girl."

"Because it likes me."

"Good answer."

"Daddy?"

"I think, um . . . Hey, it's almost two-thirty. Who's hungry?"

"Me!"

"Me!"

I say that a lot, "Who's hungry?" One reason is that I usually am, another perhaps is that the endless kilometres of the Trans-Canada allow too much time and space for thought. I am not entirely comfortable with the notions that come to me, unbidden, even hostile, wearing great big berky boots and eager to kick out the jambs. Jay often falls silent for long stretches of time. The Dodge Super Bee has an eight-track tape player and Jay has managed to acquire—I can't imagine how, other than by an odyssey through lawn sales that should have lasted years—cartridges containing the music of the French masters he so adores. Satie, Fauré and Ravel fill the cab, inducing an atmosphere of meditation and melancholy. The girls have long since stopped demanding that popular music be found on the radio. They have found whatever charms they can in the *Trois Gymnopedies*, the austere *Requiem*, the *Pavane for a Dead Princess*. Mind you, this has its downside, in that they are both often lulled into deep torpor. Ellis, it seems, is especially susceptible. She is small enough that she can stretch out along the big bench back seat, provided of course that Currer scootches to the side and presses her own face against the cool window. This Currer is willing to do maybe seventy per cent of the time.

She has done it at the time of which I write. It is nearing five o'clock, which, given the time of year and our longitude, means that the sun has begun a rapid descent. A plummet, really, as though the sun had been standing by a conveyor belt for eight hours performing some mindless task, and now that it was quitting time only wanted to go somewhere and have a few drinks. It sat on the horizon briefly and bubbled with an orange fury. Jay and I both lowered our visors, but we couldn't block it out. Signs had informed me that a service centre was coming up—thirty-seven, twenty-three, a mere five klicks away!—so I decided we needed a pit stop. That would use up five or ten minutes, during which the sun could complete this ridiculously beautiful thing it was doing. And at any rate, I had to piss rather badly. Mind you, I often, even usually, have to piss, the price I pay for caffeine addiction. So I said, "Who's hungry?"

Jay said, "We just ate four hours ago."

"I'm not following."

"I'm not hungry," he said, simplifying for my benefit.

"Neither am I," said Currer, "and anyways, Ellis is asleep."

"Wake her up."

"Phil, we're going to be in T'Bay in like three hours."

"Well, I can't wait three hours. I have bodily functions to attend to."

"Maybe if you didn't drink so much coffee . . ."

"I don't drink as much coffee as you!"

"Yeah, but you don't have my metabolism. Just because we're brothers doesn't mean we're the same or even similar."

"This is kind of a theme or motif you've developed for this trip."

"I'm just saying. We're not the same. Our histories are different. Our perspectives couldn't be further apart."

"Fine. I don't know why you think I think—"

"Excuse me, Phil. Point of clarification. I *don't* think you think."

"Curry, wake up Ellis."

"Daddy, she's really flaked out here."

"Just wake her up."

"Ellis? Ellis. Ellis!!"

The service centre arrived before the waking up could be done, so I said, "Well, fine, okay, don't wake her up. Jay's gonna stay in the car, anyway."

"I wouldn't mind grabbing a pop or something."

"Yeah, and I need to go to the bathroom too, Daddy."

"Okay, just pull the car over beside the pumps there where we can keep an eye on her."

This was done and we dispersed. Currer and I headed around the side of the gas station and found two doors brandishing cryptograms, two genderless stick figures. After some study, one was determined to be wearing some sort of traditional Slavic skirt, so Currer went through that door and I pushed through the other.

"Oh, geez, sorry!"

I'd opened it enough to see two pale thighs, blue jeans crumpled around work-boots.

"Hey, no, bro', that's okay!" He'd managed to call out before the pneumatic device allowed the door to close completely. I burped out a startled "Huh?"

"It's a double-header, bro'. If you just wanna take a leak, come on in."

"No, that's fine, I can wait."

"Come on, what's the big deal? You're not a faggot or anything, are ya?"

"Oh, no. No, that's not the issue here."

"The *issue*. That's a good fucking laugh. Come on, funny boy, get on in here. It's okay with me, we're both guys."

"Well . . ."

"No fucking biggie."

It's true, the architects—if indeed architects are responsible for service centres in Northern Ontario—had designed the washroom so that it contained both a toilet proper and a urinal, as though they anticipated that at some point two gentlemen would share the facilities. I guess. At any rate, I pushed through into the gloom.

"Ignore the fragrance. I've kind of been on a toot."

"Uh-huh?"

"Such is fucking life."

"Uh-huh."

"She gives me nothing but grief about it. Did you see her out there?"

I took up the position in front of the urinal, pulled down my zipper, extracted the little fellow. "Who?"

"Selma."

"No."

"She is fucking pissed off. Says she's gonna leave me. *How's that,*

Selma? That's what I say. *How are you gonna do that? I have the keys to the fucking pickup.* What's the matter?"

"Hmm?"

"You're not whizzing. What's the matter?"

"Oh, I . . . I've been sitting down for a long time, that's all."

"Right."

"Mm-hmm."

"That makes no fucking sense at all."

He was, I'd guess, in his late twenties, although I had not studied the man with any thoroughness, certainly not with the thoroughness with which he was studying me.

"Are you sure you didn't see her out there?"

"Selma?"

"Yeah. Blonde. Good-looking girl. Nice set of jugs."

"I can't say I noticed."

"Well, you would have noticed. Niagara Falls."

"Excuse me?"

"Try thinking about Niagara Falls. Or firehoses, shit like that."

"It's coming."

"Sorry about the fragrance. I haven't been eating anything, so I don't know what this shit is. Sure smells, though."

I tried thinking about Niagara Falls, but being me, I hadn't really stored many images in the memory banks that dealt with vast walls of cascading water. I remembered a heart-shaped hot tub, and I remembered cavorting in it when Veronica and I were naked young people, but that didn't help my situation.

"We're having a big fucking fight."

"You and, um, Selma?"

"You got that right, Sonny Jim. Still a no-go, huh?"

"What are you fighting about?"

"You know, it comes down to this: I am a man and she is a woman.

That's what it comes down to. Our natures are just not the same. Are you with me?"

"Sure, I mean, I see your point."

"There you go!"

"Yeah. Finally."

"Is that it? Just a little dribble?"

"Daddy!"

There was a pounding on the door and Currer hollered, "Daddy! Somebody stole Ellis!!"

The somebody, as it turned out, was Selma.

It was Jonathon who pieced this together. Jonathon had reacted every bit as urgently as I had when we heard Currer's alarm, leaping up from the toilet, drawing up his blue jeans all in the same motion. I burst through the door only a nanosecond or so before he did. I stumbled toward where the Super Bee had last been seen and stared at the empty square of tarmac. "The car," I moaned. "Where's the car?"

"I bet," announced Jonathon, "that Selma took it."

I looked at him. He was tall, maybe six-three or so, and slender to the point of emaciation. He had about him an air of wildness. His hair was wild, certainly, but much of the wildness was to be found in his eyes. They were surmounted by shaggy eyebrows and underscored by purple pouches. Within these brackets were pink orbs, pinpricked by black dots.

"Why would she take the car?"

"I told you, man, I told you, we were having a big fight."

"Phil, who is this guy?"

"This guy is, this guy is . . ." I didn't really know, nor give a fuck. I was trying to figure out what to do, and not really having much in the way of success.

"My name is Jonathon," the guy responded. "I'm sorry Selma took your car."

"She took," I said, "my child."

"Oh." Jonathon swallowed, producing a loud *gulp,* just like in the cartoons. "That's a drag."

I spun around on Jay. "Why the hell didn't you take the keys out of the ignition?"

"Haven't you noticed? I *can't* take the keys out of the ignition. It's like they're rusted in there or something."

Currer suggested, with a level-headedness that kind of surprised me, "We should call the police."

"That's a good idea," I said, drawing my cellphone out of my pocket.

"Hold on, man." Jonathon laid his hand over mine. It was an oddly gentle measure. "Please don't call the cops. The thing of it is, we're kind of on the run."

"*What?*"

"We like ran away. The thing of it is, her parents don't like me, so we had to run away. If you call the cops . . ."

"Listen, none of that is my fucking problem. My fucking problem is that my daughter, my child, is in that car, and your girl-friend—"

"I can help. I can find Selma. I know exactly how her mind works."

"I thought you said you and she were completely different. Remember?"

Jonathon took a deep breath. "Look. Let's get in my truck, we'll go after them. We'll find them. Trust me."

So there you have it. *Trust me.*

I guess it comes down to this: I don't trust people. I may have once upon a time. At least, I suspect I trusted my mother, and continued to do so until she died (unreasonably early in life, fifty-three years of age). But since the incident, the encounter with twisted teenaged fuckwhips, I haven't trusted a soul. Same deal with Jay, I guess. He was unable to trust any of his wives. He'd marry them, then accuse them of infidelity on the actual honeymoon. And so we ascended from the ravine, our fates sealed, our souls fated. Having discovered that human beings were bad, I decided to be worse, so that we all might look better by comparison. Having failed to do the right thing—having done the wrong thing—doing the wrong thing was staying the course. The tendency could thereby be seen as somehow congenital, not a moral failure.

But these things were mere symptoms, red spots that distracted attention from the more profound contagion. Which is to say, I didn't trust people, and accordingly made no real connections. I chose a career that allowed me to control people, to put words in their mouths, to script their actions, so that there could be no nasty surprises. Now I was being asked to trust a young man who'd been on a bit of a toot. Judging from the stench in the service centre washroom, he'd been digging up graves and devouring corpses. Or I could (as Currer kept urging me, at increasingly louder volumes) call the cops. But (aside from the fact that I didn't trust cops either) I decided I had a small chance to teach my older daughter something, some small thing, and she might go on to have a better life than I. So I looked at Jonathon and demanded, "Where is your truck?"

In a matter of minutes we were on the highway again. Jonathon's pickup had a spacious cab; still, Currer and Jay were squished in behind the two big captain's chairs. Jonathon drove with care and concentration, working the big gear lever, squinting to see into the new night. "How much gas did you have?" he asked.

"Hmm?"

"In your car. How much gas?"

"Jay?"

"What?"

"How much gas did we have?"

"Little more than half a tank."

"Okay. So she'll stop for gas when it's at a quarter. She's funny that way."

"Why is she running away?" demanded Jay. "Do you beat her?"

Jonathon tried to find Jay in the rear-view. He did, and the two men locked eyes. "Naw, I don't beat her. She just is like that. She just takes off when the going gets hairy."

Jay made one of those huffy sounds, indicating he wasn't buying any of it.

Currer was crying in the back seat. Trying not to, but crying just the same.

"Everything will be all right," I said. "This girl, this Selma, she needed a car. For whatever reason. And she didn't see Ellis sleeping in the back seat, I guess. As soon as Ellis wakes up, Selma will see what went wrong and then she'll . . . I don't know what she'll do."

"Well, she won't do anything whack," said Jonathon defensively. "She's a good person."

"So you two eloped?"

"Huh?"

"You eloped. You ran off. Her parents don't like you."

"It's a fucking rock-and-roll song," said Jay.

"Hey. Your brother is getting on my tits."

"All we did was pull into a service centre. Two men, two little girls. There were leaks to be taken. That falls soundly into the category of minding our own fucking business. This is shit we didn't ask for, and it's shit we sure don't need."

"Well, you know, shit happens."

"Ah. A philosopher."

"Jay, just leave it."

"Yeah, right. Just go along with it. Just, you know, fucking go along with it."

"What is *that* all about?"

"Hey, Philly Four-Eyes. Figure it fucking out."

I don't have to figure it out, of course. I know, although he's referring to a memory from the sludgy muck that covers the bottom of my soul, so I can't really get hold of it. It slips through my fingers and leaves behind only stain and stench. But, hey, I'm a novelist now, and as I near the end of these pages I realize that I've learned a thing or two. Dramatization, imaginative reconstruction, literary licence, stinking lies, call it what you will, it's what we writers are meant to do. So here goes . . .

Ted and Terry were doing whatever they did to Norman Kitchen. (What did they do to Norman?) I was blinded, because Terry had flicked the spectacles away from my face for no good reason. He wasn't trying to limit my utility as a police witness or anything. That would have been halfway intelligent, and Terry wasn't. (Maybe Ted was, I don't know; at some point in my life it will stop being important.) Terry flicked my glasses off as a kind of invidious grace note, a small evil embellishment. I was as blind and hopeless as poor Henry Bemis, the meek bibliophile. So I was doing what I could with my other senses, and by that I mean that I was trying not to hear what I was hearing. One of the things that pounded on my ears was the sound of Jay's grunting as he tried, in vain, to pull the ropes away from his skinny wrists. And that's when I said—in a stage whisper that Ted and Terry could surely hear, but were too occupied to care about—"Just go along with it, Jay. Just go along with it!"

—

"Hey!"

"What?"

"That was the Super Bee!"

"What was the Super Bee?"

"What just went by on the other side of the highway!"

"Are you sure?"

"Yes. Because I have been *watching*. Unlike you, totally zoned out. Not to mention the fact that you wouldn't recognize the Super Bee if it ran you over. You can recognize a Volkswagen Beetle, that's as far as your automotive knowledge goes."

"You know, for brothers you guys bicker a lot."

"Jonathon, your job is driving."

"And *turning around!* I told you, they're heading south."

Jonathon processed and nodded. "Makes sense. The kid must have woken up and now Selma's trying to find you guys—"

The highway was divided by a swale, a shallow ditch covered by patches of grey snow and even greyer grass. It was mid-November, and those of us from Southern Ontario felt that winter was yet to come. So where did that old snow come from? Was it possible that it lasted all the year round? That certainly made me feel sad and desolate, but I had only a moment to feel so, because Jonathon cranked the wheel sharply to the left and the pickup pounced into the swale.

It became mired immediately.

"What," said Jay, with ponderous gravity, "the fuck?"

"Don't sweat it," said Jonathon, pulling at the gear lever and pressing down the accelerator. There was a high-pitched wail, and muck rained everywhere.

"Oh-oh." A heartbreakingly meek sound from Currer.

"You idiot!" said Jay.

"Look, man," said Jonathon, with as much patience as he could muster, "if I had of waited for the next exit to turn around we would be on this highway for hours. This is north of Superior, baby. This is the moon!"

"So you decided to go off-road. Idiot."

"You're not being helpful."

"Helpful? How the fuck can I be helpful?"

"Ever hear of *pushing?*"

Jay and I stumbled out into the quagmire. So did Currer, although I told her to get back into the pickup. But she insisted that she wanted to help, and I'd learned not to press issues once she started insisting. Currer's got a stubborn streak, something she inherited from her mother. Jonathon rolled down the window so that he could holler instructions, even though the concept was rather easy to grasp. "Put your shoulders into it," he called, "and push!"

My brother and I placed our shoulders against the tailgate. A high-pitched whining sound came as the tires spun uselessly. There was a freshet of muck in the night. "Harder!" demanded Jonathon, but it was impossible to get purchase; our feet kept sliding backwards. "We need," said Jay, "blocks of wood, or rocks or something."

We went off through the darkness in various directions and reconvened a couple of minutes later. Currer had a handful of stones and a twig, which made me want to weep. I had two good-sized rocks. Jay had a boulder tucked under each arm, reminding me that dung beetles can haul twenty times their own weight in shit. He threw these boulders down by our feet. They sank into the muck and then we stood atop them, reapplying our shoulders to the pickup. "Give 'er!" shouted Jonathon, and the truck started to scream as the tires turned, and there was briefly a downpour of mud, and then the pickup popped out onto the highway. A transport had to veer sharply around it. The driver sounded his horn, and the countryside rang with annoyance. My brother and I were face down in the quagmire, having fallen with resounding splats when the pickup truck instantaneously relocated itself. "All right," Jonathon called, "let's get going!"

"Look," said Currer, pointing to the northbound lanes. Headlights were approaching. The Dodge Super Bee pulled over onto the soft shoulder and rolled to a sedate stop. A young woman stepped out, dirty blonde hair, blue jeans, an old blue pea jacket. She had her hands rammed into the pockets and shivered pretty much uncontrollably. "Sorry about the fuck-up," she said quietly. Ellis came around to join her.

Despite the bitter night, Ellis was sucking calmly on a Popsicle. "Told you," she said to me. "Told you the universe was a friendly place."

Well, maybe she didn't say that, exactly, but that was the lesson she was trying to teach me. You may well be asking yourself now, was that the lesson I learned?

I will try to hurry now to the end of these pages . . .

We rented rooms at the Prince Albert, a stately old hulking hotel that sat right on the shore of Lake Superior. Through our window, illuminated by the moon and made hazy by a fall snow squall, we could see the Sleeping Giant, the long, low island that the natives had decided looked like someone lying on his back, hands folded neatly across his chest.

While I stared at the Sleeping Giant, my kids watched television and bounced from one bed to the other. In the room next door, I could hear my brother's muffled murmur. He was making phone calls, he was conducting his investigation, locating coordinates. In the morning, after breakfast in the restaurant downstairs, we climbed into the Dodge Super Bee and headed for the outskirts of town. Mind you, Thunder Bay has a lot of outskirts. It's actually two cities melded together, so in a sense it has twice as many outskirts as other places. It's understandable that we got lost, and being as our municipal map had done double duty that morning as a placemat (the landmarks were huge and cartoonish, all but the dozen or so most important thoroughfares done away with), it was almost noon before we arrived at our destination, which was a United church. Jay made inquiries at the office and then ushered us through a back door and into a small graveyard.

It was a small cemetery, crowded although not crammed. Most of the local population is of Finnish descent, followed in numbers by the dour Scottish Presbyterians—the muted Anglicanism of the Canadian United Church is not a going concern in here. The stones in the graveyard were mostly old, green with tiny but tenacious lichen.

Jay had told me none of what he'd found out, saying that I needed more surprises in my life. So I stared at the orderly cenotaphs and asked, "Is he dead?"

Before Jay could answer, a man rose from behind one of the stone markers. There was first a blinding glint of light as the sun bounced off his bald head—it took a moment or two for my eyes to clear. By then he was standing up, wiping dirt from his hands onto a brown gardener's apron. He noticed us, looked first at my brother, then at me.

"Jay? Phil?"

Jay spoke first. "Hi, Norman."

Yes, gone were the golden tresses. All that remained was a band of curly white hair that embraced both of his ears. Otherwise Norman Kitchen seemed unchanged. His eyes were still half-hidden behind dark folds of skin, his lips were still pale and puckered. Oddly, his body had not run to fat. As a boy Norman had been quite plump, but as a man he was lean, even a bit muscular. And he was tall, too, well over six feet.

He lifted his heavy eyelids, nodded in our direction. "And these are . . . ?"

"Oh," I answered, "these are my daughters. Currer and Ellis."

"Did you just bury a dead guy?"

"No, no. I was just looking after the site. The man resting here has no family, except his wife, and she's very ill. So." Norman looked at us all, for a long moment, obviously trying to decide what to do. He arrived at a decision. "Let's eat!"

Norman's wife—Norman's wife!!—was a lovely woman named Elspeth. Elspeth had the kind of lean, hardened body that I associate with long-distance running, although it was easy enough to surmise whence she derived her exercise. There were no fewer than five Kitchen offspring, and although three were out of the house (two sons at the local high school, the eldest daughter at university in the Maritimes), the two who had come home from school for lunch were more than workout enough. The girl, Catherine, was eleven, and she kept her mother hopping by having a life so complicated that it made my mind whirl. Over lunch, much had to be organized: her participation in a soccer match, her costuming for the school Christmas pageant, her attendance at a party honouring the tenth birthday of one of her friends.

As for the youngest, a boy, Elspeth said, "Hamish, stop that." A lot. And Hamish never did stop that, whatever it was.

He was nine years old, and I don't think it's any exaggeration to say that he was devil spawn. Well, maybe a bit of an exaggeration. But honestly, you have never seen the like. It's not that he was hyperkinetic, he wasn't—there was even a deceptive languor to Hamish.

There was this deep smouldering energy source, which reminded me of the fierce heat that lies at the heart of compost. The kind of thing he was constantly being told to stop doing was, say, picking up a spoon and banging it against the side of a cup, banging it with a relentless stateliness, as though he were counting cadence for a funeral march. "Stop that, Hamish." Another example: by doing something with his tongue and inner cheek, Hamish could produce a high-pitched, bubbly little whistle. It sounded like a miniature teakettle boiling. Or, more to the point, it sounded like a young greaser squeezing the life out of that thing many years ago, the small monster that was neither tadpole nor frog.

The most interesting thing about Hamish, to me, was that he looked exactly as his father had at nine. He had the nose that angled out like a snowman's carrot, he had the mouth that pursed as though some unseen being were trying to force-feed him manure. And yes, he had the hair, the bangs, curls and locks. Hamish had made some concessions to his times—he already wore an earring, for example, and there were tints of odd colours in his hair—but that didn't prevent him looking (as his daddy had) like Little Lord Ponce. So I'm writing this as kind of an argument for nature, because I suppose what my brother, Norman and I are about to discuss involves the nature/nurture argument.

What we are about to discuss is the nature of evil.

We left the manse (my daughters were enthralled with Catherine and under constant attack from Hamish, so I knew they would be occupied for at least an hour) and wandered into the church proper. We sat in the rearmost pew. A shaft of light drove through a stained-glass window, but missed us by a few feet.

"What did those boys do to you?" Jay asks.

"Oh. Yes. Those boys."

"So you know what we're talking about?"

"Of course I do."

"Phil didn't remember squat about it until he was in his twenties."

"That's interesting."

"Not really. Phil squelches and squashes."

"I beg your pardon?"

"That's how he deals with emotional shit. Sits his big fat ass down on it, that's the last daylight that particular feeling is ever going to see."

"Father Norman, I keep sensing this *anger* coming from my brother."

"Is that so?" snaps Jay angrily. "Well then, you better get to squelching and squashing."

"What happened to make you remember it in your twenties, Phil?"

"Jay reminded me."

"Point of clarification. I made a reference to the event, which is something I had been doing on a regular basis for many, many years. In this particular case, Phil was drunk and momentarily let down his defences. By the way, we're both alcoholics."

"I see."

"But I have to admit," continues Jay, "even I can't remember *exactly* what happened. I mean, we worked out mostly what happened, together we can sort of piece it together. We tried to escape, they chased us, they tied us to trees. Oh, and by the way, thanks a mill, Phil."

"What are you talking about?" I ask.

"What knot did you use on Norman? An Irish Sheepshank. What knot did you use on me?"

I ignore my brother. "Norman——?"

"What knot did you use on *me?*"

"Norman, what did they do to you?"

"Oh, it doesn't matter."

"It doesn't? Why the fuck not? Sorry, Father Kitchen."

"It's all right, Jay. You may speak however you wish to speak. The walls of the church are not going to come tumbling down. And guys, it's not *Father* Kitchen. You could call me *Reverend* Kitchen if you really felt like it, but you can always just call me *Norm* like you used to."

"But . . ."

"Yes?"

"We never called you *Norm*, Norman."

"Oh. I seem to recall you calling me *Norm*."

"Norman. Please. What did they do to you?"

"They didn't do anything to me, Phil."

"What?"

"They didn't do anything to *me*. Whatever they did, they did to a ten-year-old boy. That boy is gone forever."

"Well, how did *that* happen?"

"Excuse me, Jay?"

"That's quite the stunt. Because Phil and I, man, we're the same kids that ran screaming out of that ravine."

"Surely not. You're quite an accomplished musician, Phil is a well-known writer. By the way, I enjoyed *Padre* quite a bit. It reminded me of a movie I saw at the Galaxy Odeon one time, *The Cross and the Bullet.*"

"It was *The Bullet and the Cross.* Anyway, Reverend Norm, we're not really successful. I mean, Jay plays in a little fern bar called Birds of a Feather. He *lives* there, for chrissake, and he's kind of afraid to go outside."

"And Phil isn't a writer."

"I am so a writer."

"Phil, you're not a writer like you wanted to be a writer when you were a kid. You don't write novels. You write shit for teevee, simplistic shit that really should be shot in black and white, that's how hackneyed it is. Christ, you stole your biggest idea from a movie we saw at the Galaxy Odeon!"

"I'm aware that I fall short of whatever mark you've set for me, Jay. I'm aware that I have fucked up. I'm a shit and a moral wash-up. I get it. But what I don't get is why you keep throwing it in my face. Why do you want me to live in a constant state of guilt?"

"Umm . . . it's not so much that I want you to, I guess. You *do* live in a constant state of guilt. And I suppose that sometimes I take advantage of that fact. But, another point of clarification, it's not really *guilt*, it's more like free-floating self-hatred. It's, um, general auto-damnation."

"Where does this shit come from?"

"It comes from the *ravine*. It only goes to prove the point, what happened down in the ravine has fucked us over profoundly. Look at Norman! He's a goddam priest!"

"I'm a minister, Jay."

"The point is, we weren't really looking for you, all those years ago, to become a man of the cloth. Then the thing happened."

"The incident."

"Phil likes to call it *the incident*. He likes to give things names. So, *the incident* happened, and now little Norman Kitchen is a minister. Coincidence? I think not."

"No. You're right, Jay. It's not a coincidence."

"What did they do to you, Norman?"

"Phil, you *know* what they did to me."

"Okay. Okay, I guess maybe there was part of me that was

hoping, you know, that maybe they just, I don't know, had done something less severe."

"It was very severe."

"You know, Reverend Norm, right now you seem a little pissed off. For a reverend," Jay says.

"Hmm. You're right. I'm sorry. Anger is an incredibly destructive force. And when I came out of that ravine, I was a very angry boy. Weren't you?"

"I don't think we came out angry. Do you, Phil?"

"No. We weren't angry, exactly, we were . . ."

"Afraid."

"I was going to say *confused*."

"I was afraid," said Jay. "Still am. Afraid of everything. Boys. Men. Women. So I came up with these lame solutions. I stayed inside a lot. Played the piano all the time. If I ever stumbled into a relationship, I made sure I scuppered it long before it could bite my ass."

"I was confused. I liked people, and then all of a sudden people were these evil creatures, so how could I like them any more?"

Norman says, "I feel so sorry for those boys."

"*What?*"

"What sort of desperation, what sort of pain and *hopelessness*, would drive them to do what they did?"

"Reverend Norm, surely as a minister you endorse the notion of evil," I say.

"Evil is a choice."

"Not always. Some people just pop out that way. Rabid and red-eyed."

"I disagree. Because if you're right, what would be the point of my vocation? I would have no influence. In your universe, the deck is stacked."

"Hmm."

"Reverend Norm. You came out of the ravine angry. And . . . ?"

"And I started making everyone's life hell. My mother's life, especially. Other people's lives, too, whoever I came into contact with. I was confused. I acted out quite a bit. I shoplifted. I started— this is hard to explain . . ."

"Go on, we're listening."

"I started breaking into people's houses."

"No!"

"Little Norman Kitchen?"

"I wouldn't steal things," he hastens to add. "At least, I wouldn't steal anything big, anything that might be noticed. I might take a family photograph, or a souvenir from some vacation. I wasn't there to rob anybody, I was there to, I don't know, see what it felt like to live in a normal home. I'd make a sandwich, sometimes. Turn on the television, watch for a few moments. I'd always leave the television turned on. Anyway, I got caught doing that and I was sent to reform school."

"Norman Kitchen got sent to reform school?"

"Yes. When I was fourteen. And, of course, there were many boys there like the boys in the ravine. So I thought, you know, that's it. Game over. But then I thought, no. I'm not getting tied up to any more trees."

"Guys. They *made* me tie you up."

"Philip, I've forgiven you for that."

"I haven't forgiven him for that."

"Do you think I've forgiven myself?"

"There was a gymnasium at the reform school . . ."

"Seriously," I say, "do you think there has been one night, a single night, in my entire lifetime when I have gone to bed not feeling like the worst piece of shit on the planet?"

"Phil."

"Yes, Norman?"

"I'm talking."

"Okay. Sorry."

"There was a gymnasium at the reform school. I started weight training."

"Norman, I don't like to sound rude, but . . . are you making this up?"

"I was doing the bench press one day and I lost control of the bar. I dropped it on my head and knocked myself unconscious."

"Ah! This sounds more like it."

"I woke up at the hospital. And there was a man there, a minister, Frank Ulmer, who became a very good friend of mine. He died a few years back . . . anyway, we talked about, oh, you know. Getting tied to trees."

"And he said, let me tell you about a man who was tied to a tree."

"Hmmm?"

"Segue to Jesus."

"Jesus wasn't tied to a tree, Phil. He was nailed to a cross. Big difference."

"Even I knew that," puts in Jay.

"But if he could forgive the people who did that to him, I figured I could forgive those boys. And here I am."

"Well, frankly, that had never occurred to me," says Jay. "Forgiving them, I mean."

"It seems to me, Jay, that if you play music, you're concentrating on one of the beautiful things that people do. And forgiving people, in general. Those boys get included in the mix."

"I guess if I just write shit for television, I'm not really forgiving anybody."

"You have to forgive yourself first, Philip."

"I don't know if that would do the trick," I say.

"Plus, it may not be the easiest thing to do," my brother adds.

"How's that, Jay?"

"Well, let's think about this, okay? Let's just make sure we're all on the same page, that we understand exactly what went down. You tied Norman up so he could escape. You tied me up so that I couldn't. *You tied me to the tree.* I mean, I could have gotten away, I was pulling and yanking on my ropes, I could have gone for help or . . . forget it. It doesn't matter."

"You guys. You guys never did really understand what was going on. You never watched enough television. I practically had to beg you to join me in that escape attempt and, Jay, let me point out, I myself was in the clear, I could have kept going. But I came back. The point is, I knew Ted and Tony . . ."

"Tom and Terry."

"Father Norman, what were their names?"

"Oh, I wouldn't know. It was such a long time ago."

"I knew they were going to check the knot. And they did."

"No, they didn't."

"Sure they did. It's in my book. They said, 'Philly Four-Eyes is a tricky little bastard.'"

"Just because it's in your book doesn't mean it happened," Jay says. "They never checked the knot."

"I remember."

"No, you don't, Phil."

"I'm pretty sure they checked the knot, and if it had been a trick knot, who knows what might have happened?"

"We are not discussing what *might* have happened. We are discussing what *did* happen."

"Look, Jay. I didn't want to die alone. Okay? *That's* why I tied you to a tree. Satisfied?"

"Well . . . we're getting there."

"If I was going to get slaughtered by those fuck-pigs, I wanted to be with you. I wanted you to be with me."

"I forgive you."

"What?"

"I understand. You didn't want to die alone. You wanted to die with me there. So you tied me to a tree. It's not a decision I can really get behind intellectually, but I suppose I can understand it. After all, I'm your brother. So I forgive you."

"I don't see how you can be pissed off for so long and then just forgive me."

"That's because you don't understand—*yet*—what is so wonderful about human beings."

"Well put, Jay," says Norman. "Have you ever considered the vocation?"

"In my own way, Norm. In my own way. Let us pray."

"Yes. Good idea. We in the United Church tend not to be so, um, *dramatic* about it—"

"Akela!" Jay's voice rings, golden and pure, in the empty church.

"We will do our best," chants Reverend Norm.

"Dib dib dib . . ."

"Dob dob dob . . ."

The sun has continued its journey across the sky, and the light that comes through the stained-glass window now illuminates our tear-glistened cheeks.

The timing of our departure from Thunder Bay, combined with the cruising speed of the Dodge Super Bee, meant that when we were ready to stop for the night we were just a few kilometres away from the Shady Rest Motel. We decided to stop there. At least, I decided we should stop. Jay thought we should drive through the night, allow the rusted-out land shark the freedom to prowl in the darkness. He always was a romantic at heart. The girls wanted nothing to do with that place. "Daddy," they chastised me, "the bathroom walls say *Fuck, fuck, fuck*. And the guy running it is like really, really a creepa-zoid." But I insisted. Maybe I was just exhausted, maybe—and here we're getting close to the truth—I knew that the Shady Rest had a bar attached, the Luau Lounge, and I was just a tiny bit thirsty. Whatever. My will prevailed.

When we pulled into the empty parking lot, the odometer on the mighty Dodge, the Super Bee, had rolled to 299,999 miles. The last little white roller was stuck between numbers.

There was a woman behind the check-in counter this time, a large matronly woman who clucked over the girls and made us all feel bet-ter. This woman (perhaps forty-three years of age, perhaps as many pounds overweight) wore a man's wife-beater. It was inadequate.

Anyway, the girls were tired and wanted to go straight to bed. I supervised the hair- and tooth-brushing, standing in the doorway that separated the bathroom and the bedroom. Then I pulled out the banjo and sang a few verses of "The Window."

Little Jack Horner sat in a corner,
Eating his Christmas pie.
He stuck in his thumb, and pulled out a plum,
And threw it out the window.
The window, the window, he threw it out the window . . .

What, I didn't tell you that I brought my banjo with me? I tossed it into the trunk when Jay came to pick me up, just after my wife had left on a Mexican holiday with her young lover. Look, you readers shouldn't be so suspicious at this point in the game. I'm heading toward the finish line here, and I'd appreciate your support. After all, I'm limping and stumbling and starting to lose it.

———

I went outside and trod the wobbly walkway to the door marked "114." I could hear my brother's muffled voice coming from the other side. "Jay!" I called. "Hurry up. The book's almost finished."

He pulled the door open. He held the almost antique telephone base in one hand, and had the receiver squeezed between his shoulder and his ear. He muttered, "Look, I'll talk to you later," into the mouthpiece and ejected the receiver from the crook of his neck, catching it as it hurtled toward the ground.

"Who were you talking to?"

"Ex-wife number four," he answered. "What's up?"

"Let's go get a drink."

My brother eyed me suspiciously.

"What?" I said. "Did you think that all of a sudden we wouldn't be fucked up?"

"Well, I was *trying*," he argued. "I mean, look." He gestured with the telephone. "I was reaching out."

"Yeah. But it's not over. I don't know what's supposed to happen, but it's not over. It's *almost* over."

"Say what?"

"My book isn't finished."

"Well, can't you just make something up?"

"I *am* making something up."

"Huh?"

"Let's just go get a drink, okay? You and I have had drinks before. Like you said, we're alcoholics."

"Oh, all right." Jay grabbed a windbreaker for the journey across the tarmac. "I *was* looking forward to a nice little wank."

"Now *that's* reaching out."

"Let's go."

We entered the Luau Lounge, which seemed unaccountably gloomy, and stood still and waited for our eyes to adjust from the starlit night to deep shadow. In my case the wait was fated to be long—in point of fact, my eyes are incapable of adjusting—so I was still rather blind when I heard a voice say, "Hey. It's you guys."

Todd seemed subdued, even depressed.

"Hey there, hi there, ho there," whispered my brother.

I could see that Todd stood beside the bar. He gestured with something (was that a gun?) at a figure slumped over the countertop. (It was a gun!) "Les pissed me off. He couldn't stop talking about cunts."

"Todd?" said my brother. "I think we should call the police now."

"Right," snorted Todd. "Like *that's* gonna happen. Come off it."

"I've got children," I offered meekly.

"I've got children, too," Todd snapped. "Twin girls. Fifteen years of age. I'm not allowed within a mile of them. Why? Am I some kind of monster? Well, that's what the Court of Cunts says, that I'm a fucking monster, so I figure what the hey? Les wouldn't shut up, so bango-bingo. How about you assholes?"

"We'll shut up."

"*You* might." Todd waved the gun at me. "I'm not so sure about your brother."

"He'll shut up."

"Tell you what," said Todd. "Let's shut him the fuck up."

Todd set down his beer bottle (he had been holding the gun in his right hand, a brewski in the left), reached behind and threw up the hinged leaf that allowed staff behind the bar proper. He backed up, training the gun on us with such concentration that he was actually biting the tip of his tongue, and began rooting around back there.

I could see better now, enough that I took note that Les the bartender had only half a head left.

"So like, where have you guys been for the last couple of days?"

"In, um, Thunder Bay."

Jay said, "Todd, you don't want to make this any worse than it has to be."

"How much worse can it get? I'm already going to the gas chamber."

"No you're not."

"Huh?"

"We don't have the gas chamber in Canada."

"Here we go!" Todd had come up with a roll of duct tape and some lengths of rope. He held them up in the air triumphantly and wiggled back toward us. "Let's shut your brother up, Phil!"

"I'm not going to—"

"Or . . . I could just shoot you both. Bang-bang. What do you think?" He tossed me the rope. "So I think you should just shut the fuck up and tie your brother's hands together."

"Shoot us both," I said.

"Huh?"

"Do it, Todd. Like you said. Bang-bang."

"Don't take the easy way out, Phil," Jay said. "I think you should tie me up."

I searched my brother's face. I detected a small movement in his eyes, an intense whorliness. I'd seen this before, years and years ago, when as kids we experimented with extrasensory perception and silent thought transference.

"Okay, Jay? Jay, listen. I'm going to tie you up, now. I'm going to tie an *Irish Sheepshank.*"

At this, Todd's head bounced like that of a bobble-head doll. "Don't do that, goofus," he said. "He can just pull that knot apart. Tie something good."

"Um," I asked, "were you a Wolf Cub?"

"*Dib dib dib dob dob dob get a job.* Or however that goes. So tie something good. A Buntline Hitch. That's like the best knot there is."

"Oh." I held the piece of rope up and looked at it. I imagine that my look was more than pitiful.

"You know that one, Philly Four-Eyes?" asked Todd.

I nodded. "Yeah, I know how to tie a Buntline Hitch."

"So do it. Before I shoot the both of you cunts."

"Jay, I—"

"It's okay." Jay folded his huge hands together and proffered them.

I looked at Jay and tried to communicate that I was *still* going to tie the Irish Sheepshank, but even as I did so, we heard Todd say, "And I'm going to check that knot, too! So make it a good one."

"Make it a good one, Phil," my brother told me. He winked—at least, I think I saw him wink, but it may have been a tic, or he may have been trying to dam the tears.

I bound his wrists together—

"Make it a *really* good one, Phil," said Jay, which confused me a little.

—and looped the rope between his hands, and then I took the two ends and secured them with a Buntline Hitch, which is (Todd was correct in this) the best knot there is.

"Done."

"Sit him down and tie up his feet, too."

This was done. I kept trying to think of a plan. On television, the heroes seemed able to devise plans in a trice. Indeed, Padre needed hardly any time at all to work out a feasible strategy, and sometimes circumstances were such that he had to do this twice, three times an episode. But the only plan I could come up with was to run away, and hope that the bullets lodged non-lethally in my butt-fat.

Todd checked the knots. Apparently they passed muster. "Now put some of that duct tape over his mouth."

I picked up the roll of tape and noted that it had a surprising amount of weight to it, and then, miraculously, I formulated a plan. First of all, I would distract Todd. This could be pretty easily accomplished, I thought. Indeed, I didn't think I would have to do much more than suddenly point, and exclaim, "Hey! What's that over there?" Then, see, I would hurl the roll of tape at the gun, knock it from his pudgy hand, race over and claim it, hog-tie the motherfucker—well, the rest of the plan would work itself out. The salient point was the neutralization of the gun.

Unfortunately, before I could enact any of this, a sound intruded upon our collective senses. A siren.

"Oh, fuck." Todd wrapped his arm around my neck suddenly and pulled me close. He pressed the barrel of the gun into my temple and breathed all over me, softly, intimately, as though we were lovers. "Looks like it's just you and me, Philly Four-Eyes."

We listened to the siren grow louder and louder, until it was a scream that echoed throughout the land. I kept thinking it was as loud as it could possibly get, but it kept coming, some horribly hungry beast—

Then, suddenly, there was silence, and the sound of car doors opening and slamming shut.

"Here we go," said Todd.

"Todd Benson!" The voice came from just beyond the front door. "Come out with your hands up!"

Todd put his lips to my ear. "Did you know they actually said that?"

"No," I admitted.

"Just like on television," noted Todd, to which I could only nod dumbly. Then he raised his voice. "Don't come in!"

As he spoke the words, the door to the Luau Lounge burst open and two OPP officers entered, weapons drawn. They planted their feet firmly and stood side by side, remaining as close as possible for comfort and solace. They levelled their side arms.

"Release the hostage."

The OPP officers looked terrified, which I didn't count as good news. It was pretty clear to me that neither had ever used his gun. Their hands trembled and sweat threatened to blind them.

"Release the hostage," repeated Officer A.

"No, I don't think I'm gonna do that, because then you'll shoot me."

"No we won't," said Officer B.

"Right. Like I believe that."

"Honest injun," said Officer B., which I thought might get him into a little trouble, it's kind of an insensitive thing to say in Northern Ontario.

"Back off or I'm going to shoot Philly Four-Eyes here." As though he needed to explain the epithet, Todd flicked at my spectacles with the barrel of the gun, and knocked them off my face.

So that everything became a blur.

And when that happened, I felt the same despair as poor Henry Bemis had felt on the library steps. In a post-holocaust world, he had found a reason to live—books and time enough at last to read them—and then, in an instant, everything was ruined. Even though my brother was once again tied up, even though my own death seemed likely, I'd maintained a small candle-flicker of hope. Now hope was gone forever.

I began to reach for Todd's hand, and the gun.

I heard my brother's voice—

"Don't even think about it, Phil."

—and everything went fairly crazy, although I, lost in my own blurry little universe, have a hard time relating exactly what took place. But I can report that Jay leapt from the shadows brandishing two lengths of rope, the ones I'd used to bind his hands and feet. And then—employing the lethal towel-flicking technique we'd perfected in the steamy bathroom of our childhood home—he deftly removed the gun from Todd's fat hand. "Hey!" ejaculated Todd, as the revolver spun end over end out of harm's way. Todd pushed me away and went for Jay, his face twisted with rage. Jay flicked the other rope and caught the end of Todd's nose. Todd put his hands over his face, and said, "Ouch. *Fuck*."

And then the OPP officers descended upon him.

That's almost the end, although I should relate the conversation my brother and I had back in the motel room:

"How did you get out of the ropes? That was a Buntline Hitch, probably the very best knot there is."

"I hooked my thumbs when I put my hands together. When you do that, it's pretty easy to work your hands free. It's an old magician's trick."

"What do you mean, an old magician's trick? Where'd you learn that?"

"From television!"

"What?"

"Weird, eh? I've only watched television for about nine minutes my entire life. I watched Mickey Mantle strike out when I was a kid, and then I was in some bar, I forget which, and the teevee was showing *Magic Secrets Revealed*, and they explained that trick where a magician gets tied up, you know, but he doesn't *really* get tied up . . ."

"See, I told you."

"Hmm?"

"I told you teevee was great."

"Maybe you're right. We should all get down on our hands and knees and pray to the great magic box."

"Not only should we, Jay, but we *do*."

And the next morning, when we pulled out onto the Trans-Canada Highway, the odometer on the Dodge Super Bee turned over, and there were nothing but zeroes.

———

"So . . . what did you think?"

"Well . . . I'm not sure I understood the ending. With all the zeroes."

"I just wanted to indicate somehow that my life was suddenly filled with possibilities. There is no *ending* as such."

"Uh-huh. And how much of the scene in the Luau Lounge . . . ?"

"Is true? You heard about it on the news, didn't you? A couple of weeks back?"

"I suppose. I didn't really pay attention. I don't remember anything about a hostage situation."

"Is it important that it's all *true*-true? How much of what Anthony Trollope wrote was true?"

"What's he got to do with anything?"

"Well, we're both novelists. And we're both quiet, sobersided men of considerable industry."

"Uh-huh. Give me a break."

"Let's get down to the nitty-gritty. What did you think of the portrayal of, oh, *you*?"

"Of me? Well, I thought it was, you know, fair."

"Good."

"It's not like it's a really *detailed* portrait. There are other women in the book besides me."

"But it's clear that you were, you know, where my heart lay."

"Uhhh . . . nope. Not so much."

"No, I guess you're right. Not much was clear to me as I was writing the book. Things are much clearer now. Huh. Funny, eh?"

"What's funny?"

"That my ending is the exact opposite to the ending of 'Time Enough at Last.'"

"And the novel is a little too graphic, I think."

"Really?"

"I don't think Currer and Ellis should read it for a few years."

"You'd be surprised at the things Currer and Ellis know about."

"Uh-huh?"

"Uh-huh."

"You coming over tonight?"

"Well . . . I think maybe I can finish the book tonight. I think maybe that if I sit here long enough, I should be able to come up with just the right sentence to finish the novel."

"If I were you I'd just bung something down—*I woke up, it was all a dream*—and race over here."

"All right. I'll see you soon."

I have awoken. It is all a dream.

The author of ten novels, Paul Quarrington is also a musician—most recently in the band Porkbelly Futures—an award-winning screenwriter, a filmmaker, a playwright and an acclaimed non-fiction writer. His last novel, *Galveston*, was nominated for the Giller Prize; *Whale Music* won the Governor General's Literary Award for Fiction in 1989. Quarrington has also won the Stephen Leacock Memorial Medal for Humour for *King Leary*.